SPIRIT OF THE CENTURY™

PRESENTS

KING KHAN

BY
HARRY
CONNOLLY

EVIL HAT
PRODUCTIONS

An Evil Hat Productions Publication
www.evilhat.com • feedback@evilhat.com

First published in 2013 by Evil Hat Productions

Editor: J.R. Blackwell
Art: Christian N. St. Pierre • Design: Fred Hicks
Branding: Chris Hanrahan

Hardcover ISBN: 978-1-61317-044-1
Softcover ISBN: 978-1-61317-019-9
Kindle ISBN: 978-1-61317-046-5
ePub ISBN: 978-1-61317-045-8

Printed in the USA

THIS BOOK WAS MADE POSSIBLE WITH THE SUPPORT OF...

Michael Bowman *and a cast of hundreds, including*
"The Cap'n" Wayne Coburn, "The Professor" Eric Smailys, @aroberts72, @syntheticbrain, A. David Pinilla, Aaron Jones, Aaron Jurkis, Adam & Jayce Roberts, Adam B. Ross, Adam Rajski, Adan Tejada, AJ Medder, AJT, Alan Bellingham, Alan Hyde, Alan Winterrowd, Alex, Alien Zookeeper, Alisha "hostilecrayon" Miller, Alosia Sellers, Amy Collins, Amy Lambzilla Hamilton, Andrew Beirne, Andrew Byers, Andrew Guerr, Andrew Jensen, Andrew M. Kelly, Andrew Nicolle, Andrew Watson, Andy Blanchard, Andy Eaton, Angela Korra'ti, Anonymous Fan, Anthony Laffan, Anthony R. Cardno, April Fowler, Arck Perra, Ariel Pereira, Arnaud Walraevens, Arthur Santos Jr, Ashkai Sinclair, Autumn and Sean Stickney, Axisor, Bailey Shoemaker Richards, Barac Wiley, Barbara Hasebe, Barrett Bishop, Bartimeus, Beena Gohil, Ben Ames, Ben Barnett, Ben Bement, Ben Bryan, Bill Dodds, Bill Harting, Bill Segulin, Blackcoat, Bo Saxon, Bo Williams, Bob Bretz, Brandon H. Mila, Bret S. Moore, Esq., Brian Allred, Brian E. Williams, Brian Engard, Brian Isikoff, Brian Kelsay @ripcrd, Brian Nisbet, Brian Scott Walker, Brian Waite, Brian White, Bryan Sims, Bryce Perry, C.K. "Velocitycurve" Lee, Calum Watterson, Cameron Harris, Candlemark & Gleam, Carl Rigney, Carol Darnell, Carolyn Butler, Carolyn White, Casey & Adam Moeller, Catherine Mooney, CE Murphy, Centurion Eric Brenders, Charles Paradis, Chase Bolen, Cheers, Chip & Katie, Chris Bekofske, Chris Callahan, Chris Ellison, Chris Hatty, Chris Heilman, Chris Matosky, Chris Newton, Chris Norwood, Chris Perrin, Christian Lindke, Christina Lee, Christine Lorang, Christine Swendseid, Christopher Gronlund, Chrystin, Clark & Amanda Valentine, Clay Robeson, Corey Davidson, Corinne Erwin, Craig Maloney, Crazy J, Cyrano Jones, Dan Conley, Dan N, Dan Yarrington, Daniel C. Hutchison, Daniel Laloggia, Danielle Ingber, Darcy Casselman, Darren Davis, Darrin Shimer, Daryl Weir, Dave BW, Dave Steiger, David & Nyk, David Hines, David M., David Patri, Declan Feeney, Deepone, Demelza Beckly, Derrick Eaves, Dimitrios Lakoumentas, DJ Williams, DL Thurston, Doug Cornelius, Dover Whitecliff, Drew, drgnldy71, DU8, Dusty Swede, Dylan McIntosh, Ed Kowalczewski, edchuk, Edouard "Francesco", Edward J Smola III, Eleanor-Rose Begg, Eli "Ace" Katz, Ellie Reese, Elly & Andres, Emily Poole, Eric Asher, Eric Duncan, Eric Henson, Eric Lytle, Eric Paquette, Eric Smith, Eric Tilton, Eric B Vogel, Ernie Sawyer, Eva, Evan Denbaum, Evan Grummell, Ewen Albright, Explody, Eyal Teler, Fabrice Breau, Fade Manley, Fidel Jiron Jr., Frank "Grayhawk" Huminski, Frank Jarome, Frank Wuerbach, Frazer Porritt, Galen, Gareth-Michael Skarka, Garry Jenkins, Gary Hoggatt, Gary McBride, Gavran, Gemma Tapscott, Glenn, Greg Matyola, Greg Roy, Gregory Frank, Gregory G. Gieger, Gus Golden, Herefox, HPLustcraft, Hugh J. O'Donnell, Ian Llywelyn Brown, Ian Loo, Inder Rottger, Itamar Friedman, J. Layne Nelson, J.B. Mannon, J.C. Hutchins, Jack Gulick, Jake Reid, James "discord_inc" Fletcher, James Alley, James Ballard, James Champlin, James Husum, James Melzer, Jami Nord, Jared Leisner, Jarrod Coad, Jason Brezinski, Jason Kirk Butkans, Jason Kramer, Jason Leinbach, Jason Maltzen, Jayna Pavlin, Jayson VanBeusichem, Jean Acheson, Jeff Eaton, Jeff Macfee, Jeff Xilon, Jeff Zahnen, Jeffrey Allen Arnett, Jen Watkins, Jenevieve DeFer, Jenica Rogers, jennielf, Jennifer Steen, Jeremiah Robert Craig Shepersky, Jeremy Kostiew, Jeremy Tidwell, Jesse Pudewell, Jessica and Andrew Qualls, JF Paradis, Jill Hughes, Jill Valuet, Jim "Citizen Simian" Henley, Jim & Paula Kirk, Jim Burke in VT, Jim Waters, JLR, Joanne B, Jody Kline, Joe "Gasoline" Czyz, Joe Kavanagh, John Beattie, John Bogart, John Cmar, John D. Burnham, John Geyer/Wulfenbahr Arts, John Idlor, John Lambert, John Rogers, John Sureck, John Tanzer, John-Paul Holubek, Jon Nadeau, Jon Rosebaugh, Jonathan Howard, Jonathan Perrine, Jonathan S. Chance, José Luis Nunes Porfírio, Jose Ramon Vidal,

Joseph Blomquist, Josh Nolan, Josh Thomson, Joshua K. Martin, Joshua Little, JouleLee Perl Ruby Jade, Joy Jakubaitis, JP Sugarbroad, Jukka Koivisto, Justin Yeo, K. Malycha, Kai Nikulainen, Kairam Ahmed Hamdan, Kal Powell, Karen J. Grant, Kat & Jason Romero, Kate Kirby, Kate Malloy, Kathy Rogers, Katrina Lehto, Kaz, Keaton Bauman, Keith West, Kelly (rissatoo) Barnes, Kelly E, Ken Finlayson, Ken Wallo, Keri Orstad, Kevin Chauncey, Kevin Mayz, Kierabot, Kris Deters, Kristin (My Bookish Ways Reviews), Kristina VanHeeswijk, Kurt Ellison, Lady Kayla, Larry Garetto, Laura Kramarsky, Lily Katherine Underwood, Lisa & M3 Sweatt, Lisa Padol, litabeetle, Lord Max Moraes, Lorri-Lynne Brown, Lucas MFZB White, Lutz Ohl, Lyndon Riggall, M. Sean Molley, Maggie G., Manda Collis & Nick Peterson, Marcia Dougherty, Marcus McBolton (Salsa), Marguerite Kenner and Alasdair Stuart, Mark "Buzz" Delsing, Mark Cook, Mark Dwerlkotte, Mark MedievaMonkey, Mark O'Shea, Mark Truman of Magpie Games, Mark Widner, Marshall Vaughan, Martin Joyce, Mary Spila, Matt Barker, Matt Troedson, Matt Zitron & Family, Matthew Scoppetta, Max Temkin, Maxwell A Giesecke, May Claxton, MCpl Doug Hall, Meri and Allan Samuelson, Michael Erb, Michael Godesky, Michael Hill, Michael M. Jones, Michael May, michael orr, Michael Richards, Michael Thompson, Michael Tousignant, Michael Wolfe, Miguel Reyes, Mike "Mortagole" Gorgone, Mike Grace (The Root Of All Evil), Mike Kowalski, Mike Sherwood, Mike 'txMaddog' Jacobs, Mike Wickliff, Mikhail McMahon, Miranda "Giggles" Horner, Mitch A. Williams, Mitchell Young, Morgan Ellis, Mur Lafferty, Nancy Feldman, Nathan Alexander, Nathan Blumenfeld, Nestor D. Rodriguez, Nick Bate, Odysseas "Arxonti" Votsis, Owen "Sanguinist" Thompson, Pam Blome, Pamela Shaw, Paolo Carnevali, Pat Knuth, Patricia Bullington-McGuire, Paul A. Tayloe, Paul MacAlpine, Paul Weimer, Peggy Carpenter, Pete Baginski, Pete Sellers, Peter Oberley, Peter Sturdee, Phil Adler, Philip Reed, Philippe "Sanctaphrax" Saner, Poppy Arakelian, Priscilla Spencer, ProducerPaul, Quentin "Q" Hudspeth, Quinn Murphy, Rachel Coleman Finch, Rachel Narow, Ranger Dave Ross, Raymond Terada, Rebecca Woolford, Rhel ná DecVandé, Rich "Safari Jack Tallon" Thomas, Rich Panek, Richard "Cap'n Redshanks" McLean, Richard Monson-Haefel, Rick Jones, Rick Neal, Rick Smith, Rob and Rachel, Robert "Gundato" Pavel, Robert M. Everson, Robert Towell (Ndreare), Ross C. Hardy!, Rowan Cota, Ryan & Beth Perrin, Ryan Del Savio Riley, Ryan E. Mitchell, Ryan Hyland, Ryan Jassil, Ryan Patrick Dull, Ryan Worrell, S. L. Gray, Sabrina Ogden, Sal Manzo, Sally Qwill Janin, Sam Heymans, Sandro Tomasetti, Sarah Brooks, Saxony, Scott Acker, Scott E., Scott Russell Griffith, Sean Fadden, Sean Nittner, Sean O'Brien, Sean R. Jensen, Sean T. DeLap, Sean W, Sean Zimmermann, Sebastian Grey, Seth Swanson, Shai Norton, Shaun D. Burton, Shaun Dignan, Shawna Hogan, Shel Kennon, Sherry Menton, Shervyn, Shoshana Kessock, Simon "Tech Support" Strauss, Simone G. Abigail C. GameRageLive, Stacey Chancellor, Stephen Cheney, Stephen Figgins, Sterling Brucks, Steve Holder, Steve Sturm, Steven K. Watkins, Steven McGowan, Steven Rattelsdorfer, Steven Vest, T I Hely, Tantris Hernandez, Taylor "The Snarky Avenger" Kent, Team Milian, Teesa, Temoore Baber, Tess Snider, Tevel Drinkwater, The Amazing Enigma, The Axelrods, The fastest man wearing a jetpack, thank you, The Gollub Family, The Hayworths, The NY Coopers, The Sotos, The Vockerys, Theron "Tyrone" Teter, Tim "Buzz" Isakson, Tim Pettigrew, Tim Rodriguez of Dice + Food + Lodging, TimTheTree, TJ Robotham, TK Read, Toby Rodgers, Todd Furler, Tom Cadorette, Tom J Allen Jr, Tony Pierson, Tracy Hall, Travis Casey, Travis Lindquist, Vernatia, Victor V., Vidal Bairos, W. Adam Rinehart, W. Schaeffer Tolliver, Warren Nelson, Wil Jordan, Will Ashworth, Will H., William Clucus Woods...yes, "Clucus", William Hammock, William Huggins, William Pepper, Willow "Dinosaurs and apocalypse? How could I NOT back it?" Wood, wufl, wwwisata, Wythe Marschall, Yurath, Zakharov "Zaksquatch" Sawyer, Zalabar, Zalen Moore, and Zuki.

CHAPTER ONE

"Of course, this little beauty is not for racing, you understand. It has nothing on those J-class *monstrosities* you see in the America's Cup nowadays. We don't even have the Bermuda mast."

Professor Khan nodded and smiled, being careful not to show his teeth. If there was anything more tiring than listening to Lord Blinkersly complain about the inadequacy of his fifty-foot yacht, it was his oft-repeated confession that he found Khan's teeth "damned disconcerting."

"Daddy!" Bertie Blinkersly called. He pronounced it *Duddy*. "You mustn't bore the Professor talking about yacht races we won't even enter!"

Bertie was a tall lad, topping six foot four inches, but despite being old enough to take up arms in defense of king and country, he still seemed unfinished, more of a gawky boy than man. Khan liked him the way one might like an enthusiastic puppy: near enough to make one laugh but not close enough to accidentally muss one's tweed. Sadly, while the yacht was quite impressively long, it was also narrow. Bertie, clambering toward them in the bow, would soon be very close indeed.

Following carefully behind him was his fiancé, Petunia. She was a painfully shy young woman, but pretty in a colorless, self-effacing way. Khan had politely inquired after her health before they had set sail, but she had simply squeaked in response, then stared at the toes of her deck shoes. No matter. He had become accustomed to the unfortunate effect he had on people.

The bow struck a wave, raising a salty spray that soaked them all. Bertie and Lord Blinkersly did their best to bear it manfully. Petunia shielded her face, blinking down at the deck.

"Dear boy," Lord Blinkersly answered. His jowls started at his lower eyelashes and stopped at the collar of his shirt. They jiggled hypnotically whenever he spoke. "I'm only talking about larger, more comfortable vessels! I do believe your professor is feeling a widge out of sorts, don't you know."

Khan realized his hands were gripping tightly to the wooden bench upon which he was seated. What's more, he had not moved from the spot since they had first glided away from the dock.

"I'm fine," he lied. "The sun is wonderful and I've always loved the smell of the sea."

Lies were expected. Lies were polite. It was also expected that, when one of your most mediocre students invited you to go sailing with his father, a Lord Temporal who had endowed a chair at Oxford, you accepted. It wouldn't affect Bertie's grades one jot, no matter how much the Blinkerslys hoped otherwise, but still, the Professor could not bring himself to refuse Bertie's offer.

He should have. Khan had been on the water before, but familiarity had not made the experience any easier. He was still terrified.

"I say, the water's not particularly rough today, don't you know, but I could always ask the fellows to turn us back in toward land." *The fellows* were a pair of Portuguese sailors who actually did the business of sailing the yacht. Khan hadn't been introduced and he half expected that the Blinkerslys did not know their names. "It would be no problem at all, my good fellow."

"Oh! By Jove, Daddy, I think I've tackled it! It's the life jacket."

They all turned toward Professor Khan. He was, indeed, wearing his life jacket. Yes, he was the only one. Yes, he'd put it on before they'd even untied from the dock.

Lord Blinkersly harumphed and looked vaguely put out. "We haven't sunk ourselves so far, and the fellows are quite skilled at fishing unfortunate passengers out of the drink. They've certainly hooked Bertie here back into the boat enough times."

"Ha ha! I'll say! There's really nothing to fret about, Professor. Truly."

Khan felt a chill run down his back. Would propriety require him to remove his life jacket, too?

"No," Petunia said.

As they turned to her, she seemed to shrink in on herself. Bertie stood beside her but didn't offer a comforting hand. In fact, he never seemed to touch her at all. Khan felt a sudden flush of anger he dared not show: They were engaged to be married, for pity's sake! Yet Khan had never seen them so much as hold hands. Did they love each other at all? Or were public displays of affection "simply not done"?

By God, the boy mustn't make the same mistake that Khan had, but of course it wasn't his place to speak.

"You see..." Petunia forced herself to continue. "When Bertie told me we would be sailing with the Professor, I went to my library—"

Professor Khan felt his heart break a little. She was engaged to Bertie and she was bookish, too? Good Lord.

"... And did a little research. You see, the fellows would never be able to rescue Professor Khan if he fell overboard, because he's not as buoyant as we are. Because he's..."

Petunia couldn't bring herself to say it, even though the fact was evident to anyone with eyes: *because he's a gorilla.*

An intelligent gorilla, created by Doctor Methuselah as part of one of his obscure plots. In fact, there was an entire small nation of his kind out there in the world, ruled over by the iron hand of the Professor's "father," Gorilla Khan. The Professor could have lived among them as a prince, if he were willing to devote his life to carnage and war rather than science and learning.

But Professor Khan had turned his back on conquest. He had sided with the humans against his own people to protect innocent lives. Now he was both hero and exile, Englishman and ape, Oxford professor and barely-tolerated freak of nature.

Lord Blinkersly turned to Khan with a shocked look on his face. "I say, old boy, is that true?"

The Professor shrugged and glanced down at his bare feet. No one in all of England made shoes to fit those feet. "I weigh about four hundred pounds and, although I do prefer traditional English foods like bangers and mash, I don't carry the same level of body fat humans do. If I were to lose my footing—"

"I say! You'd sink like a stone, jacket be damned! Fellows!" Lord Blinkersly began to wave toward the low, green shape of England off the starboard side. "Back-o to dock-o!"

The fellows trimmed sail and brought the boat about. Bertie knelt beside the Professor's bench. "I had no idea, Professor. I wish you had popped the cork on this one when I lobbed the invitation toward you."

"Nevermind that, boy," Lord Blinkersly interrupted. "I understand why he didn't say anything, although I can't say the same for my *future daughter-in-law*." Petunia drifted toward the stern, out of earshot of whatever scolding the old fellow had in mind. Everyone gripped the rails tightly as the ocean swells hit the yacht broadside, making her roll. "I imagine the Professor felt obliged by our name and title. It's not unheard of for... er.... *immigrants* to put a greater weight on the English system than we do, wot? Still, Professor, your life jacket looks better than that whorehouse window curtain my son is wearing."

Bertie stroked the sleeve of his tangerine checked jacket. "Now, Daddy."

Lord Blinkersly bent down to Khan. "Professor, how do you feel about sitting *by* the sea, wot? Would you enjoy feeling the sand between your... toes?"

Khan tried to hide his relief. The rolling yacht made him queasy and he had to relax his grip on the bench for fear of breaking the wood. "I would very much, thank you."

Lord Blinkersly clapped him on the shoulder, looking more comfortable now that he was in a position to ease or exacerbate his guest's fears. The yacht rolled hard to the port side, then back the other way. It was when the mast was pointed farthest to the west that the gleaming arrow flashed out of the sky and struck the boat, nearly neutering Professor Khan.

CHAPTER TWO

By Jove! It was bally chaos at first. Daddy began shouting orders as if he was back fighting the Boers. Petunia began shrieking about holes in the sky. As for Bertie himself, well, he would have to accept that there are certain occasions when a fellow—even a jolly solid English fellow of the best stock—occasionally panics like a chicken in a fox's den. Even Miguel and Miguel 2, or whatever the fellows called themselves, abandoned the lines and rudder to come see.

Only Professor Khan seemed to hold himself together. In fact, it almost seemed to calm him, as though a mysterious attack out of nowhere was a comforting return to his normal routine.

The arrow was made of gleaming metal, bright like chrome, but Bertie could see it wasn't, not really. It had struck while *Manor Born* was heeling to port, practically on her beam ends, piercing both the hem of Professor Khan's kilt and the wooden bench below it. Right between his blinking legs.

Bertie felt positively wobbly at the idea, but the Professor scanned the western sky coolly. There were no other ships in evidence, no planes, nothing that could have harbored a bellicose archer.

"Intolerable!" Daddy shouted. "Intolerable! Intolerable!"

Professor Khan splintered the bench without apology as he withdrew the arrow. Not only was the shaft made of metal—and as thick as a pinkie finger, much larger than average—but so were the head and the feathers, too.

Bertie realized he was blubbering and slapped his hand over his mouth to shut himself up. "Petunia!" he said, his voice still high with panic, "Stop shrieking like a silly fool!"

"My dear," Khan said, turning around to address her. Bertie could not imagine how the Professor kept his head. "What was that you said about a hole? I'm afraid you're the only one of us to have seen it."

She took several gasping breaths. "A hole," she said, pointing above Khan's head to the port side. The flush in her cheeks made her look almost pretty. "Right there above you. The arrow just... flew out of it."

"Intolerable!" Daddy shouted again. "Not only that you should be... But to have one of my guests attacked! And the blasted thing just missed me, too!"

The Miguels had come forward to eyeball the arrow for themselves. A wave took the stern at an angle and soaked everyone to the skin.

"Intolerable!" Daddy shouted at them, his whole face wobbling. "Get back to your jibs and things, damn you! Climb the mast-o and tell me who could have attacked our guest-o!"

The Professor cleared his throat. "I don't think it was an attack, Lord Blinkersly. I think it was a message."

Bertie leaned in close. By Jove, there was a note tied to the front of the arrow, just behind the head. Professor Khan undid the slipknot—it was a black shoelace of all things—and put it in his pocket. Then he unfolded the note. Fine lavender paper, Bertie noted, the sort his aunts gave him at Christmas when they wanted to extort letters from him.

The Professor put on his reading glasses. "*Come to Los Angeles immediately. Anselme Leveque is in terrible danger.* There's even an address."

Daddy snorted. "Leveque? Sounds Frenchy. Why would someone send me a message about a Frenchy?"

"I daresay this note is for me, Lord Blinkersly. Professor Leveque is a brilliant theoretical physicist. He is also a friend and colleague of mine."

Daddy snorted again, this time in relief. Bertie had never met a man who could be so incapable with words but so communicative without them. "Not terribly informative. Who is it from?"

The Professor folded the paper back up. "The forger didn't sign it."

"Forger? What do you mean by that?"

"What I mean," the Professor said calmly as the Miguels turned them back toward the shore, "is that it appears to have been written in my hand."

CHAPTER THREE

The dean had let his desk get out of control again. Damnation. His hatred of his own messiness was matched only by his inability to do anything about it. Where was Mrs. Evermore? She was supposed to be keeping him under control to avoid this sort of embarrassment.

As he pawed through the papers on his desk, he muttered: "Where did that fool woman put that—"

"AWAY!" came Mrs. Evermore's voice from the front office. Good Lord, that woman had the ears of a barn owl.

Sure enough, the requisition approval forms were in the cabinet, just where they were supposed to be. The dean pulled out the folder and promptly spilled them across the window seat.

Damnation doubled. It was summer term! This was the time the university was most pleasant, when the teachers and students were supposed to be absent. Why couldn't the professors go on holiday like sensible people? Couldn't the physics department do their nuclear experiments without... He scanned the form in front of him. Lead shielding? Frivolous! Denied.

And the archaeology department, with their sealed rooms and their secret "special collection." Not only was there no room in the budget for silver bullets, but to ask the Archbishop of Canterbury to bless them? The scandal would be humiliating! Denied.

The dean glanced out the window. "Speaking of scandals..." he muttered. That infuriating Professor Khan was coming up the walk with... Was that Lord Blinkersly's son? Damnation, it was. As much as he wished otherwise, the dean knew they were coming to see him.

His first order of business when he'd started this job had been to force Khan out of the school, but the backlash he'd faced had been outrageous. The dean considered Khan little more than a circus freak, little better than a tenured horse that could do arithmetic, but the staff and faculty genuinely liked him. Even the students admired him, if that mattered.

Of course, the dean was no neophyte when it came to school politics. If he couldn't force a teacher out directly, he knew how to make his position too uncomfortable to retain. Unfortunately, his order to move Khan's office to the basement seemed to vanish from his outbox, his requirement that all staff shave daily never turned up in the day's typing, and his rule that all male staff wear trousers... Well, that was the one that brought Mrs. Evermore into his office, her shrill voice rattling the windowpanes. Poor Professor Khan, she said, couldn't be expected to wear *human* trousers because he wasn't human (as if the dean had forgotten there was an Honest to Heavens mountain gorilla on the faculty). Besides, her maternal grandfather had been North Country, and he'd worn a kilt every day of his life. With pride.

The dean had admitted defeat at that point. Still, it had all been so embarrassing—for the institution.

However, there was hope. If Khan was coming here, it was because he needed research money—which he wasn't going to get—or he needed to take leave for another of his adventures. As far as the dean was concerned, the only problem with Khan's adventures was that he came back afterward.

Please, please, don't let this visit be about money.

CHAPTER FOUR

Sally Slick had put on her clean coveralls and washed her face, too. She'd even looked in a mirror to make sure she hadn't missed a spot of engine grease. Yes, she was only going to New Jersey, but even so she had a special guest to meet.

The auto-gyro rumbled from out over the water with the rising sun behind it, then swung around toward the landing strip. Sally drove out onto the field to meet it. Before she clambered from her convertible, she checked herself in the rear view mirror one last time.

There was a smudge of black grease on the side of her nose. Aw, what was the use?

Professor Khan and his assistant climbed awkwardly down the auto-gyro's ladder. The old gorilla looked just as he always did, bundled in his professorial tweeds, tartan kilt and bare feet, with his reading spectacles poking from his pocket. His assistant wore a green bowler over a green jacket and pants. If he'd tripped and fallen, someone might have stuck a golf flagstick into his gaping mouth.

In a few hours, the July temperatures in New York would make them regret those sport jackets, but for now it was still early enough to be cool.

"Professor, it's so good to see you!" Sally rushed forward to embrace him, which he returned warmly. Boy, was he big. He was no taller than Sally, but beneath that thick black body hair, he was as solid as the prow of a tugboat. "Wasn't it nice to be met at sea and flown in, rather than wait in line to have your passport stamped?"

"You mean 'be refused entry into the U.S. because my kind are still deeply distrusted.'"

"That, too," she admitted.

"Thank you, Sally. I really am terribly grateful."

How sad he seemed! She'd heard that he was still haunted by a previous adventure—a war on another planet, in fact, and a woman he left behind—but she didn't know the details. Considering her own romantic history, better if she didn't broach the subject at all. "The others asked me to tell you they're sorry they couldn't meet you. They're out of the country."

"My dear, never mind the others; what are you doing here? You shouldn't be interrupting your work just to chauffeur an old gorilla around New York."

"Hah! As if I'd let you pass through my city without seeing you. I don't think so. We have a few hours before your train so I'm taking you someplace nice."

As it turned out, *nice* meant a table at Katz's Delicatessen. The room fell silent as Khan stepped through the door, but Sally called the owner's name and he hustled two couples who were obviously finishing a night on the town out of a back booth.

Sally watched Benny closely as he placed plates and napkins on the table. He understood a little of who and what she was, and he'd always treated her well, but the gorilla obviously made him uneasy. The memory of the recent failed gorilla invasion was still strong, even if most people had no idea just how close things had been. Would he have thrown the Professor out if he'd come in alone? Considering everything Khan had done to save the city—against his own people, no less—it seemed unfair.

Khan's assistant grimaced at the menu. "Is this... Jewish food?"

Sally turned away from him. "Professor, tell me about this mission of yours."

He tried to insist that it wasn't anything of the sort, but the more he described it, the more it sounded like exactly the sort of trouble the Centurions investigated. The Professor didn't want her help, though. This was his friend, he insisted, not an invasion from outer space or an evil mastermind with a death ray.

There was something different in his voice and in his expression; it worried her. She'd known him to be fussy and she'd known him to cut loose like a wild animal, but she had never known him to look downcast. "Are you missing... that other place?" She couldn't bring herself to say *Mars*.

Khan gave her a steady look. Bingo. "Not the place so much as... Well, the place, too." He rubbed his face with a hairy paw. "You must understand, Sally: Oxford is my home. It was the first place I truly belonged. When I'm teaching a class and it's going well, I feel a tremendous sense of *connection* with my students. The same is true when I'm doing research in my library. The books on my desk and on my shelves, the information contained in them... I feel as though they are a part of me."

Sally stared deeply into Khan's small, dark eyes. "I think I know what you mean, Professor. When I'm in my shop, inventing something, I feel like I'm connected with everything at once. Sometimes I imagine I can feel the movement of the earth and the fury of the sun, the swirl of electricity all over the city, the warps of magnetic fields. That's when I know I'm about to solve a sticky problem or come up with something new and amazing."

Professor Khan stared back with a frankness that made her slightly uncomfortable. "That must be incredibly profound," he said at last. "But then, I imagine that's what makes you who you are."

The gangly assistant interrupted with the casual confidence of someone who believes everything he says is worth hearing. "I must say, I don't think much of this talk of 'connectedness.' It doesn't seem very full of veryness."

It was time to place their orders, and within a few hours Sally put the Professor and his ridiculous assistant on a westbound train.

CHAPTER FIVE

All the way to Wilshire she'd driven, just to buy those special Russian sausages for her Horst. Berta wouldn't tell him they were Russian, of course. Horst had no love for people he now called "Soviets," even if they'd come to America while the tsars were still in power, or had fled the Bolshevik armies... even if they were Jews fleeing pogroms.

Horst, her big, hairy bear of a man, was not fond of nuance.

But the sausage was fatty and had no sugar in it, which he liked, so Berta never told him it was made by former White Army deserters. Fifteen years of marriage had taught Berta a great many things, but chief among them was that little lies made life tolerable. She remembered all too well the imperious lecture he delivered when she'd told him she'd attended his Home State Picnic because she was tagging along with a friend, not because she'd moved here from Wisconsin as she'd claimed. What did it matter, four years later, to discover that she'd actually been born in Iowa? Why couldn't he just laugh about it like a sensible person?

So she never told him about the sausage, or how much time she spent in the auto fetching it. She certainly never told him about the lunchtime visits to restaurants that served food from all over the world.

How he would have fussed at the idea of her eating this way! For Horst every meal was wurst, spaetzel, potatoes and pickles; if he'd discovered that, for three months running, she had lunched twice a week at a family bodega because she loved their mole sauce, he would have taken her car keys away.

Today she had stopped at a tiny Filipino place, and her meal was made all the more delicious when she imagined Horst's outrage if he'd ever learned it had been prepared by a Malay family.

Luckily, he never asked. The thought brought a familiar tinge of loneliness, but she brushed it off as she gathered her groceries from the trunk of her car. Horst had his research and his lectures. The university kept him quite busy and his work was so very important. When a man spent long hours searching for "the mathematical name of God," well, was it any wonder that he wasn't interested in discussing the price of pickles?

Berta was startled out of her reverie by the sight of a car parked behind her husband's at the curb. A Renault Primaquatre may not have been an extravagant car, but it was probably out of the price range of most of the university employees who lived on the block.

Stranger still was that a young woman sat unmoving behind the wheel. She was pretty enough but otherwise unremarkable. However, she seemed to be in some sort of trance; her eyes were wide open and her head was held upright but she was so still she could have been sound asleep.

It was possible the poor woman was simply lost in thought, but there were other, more worrisome causes for such a trance, too. Berta resolved to slip her groceries into the icebox and come back out to check on her.

But when Berta stepped through her front door, she forgot about the woman in the car. Something about the house felt wrong. Everything looked in order, but nonetheless goose pimples ran down her arms and back.

"Horst?" she called, but there was only silence in return. His car was out front, so he had to be here, and he could never become so absorbed in his work that he would ignore her, not this close to suppertime.

She carried the shopping bags into the tiny kitchen and dropped them onto the table. A sudden certainty overcame her that he'd suffered a heart attack and collapsed somewhere in the house. Too many pastries, she thought bitterly as she hurried toward the back of the house.

What would have been a den in most homes had been turned into Horst's workshop. If he wasn't in the bath—and the door was open, so she knew he wasn't—that was where he would be. Why he needed a place to build and futz and blow out their fuse box at home when he had access to his university labs, she would never understand.

She opened the workroom door. "God in Heaven!"

Someone had torn the place apart. Horst had never been a tidy man, but he wouldn't have thrown his equipment about, shattering vacuum tubes and tearing out wires. He just didn't have the temperament to throw a tantrum.

Had something been stolen? The way everything was strewn about, she wasn't sure how a body could tell. But where was—

A shoe. One of Horst's sensible brown shoes stuck out from behind the workbench beside the far wall. Berta rushed to him, not caring about the equipment she broke beneath her heavy tread. She caught hold of the workbench and, with a mighty heave, toppled it and everything on it to the side, revealing—

Who was this? She'd expected to find her great hairy bear of a husband, but this fellow was as bald as an egg.

A wave of revulsion ran through her as she looked at the intruder's soft, pink, hairless flab. He was not dead, only comatose. Was he a burglar, who dressed himself in her husband's clothes? What madness was this?

A rush of footsteps passed in the hall behind her, and Berta turned and raced after them. By the sound, the shoes were made of metal. More madness. She reached the front room but found it empty. The front door was still shut and of course she would have heard it open.

Whoever had run by her was trapped in the house. It suddenly dawned on Berta that she was alone and had nothing to use as a weapon, not even the fish boning knife from the cutlery block. Maybe, whoever this intruder was, she ought to let them escape.

There was a metallic footstep behind her. When she turned toward it, she saw nothing but a brilliant turquoise light. Her mind was suddenly filled with numbers.

CHAPTER SIX

It was after sunset when Khan and Bertie arrived at Central Station, well past business hours. Nonetheless, Bertie was able to procure the Wanderer W22 the Blinkersly solicitors had arranged as well as a map of Los Angeles.

The route to Anselme's home took them through a small part of the Sunset Strip, making Professor Khan's first glimpses of the city contradictory and unpleasant. There were squat stone office buildings that lacked the art deco charm of Manhattan. There were intersections with pleasant little houses on one side and desolate scrub lots on the other.

And there was the strip itself: filled with neon advertisements for gambling and music, along with more subtle suggestions for other, less legal entertainments.

"I say," Bertie chattered nervously. "Sin city, wot?"

He wasn't wrong, Khan knew. Los Angeles seemed haphazard, self-indulgent, and flimsy. It looked as if it had been created to indulge the moment, without care for the long-lasting effect.

And yet, while he was waiting on Bertie at the station, or when they sat at a red light, the locals did no more than glance at him, raise an eyebrow, then look away. He felt none of the hostility he had grown accustomed to in New York and on the train ride west. No one scowled. No one stared at him while muttering to a companion. No one hurried away at his approach. It was almost refreshing.

"I'm awfully glad that the locals are not giving us so many awful looks," Bertie said. Khan was surprised he'd noticed. "Much better than in Oklahoma; I thought those fellows were going to draw their six-shooters and OK Corral us! Do you remember those fellows, Professor? They were dressed as cowboys even though they weren't from Texas."

"Bertie, I'm pretty sure there are cowboys in places other than Texas."

"Possibly, Professor, but they don't seem proper cowboys if they're not from Texas. I'm simply goggled that you haven't been treated more warmly. I thought you were famous, sir."

"Fame isn't all it's put up to be, my boy."

"Quite," Bertie said. "I say! Perhaps they think you are a movie actor! Or that we are driving around the city in costume to promote a new film! Wouldn't that be exciting! Tell me, sir, did you see that cracker about the colossal ape fellow? The one where he climbed that building in New York to win the heart of a beautiful woman?"

"I walked out of that film, Bertie."

"Ah. Yes. I'm sure she wasn't his type. My goodness! Is that a woman of ill-repute just standing out on the corner?"

"Er, I suspect not, Bertie." Khan checked his map. "Make a right at this corner, my boy."

He did. Like so much else about Los Angeles, it surprised them by changing rather suddenly. After a short block, the street began to wind up a steep hill and they found themselves almost lost among stands of trees.

Leveque's home wasn't far up the hill, but the trees were thick enough to obscure most of the garish light from the strip below. Bertie pulled off the narrow, winding road into a parking space in front of the house. "Pleasant-looking little place," Bertie said.

Professor Khan almost laughed. The house before them was a two-story Italian villa with a tall privacy hedge, a wrought-iron gate, and a picture window with leaded glass. It was a beautiful place, and should have been far outside the budget of a university professor. Only Bertie would describe it as if it was a vacation cottage.

The doorbell rang like chimes. Someone switched on a light above the lintel, and then, after a series of locks were thrown, the door swung open.

A young woman of about twenty-four stood in the entry, framed by the light behind her. Khan heard Bertie catch his breath; yes, he supposed she was pretty by human measures. Her blonde curls had been cut to show off her long, pale neck. She had Leveque's long, narrow nose but her blue eyes were large and expressive.

She was wearing a sleek, elegant dress. In black.

While Khan was considering his own gray tweed and Bertie's jaunty lemon yellow jacket and bowler, Bertie spoke up. "Pardon me, but we've come a long way to speak with Doctor Anselme Leveque."

She glanced back and forth between Khan and Bertie several times, then bared her teeth. "Is this supposed to be a joke? Am I supposed to be laughing? Are you bringing the circus to my house? Damn you!"

She slammed the door in their faces.

Bertie turned toward Khan with a bewildered expression. In all likelihood, no one had ever slammed a door on him before. "Does this mean we start back to England now, Professor?"

Khan laid his hand on Bertie's elbow and pulled him aside so he could reach the doorbell. When it rang again, the woman called through the door: "Go away!"

"I'm sorry to trouble you, but we have come all the way from England on a matter of some urgency about Doctor Leveque. I received a message saying he is in terrible danger." Khan had almost said *was in terrible danger*, but he corrected himself at the last moment. That black dress...

"One moment."

Khan and Bertie stood on the front steps for quite a little while, waiting. At first, the Professor thought the woman had gone to fetch a gun, but the delay was much too long for that. Finally, when the door swung open, the woman's cheeks were covered with tears. "What message?"

"Please let me take a moment to introduce myself. My name is Professor Khan. I corresponded with your father often over the last three years and I consider him my friend. This is Bertie Blinkersly, one of my students. We have come all the way from Oxford University to see him."

The woman sniffled. "Well, he never mentioned you to me. Let me see the message."

Professor Khan reluctantly took the folded sheet of paper from his jacket pocket and handed it to her. She glanced at it, then gave it back. "He didn't write that note."

"Certainly not. I should mention that it wasn't delivered in an envelope. It was tied to this."

Professor Khan took the metal arrow from his breast pocket. The young woman stood utterly still, staring at it as if it were a ghost. Finally, she took a long look at Khan and Bertie. It was clear she recognized the arrow, just as it was clear she was not sure what to do.

"Come inside," she said finally.

"Gosh, it's about time," Bertie said. "I thought we were going to be turned away like peddlers."

She led them down a few steps into a sunken living room. The couches were low and flat, almost like beds, and the walls were dominated by more picture windows. How much were university professors paid in the United States?

Professor Khan gripped his hat nervously in both hands. The young woman's eyes were wide and glistening, but she would not look directly at him. Her lips were pressed tightly together. Khan thought she might start crying right in front of them, or pull a gun.

Bertie threw his hat carelessly onto the nearest sofa as though he owned the place. "Is Dr. Leveque at home? We've come an awfully long way to jabber at him."

"This isn't his home," the woman said. "It's mine."

"Oh!" Bertie suddenly seemed utterly flummoxed.

Professor Khan laid a hand on his arm to silence him. "In that case, forgive us for calling at this hour. I'm sure it must have been a shock to open the door and see me standing there."

She drew a cigarette from a case, then returned it unlit. "This is Los Angeles. It's not that late and you aren't that shocking. How long has it been since you saw Dr. Leveque?"

Khan noted the pause before she said the name. "You're Sylvia, aren't you? Anselme's daughter."

She began to drum her fingers irritably on the metal rim of the case. "That's not what I would call an answer to my question, is it?"

"Three years ago," Khan answered. "It was a convention in Salzburg. I thought I had been invited to deliver a paper, but in truth the attendees wanted to gawp at me as if I were a circus performer. Your father was the only one who treated me with respect. We spent several hours in his room that first night enjoying a very fine brandy and discussing the most fascinating topics. He really was the most brilliant theoretical physicist I've ever met."

Sylvia's tone was colorless and flat. "All right, maybe he did mention you. He told me that your letters helped advance his work."

"Pish," the Professor responded uncomfortably. "Tiny suggestions."

"But he didn't write that note," she insisted.

"No," Khan said. "Neither did I, although the handwriting is supposed to resemble my own. Obviously, your father would never use one of my letters to mimic my script, but someone who had access to them must have. That person was anxious for me to come here, to help him."

"Well, he's dead." She tossed the case onto the end table as though it had disappointed her. "I'm sorry to say it so abruptly but the whole thing has been sudden. Everything is sudden. My father is dead."

Bertie took an impulsive step toward her. "You poor old thing—"

She froze him with a glance. "What did you call me?"

"Forgive my student," Professor Khan interjected. "It was not meant unkindly."

"I'd hate to see what he'd say to someone he didn't like. Look, I know you came a long way, but you're too late."

"My dear girl," Professor Khan said gently. "I'm so terribly sorry for the tragedy you've suffered. I wish there was something I could say to ease the loss of a man like your father. Truly, if there's anything I can do, please ask."

Sylvia was quiet a moment as she considered Khan's words. "You're actually a decent sort, aren't you? Boy, have you come to the wrong part of the world."

Professor Khan accepted the compliment with a nod. "I'm sorry to ask, but considering the circumstances, I feel I must. How did it happen? And when?"

Before she could answer, there was a heavy pounding at the front door.

CHAPTER SEVEN

Sylvia looked mildly alarmed for a moment, but she excused herself and slipped into the foyer. Bertie looked at the Professor and said: "Not a bad looker, eh? If she stopped clipping her nails and put a splash of color on them—"

"Pick up your hat, Bertie." The boy had not mentioned Petunia once since the start of their trip, even though she was only an ocean and a continent away. Khan couldn't help but be sharp with him. It was such a short distance!

"Ah. Quite." He stroked the yellow sleeve of his jacket, realizing too late that he was inappropriately dressed.

Professor Khan scanned the room again. There was a well-stocked bar but few bookshelves. Not what he would consider a comfortable home. At the back of the house was a large window that looked onto a deck, a smallish back yard, and the lights of another house on the far side of the fence. It would have been pleasant to sit out on that nice deck and talk in the cool evening breeze.

From out in the entryway, they heard a man's voice, smooth and assured. "Don't worry your pretty head about it, doll. I'm here."

Two men strode into the living room. Both wore dark blue double-breasted suits with wide-brimmed fedoras. The one in the lead was in his early thirties; good-looking the way movie-criminals were, with a pencil mustache and an expression that suggested everything he saw was his for the taking. The crease in his pants looked sharp enough to slice an orange.

The man beside him was shorter, older and fatter, with a pug face and beady, mistrustful eyes. His mouth curled downwards in a contemptuous frown that Khan sensed was a permanent fixture. The hairs on Khan's arms prickled; both had the look of evil men.

They took badges from their jacket pockets. "LAPD Homicide," the younger one said, smiling like a shark. "I'm Detective Waters and my partner is Detective Cross. Who are you?"

Khan answered quickly, before Bertie could open his mouth. "This is Bertie Blinkersly. My name is Professor Khan. We've—"

Waters rolled his eyes. "Off with the mask, wise guy."

Professor Khan grew warm. "It's not a mask. This is my true self."

Waters put his hands on his hips. "You wanna play games with me? Because I play rough."

"Jim," Sylvia cut in. "It's true. He's one of the talking apes you read about in the paper."

"Oh!" Waters's expression became amused for some reason. "Like that crew invaded New York a couple years back. You're one of them?"

The Professor's memory of the invasion was quite different from most, of course, but there was no denying it. "I—"

"I say!" Bertie interjected. "Professor Khan was certainly not one of them. He fought on our side!"

Waters leaned forward even further. Khan was standing a couple of steps below him, giving the detective the illusion of physical supremacy. "Betrayed your own people, eh?"

Cross spit out the word "Traitor," with more venom than Khan had thought possible. Part of him marveled that humans would hold him in contempt because he'd risked his life to protect other humans, but they were going to bully him no matter what.

"So, Mr. Monkey," Waters said. "Where were you four nights ago at about 10:30?"

"Is that the night Anselme was murdered?"

Waters stuck a toothpick in the corner of his mouth. "Who said anything about murder?"

"You're homicide detectives, aren't you?"

Waters jabbed his finger into Khan's lapel. "Don't get cute with me. Where were you?"

"Somewhere near Albany, NY," Khan answered calmly. "We only just arrived in this city about two hours ago. Bertie has our tickets."

"Why, of course!" Bertie stuffed his hand into his jacket.

Detective Cross came forward like a shot, much faster than anyone might have expected from someone his age and shape. He bounded off the top step and bowled into Bertie, striking him across the forehead with a blackjack.

The young man sprawled across the couch, ticket stubs flying into the air like wedding confetti.

"Bertie!" Khan shouted, stepping toward the boy, but Cross was already holding a gun in his other hand, and it was already pointing at the Professor's belly.

Would it be worth taking a slug to tear off Cross's arm? If the detective planned to murder them in cold blood, he didn't see what choice—

"Now now," Waters said. His gun was drawn, too. Khan let his arms fall to the side. "Let's not get all excited. It's just that when my partner here sees someone stuff a hand under a jacket, he gets all anxious. Get it? Your pal there ain't what you call a savvy operator."

Khan looked between them. While Waters talked tough, it was Cross who would murder them both in cold blood and never lose a wink of sleep. "You're correct," Khan said. His voice sounded steadier than he felt. Bertie, his eyes wet and shining, stared up at Cross in astonishment. "He's led a sheltered life, but he's basically good-hearted."

Waters seemed to consider that the way Khan would consider a menu option. Sylvia stepped toward him. "Jim, they have one of my father's arrows."

Detective Waters turned a questioning look at Khan. He didn't wait for the inevitable question. "Someone shot it at me."

Waters rolled his eyes again, then holstered his revolver. He stepped down into the living room like a prizefighter heading into a fixed match. When he was just a few inches from Khan's face, he spoke very quietly.

"*Professor*, huh? Mr. Talking Monkey is a professor? Let me ask you, Monkey: Do you think you're better than me?"

"At what?" the Professor responded.

Bertie sat up, his hand over the growing lump on his head. Cross moved to the side, stepping up one stair for a better look out the window. His pudgy sneer had a tiny twist of confusion. "What the hell is that?"

They all turned to look out the front window. The ocean breezes made the trees shimmer in the faint light, but there was something else, too. Faint figures that seemed to bounce toward them.

The front door crashed open, and an Asian man hopped into the room, his arms stretched out in front of him. His face had the ghastly pallor of death.

"Jiangshi!" Bertie shouted. "By golly, it's a jiangshi!"

The front window shattered as more corpses hopped through.

CHAPTER EIGHT

This was no act, no costume. By their horrifying pallor, the whites of their rolled-back eyes, their slack gaping mouths and protruding black tongues, Professor Khan could see they were dead. It was unmistakable.

The man at the door turned toward them and hopped in their direction, as though his knees were too stiff to bend. Two more men hopped through the broken picture window. Their tongues hung out of their gaping mouths and their bare feet left no blood on the broken glass.

"Hold your breath!" Bertie shouted, his voice high with fear.

Whatever he'd planned to say next was drowned out by Waters. "Stand clear, doll. I'll take care of this. Hey, mutts! Get on the ground! No Chinee is gonna break into a white woman's home when— Get down on the ground!"

The jiangshi, as Bertie called them, did not obey.

Khan knew it was impossible to defeat the dead unless you were properly prepared. "Detectives," he called, "we must withdraw."

Waters spat out an impolite word, but it was Cross who shot first.

No matter how often Professor Khan was exposed to gunfire, he was always startled by the overwhelming sound of it, especially in enclosed spaces. He gently shoved Bertie toward the back of the room. The young man, still unsteady on his feet, stumbled against the sofa and rolled onto his back.

Bertie's eyes were wild with fear, but his cheeks were bulging. He was holding his breath.

The gunfire had already stopped. As Bertie struggled to his feet, Cross bowled into him again, knocking him to the floor. As the detective ran for the door behind the bar, Khan lifted Bertie to his feet and turned back toward the invaders.

Waters had swung open the cylinder of his revolver and shaken the shells onto the carpet, but it was clear he would never reload before the dead men fell upon him. By Jove, there were so many—eight by the Professor's count. All of them hopped toward Waters. The way they bounced reminded him of the figures in a child's music box.

"Nuts!" Waters hissed. "You think a little ghoul makeup is gonna make me soil myself in front of a dame?" He spun the gun around and swung the butt hard against the nearest man.

It struck hard on the front of the skull—a killing blow—but it had no effect on the dead man at all. He grabbed Waters by the shoulders and pulled him close, almost as though they were about to kiss. Another grabbed the detective, then another.

Waters, finally close enough to see—and believe—that the dead men were real, screamed in terror.

Professor Khan took a deep breath and leaped forward. He grabbed hold of the nearest of the jiangshi, the third to grab hold of the detective, and tried to lift him off the ground and throw him.

It wasn't a subtle move, but for all his books, tweed, and professorial bearing, Khan was a mountain gorilla at heart.

Except this time it didn't work. The dead thing he had taken hold of, though he was a slender man of no great height, was as immoveable as a rooted tree.

The lead creature pressed its face near Waters's mouth. Their lips did not touch, but when they were inches away Khan could hear the dead man sucking air.

By Jove, it was breathing in the living man's breath. Worse, the others were leaning close to do the same.

As Khan watched, struggling futilely to break the grip of one of the creatures, Detective Waters of the Homicide Division of the Los Angeles Police Department shriveled up like a leaf in autumn.

The creatures released him and he fell against the carpet, where he broke apart in a pile of bones and dust.

Khan gasped in horror.

The crowd of dead men turned as though noticing him for the first time.

CHAPTER NINE

Luckily, they were slow creatures. Powerful. Undeniable. But not quick.

Khan leapt backward, stumbling against one of those silly flat couches. He grabbed it in both hands and flung it at the creatures.

One, struck at the top of its hop, was knocked backwards. The others paid it no more attention than if he had tapped them with a Norfolk reed.

Khan turned and ran toward the door behind the bar. Bertie! He couldn't return home without Bertie. Lord Blinkersly would be crushed and the Professor... Well, he wasn't sure what would happen to him, but he would certainly lose his position, at minimum.

He found Bertie in the next room, which was an honest-to-goodness library. Professor Khan's footsteps slowed involuntarily as he crossed the room; it was so *comfortable* in here.

Bertie stood beside an open back door, and he looked ready to come apart.

"I spent a year in Peking City as a boy, Professor," he said so quickly that Khan could barely understand him. "I saw jiangshi in their puppet plays and folk tales. I had nightmares for months, sir. Months!"

"How do we defeat them, Bertie?"

"I can't remember!"

"They've killed Detective Waters already."

Bertie pointed through the door into the darkness outside. "The other constable has long fled."

They looked at each other. At once, they said: "Sylvia Leveque!"

CHAPTER TEN

"Get out there, boy," Khan ordered. "Stay downwind of them, but keep them in sight."

He didn't wait to see if Bertie did as he was told. He yanked open the door to the living room and charged inside, not at all sure how he was going to aid his host. One of the jiangshi was nearly at the bar—by Jove, these hungry corpses were an absolute horror. Khan felt his animal nature rising, along with the sudden urge to roar.

He snatched a beautiful crystal decanter off the bar and threw it. The dead man was so close it would have taken honest effort to miss him, but he didn't. The decanter shattered against the jiangshi's forehead with the sound of an orchestra cymbal clash, but the only effect was to soak it in brandy.

It hopped forward, driving Khan back. He couldn't fight these things the way an animal would. Raw ferocity would not do, not against the supernatural.

He saw Sylvia crouching low beside a wooden lamp stand. She, too, was holding her breath, but by the color of her face could not do so for much longer.

If Khan was going to save her, he was going to have to think tactically.

He snatched the nearest barstool and stepped back, almost retreating through the doorway. The feet of the stool were capped in metal, but he wasn't going to defeat this enemy with a bludgeon. He turned the padded seat toward the jiangshi and, when it hopped forward, he struck with all his strength, knocking it fully across the room.

The other creatures turned toward him, and he heard Sylvia gasp for a fresh breath.

The jiangshi all turned back toward her. She took another deep breath and scrabbled away from her hiding place, but they turned toward her as she moved, tracking her.

Khan shouted, then panted several times like... well, like the ape he was. Five of the dead men turned toward him, but the rest continued after his host.

The Professor continued to strike them as they hopped toward him. His incredible strength could not win this rescue on its own, but it was still useful. Within a few seconds, he'd created a path along the wall to reach Sylvia, and he rushed toward her.

"Quickly!" he hissed. This time, all the dead men turned toward him.

Sylvia used the distraction to scramble toward the front door, and he raced after her.

She stopped dead in the doorway, making Khan nearly bowl into her. There was another jiangshi hopping up the front steps toward them.

"Up the stairs," Sylvia ordered, and she bolted around Khan toward the second floor. The Professor wanted to object—retreating upstairs would leave them trapped—but before he could speak she was almost to the first landing. The jiangshi were close behind, and he had to follow or abandon her.

He followed, bounding up the stairs. He supposed he could make a stand at the very top, shoving back the dead men as they jumped at him. As long as his timing was perfect and the dead grew tired before he did.

Was this how Leveque lost his life? Good heavens, how awful.

It was not yet midnight, and he did not think he could fight a tireless enemy until dawn, assuming the dawn would be some sort of deterrent to these creatures.

The key to defeating a supernatural enemy was to know its weakness. Ignorance was death, and Khan had no idea how to win this fight. The jiangshi gained the landing below. Khan braced himself. If only Bertie had told him... No, there was no point in dwelling on that. It was hopeless.

Sylvia emerged from a back bedroom carrying something that looked like a cross between an amateur telescope and a vacuum cleaner. "Out of the way, please. This is even heavier than it looks."

Professor Khan stepped aside, letting Sylvia stand at the top of the stairs. She aimed the device at the landing below—and the undead men coming toward them—and pressed a button on its side.

The device let out a high-pitched shriek; it was quite disturbing, but mercifully short-lived. At the same moment, a pulse of blue light washed over the jiangshi, the stairs, the wall, everything. The shriek faded to nothing, and the indicator light above the on button grew dark.

But there was no effect. The jiangshi were not destroyed, not flung backwards, not anything.

One hopped up the stairs and grabbed hold of the end of Sylvia's device.

CHAPTER ELEVEN

As the dead man landed on the stair, the step slid out from under him. He fell hard against the wood, making the stairs come apart as though they'd been constructed by a child's wooden blocks. The wood didn't splinter or break, but the whole stairwell collapsed like a house of cards. Even the landing slid in several directions at once. The jiangshi recovered quickly, but there was no longer a way to the second floor.

"That was brilliant, my dear! How...?"

Sylvia looked down at the device, lying amid the pile of wood below. "My... It was a prototype. It dissolves metal in a wink, but only metal. That's why the stairs collapsed: no nails. Oh well. It was only good for the one shot, anyway."

"Astonishing," Khan said, staring down at the jiangshi as they milled about below. "Your father was an amazing man. Is there another set of stairs?"

"By the kitchen," Sylvia said, scowling, "but the de-metal pulse will have hit there, too. We'll have to climb out the window onto the front porch. Hey, Professor Khan, is it?"

"It is."

Sylvia's expression was utterly blank, but her bright eyes were wide. "I was in a bad spot there, Professor. They caught me by surprise and if your pal hadn't said what he did about holding my breath, I might have gotten the same treatment as Jim." She shuddered and closed her eyes for a moment.

She seemed reluctant to continue, so Khan prompted her by saying: "Bertie does have his uses."

"But you're the one who came back for me. That means something, and I'm not going to forget it. Come on."

She led him into her bedroom without a moment's hesitation. Professor Khan did his best not to look at the unmade bed or the private things hanging in the closet. Goodness, if it was discovered he'd entered an unmarried woman's bedroom, he might lose his position.

Sylvia threw open her French doors and rushed onto the balcony. The Professor followed happily. He suddenly realized he didn't have the bar stool any longer. When had he set it down? It didn't matter. He certainly wasn't going back for it.

Sylvia looked about uncertainly for a way down but jumping seemed to be the only option. After making sure the jiangshi were not nearby, Khan lowered her onto the lawn. He climbed down the support post and they ran for the iron gate.

Beside the parked cars, they came upon Detective Cross, gun drawn, standing over a man kneeling in the gravel. There was an old canvas satchel beside him. The prisoner had his hands behind his head, and he was pleading for his life.

"I swear, none of this is my fault!"

"Tell that to my partner!" Cross shouted, then he let loose a string of invectives that nearly made Professor Khan trip.

"Wait!" Khan shouted, hurrying forward and waving his arms. The idea that the old detective would add more violence to what they'd just witnessed make the Professor queasy. Cross did not squeeze the trigger, although he didn't turn his weapon away from the back of the man's head. "Detective, please don't shoot!"

When the man saw the Professor racing toward him, his eyes went wide and all the strength seemed to go out of him. "Ho no," he said in a breathless whine. "I've died and gone to hell. I never would have quit drinking if I'd known I was going to hell anyway."

"Cross, put it away," Sylvia barked with authority. "You! What's your name?"

The prisoner looked up at her. He was a middle-aged Chinese man, his hair thinning at the front, his nose crooked from a long-ago injury. "Jameson Lee."

"Mr. Lee," Sylvia said, her tone soothing. "Now, how did all this happen?"

"I swear, none of this is my fault!" Jameson blurted out, in exactly the same tone as before. He looked to the side as though he wanted to see if Detective Cross was still holding a gun on him but was too nervous to turn all the way around.

"We believe you," Sylvia said. "But we need to know what happened."

"There was an accident," Jameson said. "Men died. I was supposed to be getting their bodies ready to ship home, when..."

Jameson glanced over at Professor Khan and stopped talking. He just stared in stunned silence.

"Mr. Lee. Jameson!" Sylvia said sharply. He snapped out of it.

"They're jiangshi now! Hungry dead! Mary and Joseph, they just rose up and started hopping around! But I swear I didn't cause this."

Professor Khan kept his voice low. Considering the adrenaline running through his body, it took an effort. "Tell us who did."

"In the satchel," he answered. "I'm not going to take it out because he'll shoot me, but it's in the satchel."

Sylvia was closest. She threw back the cover and looked inside. Jameson said: "Whoever shot that. That's who's responsible."

Sylvia drew a metal arrow from the satchel. It was identical to the one that had been shot at Khan.

CHAPTER TWELVE

Professor Khan knelt in front of Jameson. "How do we defeat the jiangshi, my good man?"

"I don't know!" Jameson's eyes were welling up with tears. "They're just children's stories!"

"If you insist. Mr. Lee, how were they defeated in those children's stories? Mr. Lee? Tell us what we can do to put them to rest again."

"I don't know! I—wait!" Jameson finally said. "Peachwood. You need to stab them with a peachwood sword."

"And how many are there?"

"Eleven," he answered, his voice bitter.

Khan turned back to the house, staring at the broken front door. Sylvia came near him.

"What are you doing in this neighborhood at all?" Cross snapped at Jameson. "Why aren't you stacking your corpses in Chinatown where you belong?"

Jameson answered through clenched teeth. "You kicked us out of Chinatown to build your damn train station."

Cross's voice turned to a hiss. "You shoulda gone all the way back to China."

"Pasadena, you mean."

"Detective," Sylvia said sharply, "can we have a moment here?" She turned back to Khan. "I'm sorry to say, Professor, that I don't have a stick of peach-wood furniture in the house."

"Hm? Oh, no, I suppose not. The creatures seemed to be drawn to noise and breath, haven't you noticed?"

"I suppose I have. What of it?"

"So where are they?"

"My God," Sylvia said. "They must be moving through the neighborhood. We're going to have to stop them. Somehow." She turned to Detective Cross. "Detective, we're going to need your help."

Cross answered out of the side of his flabby mouth. "Forget it. Jim Waters is dead. I'm gonna do something about that, but I gotta find out who unleashed these things, not fight them myself. I ain't suicidal."

"Jameson? You're the closest thing we have to an expert."

"I'm not suicidal either!" Jameson exclaimed. "I'm a veterinarian. If you want someone to fight monsters, you should get a monster." He waved vaguely in Khan's direction.

"I guess we're on our own, Professor."

"Apparently so." Professor Khan started back up the front stair. The door was still lying on its side in the foyer.

The house appeared empty. They hurried into the living room. Wooden moldings lay scattered on the floor where they had fallen from the walls. Water ran from under a door and all of the lights had gone dark. No metal, the Professor realized.

The window at the back of the house had been shattered outward. A woman's scream came from somewhere nearby, and when they hurried to the broken window, they saw the back fence had been knocked down.

"Mrs. Flewellyn!" Sylvia stepped through the broken window and ran across the deck, heedless of the danger. Professor Khan almost called to her to wait: without shoes, he couldn't follow. He ran through the library out the door he'd told Bertie to use.

Sylvia was in sight but not close enough that he could help her if she needed it. He raced forward, letting himself go on all fours to catch up. She crossed the flattened fence into the other yard, then began jumping and waving her arms.

There was an old woman in the upstairs window, frantically going through some kind of cabinet. Khan quickly noted the back door had been smashed in. Where was Bertie?

Sylvia spun toward him. "Professor, we have to get up to—"

Khan was already ahead of her. He raced toward the edge of the porch, knitted his fingers together and bent low for Sylvia to step onto his hands. She did, and he practically flung her up onto the little back roof. Sylvia gasped in surprise at his strength but she managed to keep her balance. A moment later, the old woman practically screamed.

The gutter above didn't look like it could hold his weight, so Professor Khan hurried to an oak tree growing by the side of the house.

He heard the sound of a window rattling open. "My goodness, Sylvia! What are you doing on my roof?"

"SSHH! Mrs. Flewellyn, come on. We can get out through here."

"Psh! I'm not going to be run out of my house by some damn Chinamen. Not with Emmaleen here. Somewhere."

"Mrs. Flewellyn!"

"Oh, Sylvia, I wish I'd had a chance to say how sorry I am about your daddy. I saw him do it, you know."

When Sylvia answered, her voice was very small. "You saw—?"

"Not deliberately. My window looks right up to yours, you know. I saw what he did to himself. Terrible. And the men with him didn't even try to stop him!"

Khan had finally gained the porch roof. He crossed toward the window, feeling the structure bow under his considerable weight. The inside of the Flewellyn home was a clutter of lights, light stands, and photography equipment.

"What men?" Sylvia said in that same strange little voice.

"We can discuss that," Khan said, "when your neighbor is safely away from here."

Mrs. Flewellyn took one look at Professor Khan and screamed at the top of her lungs. Her shriek was high and loud enough to rouse everyone in a half mile, living or dead. She staggered back, half-tripping over a camera tripod and falling against the armoire; it banged loudly against the wall.

"Mrs. Flewellyn!" Sylvia hissed. "They'll hear you!"

But the old woman had something else in mind. Possessed by a sudden idea, she swung the armoire door open and jammed her hand deep into the pocket of the bathrobe hanging inside. When she turned around, she held a gigantic revolver in her trembling hand.

Sylvia stepped in front of Khan, her hands raised. "No!"

Khan had a powerful urge to grab Sylvia's shoulders and move her away. It wasn't right for him to use another person as a shield but he couldn't just grab this woman and shove her aside.

The old woman didn't point the weapon at them. Instead, she bared her yellow teeth. "You and your... friend don't have anything to fear from me, Sylvia. Now excuse me while Emmaleen and I clear my house of intruders."

"Please, Mrs. Flewellyn. That won't work."

The old woman scowled at her as she reached for the doorknob. "Psh. It's loaded."

Khan's voice was low and calm. "There's nothing we can do. We can't force her to let us help her."

Sylvia laid her hands in the open window sill. "Mrs. Flewellyn, who was there with my father when he killed himself?"

The old woman frowned. This was a question she couldn't ignore. "One was just a silhouette, you understand, but I saw the other pretty clearly. He was a sharpie in a black shirt and red suit. That's all. Come around tomorrow and I'll give you a photo of him."

She backed toward the door. Sylvia opened her mouth but Mrs. Flewellyn wouldn't let her speak. "I've always considered you a good neighbor, dear—" She pointed the gun at Professor Khan. "—until you started climbing on my house like a burglar. Get yourself home and call the police if you want, but if you sic your pet on me, I'm going to shoot it." She yanked open the door and stepped into the hall. Her revolver boomed inside the house.

Khan grabbed Sylvia around the waist and carried her toward the old oak and safety.

CHAPTER THIRTEEN

Bertie didn't think it was fair at all. It was jolly good for Professor Khan to be brave; he was a gorilla, after all. It was in his nature to challenge death and all that rot.

But Bertie was just a regular fellow—actually, not even all that regular, when it came to the bravery department. How many hours had he hidden in his boarding school's air duct when Arsfield Peck had come looking for him? Enough that he began bringing his homework with him just to have something to do. And what had Daddy, who had been a war hero, probably, done when he'd found out that Bertie hid from the playmates Nanny corralled for him? He'd made the Disappointment Face.

He had steeled himself to risk the American frontier, with its Tommy-gun-wielding rum runners and hordes of wild Red Indians, but nothing had prepared him to come face to face with the hopping dead nightmares of his childhood.

Surely, Professor Khan *expected* him to be crouching here among these low trees, feeling the smoggy, salty breeze on his face while he watched the jiangshi hop out of the old woman's house in search of someone new to clutch at. Someone like him.

Where was the Professor, anyway? Bertie would much rather have been standing behind him than this bit of shrubbery. The Professor had *fangs* for goodness sakes. Or perhaps that Detective Cross person; there was a certain comfort to be taken from the notion that the chaps in your circle were capable of sudden violence.

The ghosts moved downhill toward the city lights. Had their numbers grown?

He had been planning to stay hidden until dawn, but firelight flickered inside the house the jiangshi had just left, and Professor Khan came around the side and bounded up the front steps. Bertie had been content to let his teacher explore the house on his own, but then he saw that Leveque woman running close behind him, directly into the burning building as bold as anything.

Well, sod all this hiding then. If that little blonde thing could risk her life, he and his shame could take the odd chance or two. He slid down the hill out of his hiding place and ran toward the front of the house.

He had just reached the top of the front steps when his teacher charged out, almost bowling him over. "Lost!" the Professor exclaimed. "The fire is already beyond us and the photograph is lost."

Sylvia rushed out just behind him. "It's the developing chemicals. We have to get away before it gets worse."

"But the picture!"

"It doesn't matter," Sylvia insisted. "Come on."

Bertie happily followed them away from the house. He wasn't sure about this bally picture the Professor was so concerned about, but it must have been pretty important if he went into a burning building for it. "I say, Professor, but it's a good thing that house was empty, eh?"

"I wish it had been," Professor Khan said. "Where did they go?"

Bertie knew the answer to this. He pointed downhill toward the city. Sylvia and Khan raced off after them, and Bertie did his best to keep pace. Events were moving at a jolly good clip. He wasn't accustomed to so much hurrying about; it felt vaguely obscene to run away from a burning house with a dead bloke inside. They ought to have loitered about a bit, telling each other it was a terrible tragedy.

But... no. Of course that was wrong. More lives were in peril, and Something Had To Be Done.

They hurried down the road, rounding a curve that left the wooded hills behind them and displayed the lights of West Hollywood below them. By golly, it was ugly. Vibrant and ugly as sin.

"There!" the Professor called.

The jiangshi were much farther along than Bertie had expected. They had almost reached the parking lot of a nightclub at the bottom of the hill. "We'll never catch up to them in time!"

A long black car screeched to a halt beside them, and for one absurd moment Bertie was convinced a jiangshi was going to run them all down. But no, it was only Detective Cross, his pale, flabby face greenish from the dashboard lights. Somewhere he had acquired a Chinese fellow to ride in the back.

"Where are they?" Cross barked.

Khan leapt onto the driver's side running board. "Down there! They're about to enter that building. Get me down there quickly!"

"No," was all Cross said.

If outrage was part of the visible spectrum, Professor Khan would have struck them all blind. "What do you mean, *No?*"

"That's Whispering Sally's down there. If those dead men want to ease their hunger, that's the place for it."

"How can you say such a thing?" Khan's fangs were bared, purely unintentionally, Bertie was sure.

"I ain't risking my life for anyone, least of all those freaks down there."

The Professor was utterly baffled. He looked to Bertie—as though he would have any answers—then to Sylvia.

"Professor," she said hesitantly, "have you heard of the Pansy Craze?"

"No. What does it signify?"

Sylvia shuffled her feet as she spoke. "It's the latest nightclub fashion out of New York. You know, female impersonators on stage, waiters wearing eye shadow. See the parking lot to that club? There's a wall around the parking lot of hide the license plates of the cars parked inside, and those low trees..."

"Perverts," Cross said, "deviants. If the dead men weren't already heading there, I would have pointed the way. Let those freaks—"

The Professor roared and yanked the driver's door open. Bertie felt goose bumps run up and down his body, and his guts felt watery. Khan yanked the detective from the driver's seat and dropped him in the street, then climbed behind the wheel.

"Bertie!" he snapped. "Let's go!"

Bertie wasn't sure what to do. Everyone was looking at him; did he really want them to see him hurry toward a hotspot full of pansies? Not that he wasn't a man of the world, but—

"Bertie!"

He hopped onto the passenger side running board, and Sylvia leapt on just behind him. At least this time he was rushing toward danger slightly ahead of the gal.

Cross stood in the street, his suit rumpled, his fists balled up at his side, as the car raced off. The look in his eyes was murderous.

CHAPTER FOURTEEN

Khan hated to drive. Cars were not designed to accommodate the proportions of a mountain gorilla. He had to slide his bottom all the way forward to reach the pedals with his long toes, which meant that the steering wheel rubbed against his prominent belly and his kilt rode embarrassingly high on his thighs. No matter. No matter. He had to stay focused.

Bertie stuck his long face through the passenger window. "Professor, we haven't really abducted a police car, have we?"

Oops. It seemed that he had. He glanced at Bertie and decided not to respond. He couldn't think about that now. Not now.

The jiangshi had nearly reached the parking lot—two young men in matching white shirts were already fleeing from them. Khan could see a fire exit along the side of the building. That's where they were headed. He pressed the accelerator.

"I wish you guys had left me behind," came a voice from the back seat. Khan glanced into the rear view, but the angle didn't let him see Jameson.

They were almost at the front door. Khan had to look down to see the brake, and despite the panicky way Bertie cried out his name, he did a fair job of bringing the vehicle to a screeching halt near the front of the entrance.

As Khan hopped out of the car, the bouncer at the door—a big man with a face like a steam locomotive—looked him over. "Oh, tonight is going to be a rare one. Get in line with the rest, fella."

He held out his hands to block the doorway, but Khan lifted him bodily off the ground and spun him, never breaking stride, as he rushed into the lobby and coat check area.

"You're in danger!" Sylvia was saying. "There are men coming to attack you!"

The slender, balding man in the coat check drew a meat cleaver from behind his desk, and the maitre' d moved close to his podium. A tall, dapper man in a broad-shouldered suit looked the three of them up and down. "No, there isn't. What kind of clown show is this?"

These people were wasting his time. Khan dropped the bouncer onto his feet, letting him fall back against a cushy red velvet couch, then bulled through to the entrance.

The room was not as spacious as he'd imagined from outside. There were roulette wheels along the back and a bar along one wall. Small round tables filled the room up to the smallish orchestra pit, which held about ten musicians. On the stage was a slender figure in a blinding white gown, complete with silver spangles and long white feathers.

The man—of course it was a man in that gown, Sylvia had told him as much—faltered mid-note at the sight of him. Khan took advantage of the momentary silence to shout: "Danger! You're all in danger from—"

Sylvia grabbed his arm and shook it. "Professor, no! You can't tell them the truth, they'll never believe it."

For a moment, Khan was flummoxed. Was he supposed to lie to them? He always thought it was best for people to operate with as much accurate knowledge as possible. It seemed like a betrayal to lie.

The tall man in the excellent suit appeared beside him, a pistol in hand. Before he could speak, there was a series of thunderous bangs on the fire exit door beside the bar.

"Gangsters!" Bertie suddenly shouted, for no reason Khan could figure out. "Rum-running gangster assassins are coming!"

The metal side door suddenly buckled, and jiangshi streamed inside. Panic broke out as people leaped screaming from their seats and rushed toward the exits. The man with the pistol turned toward the commotion.

"No!" Khan barked, holding the man back.

"This is my place! If I don't defend it—"

"Look at what they're doing! Look!" Four people had already been caught by the jiangshi and were being drained. "Bullets are useless here! You must help people evacuate!"

He did, and so did Sylvia and Bertie. Professor Khan stood in front of the empty coat check window and snarled at anyone who tried to retrieve their things.

"But my name is in the lining!" one middle aged man pleaded. "People will know!" A waiter dragged him outside.

The last of them made their way out just ahead of a trio of hopping corpses. The owner fired off a few rounds into the belly of the nearest corpse, but he wasn't surprised when it didn't work.

Sylvia and Bertie were already outside. Khan and the owner were the last. They slammed the entrance shut.

Patrons fled in every direction on foot. Three waiters stood beside the parking lot, turning away anyone trying to reach their cars. The other employees had gathered in the corner of the lot beneath the shelter of the trees.

"Bill!" one of them cried as Khan and the owner approached. "Tristan is still inside."

"Who is Tristan?" Khan snapped.

"Our main attraction," Bill answered. "But we can't go in after him until we know how to fight these things."

"Peachwood," Professor Khan said. "We need to find peachwood weapons somewhere."

"Peachwood?" Bill responded. He waved his arm at the long row of low trees lining the parking lot. "You mean like this row of peach trees here?"

"Let me fashion a spear—" Professor Khan said, but the others had already gotten in his way.

"This is our place," one of the waiters said. "We can defend it ourselves." They began hacking branches off the tree, sharpening them into stakes.

Khan backed away. It wasn't his place to step between them and danger. Besides, if someone was still inside, there wasn't time to make weapons. "Bertie, see to Jameson. I'll check on your singer."

Bill said: "Right behind you, Mr. Ape," as Khan raced across the lot toward the broken fire door.

CHAPTER FIFTEEN

There was no pounding at the front door when Khan approached. He was glad. That meant the dead men were still together. Unfortunately, it also meant all of them were after Tristan.

The singer stood near the edge of the orchestra pit, holding a long, narrow mirror. As he turned it from one jiangshi to another, the creatures reeled back in fear and horror. It was a good strategy, but it wouldn't protect him for much longer. The dead men were pressing him close.

"Tristan!" Khan shouted. "Hold your breath!"

Khan saw him gulp down a lungful of air just as one of the creatures smashed the mirror out of his hands. The singer dropped low and rolled across the stage, landing quietly among the instruments of the orchestra pit.

Khan breathed loudly, hooting and making as much noise as possible. He climbed onto the bar and heaved a full bottle of vodka at the jiangshi nearest Tristan. His plan, if it even deserved the name, was to distract the creatures from the singer until the cavalry arrived with their impromptu peachwood weapons.

The dead men turned toward him. Not all of them, but most. If he could only catch the attention of the others—

A hand gripped his ankle. Khan spun. The bartender lay dead behind the bar, and a jiangshi had come up behind the Professor and caught him by the ankle. By Jove, just the thing's touch seemed to steal his life away, filling him with despair and exhaustion. The creature yanked him off the top of the bar.

In desperation, Khan threw his body toward the wall of drinks behind the bar. As the jiangshi leaned its face close to his, it saw its own reflection bar mirror and staggered back, releasing its grip.

There were only seconds for Khan to make use of his reprieve. He leaped onto the bar again, fighting the inexplicable urge to surrender—the creature's magic was powerful and terrible—and slid across out of its reach. The singer was being trailed by three of them as he made his way through the pit to the side of the stage. Khan didn't dare try to follow him; that would only trap him amidst the dead men. Instead, he circled around toward the stage. It seemed that Tristan was headed that way himself, and it would probably be best if the jiangshi had their backs to the door when the staff finally charged through with their weapons.

My God, there were so many bodies.

Khan pushed his way through the overturned chairs and tables, not worrying about the amount of noise he made. Leaping onto the stage, he stamped on the hollow floorboards. He wanted to draw the last three creatures from the singer, but it didn't seem to be working.

The jiangshi were close, and Khan had no weapons at hand. As he backed away from the dead men, he felt something brush against his back and he cried out in raw terror. Damned embarrassing, but it was just the edge of the stage curtain.

The singer had found a ladder set into the wall, and begun to climb it. What a damned fine idea. Khan grabbed the cloth as high as he could, then gripped it hard with his feet. Hand over hand, he climbed up the side of the curtain, feeling his weight straining the heavy cloth.

He was out of reach of the dead men just in time, but he kept climbing. He needed to reach a balcony or something. The jiangshi were not intelligent, but they might tear down the curtain in their attempts to get at him.

Then again, they might not have to; he could hear the cloth tearing above. A sudden image of himself lying broken-backed and helpless on the stage below while the jiangshi drained his life spurred him to climb faster.

The curtain hung from a long metal rod covered with pulleys and ropes. Khan held on carefully. He glanced over at Tristan; the singer had climbed higher on the ladder, and the jiangshi with their stiff limbs obviously found it too difficult to follow.

But they had begun to shake the ladder, breaking it out of the concrete wall. Tristan had wrapped his arms through one of the rungs and was holding on as best he could amid the showers of concrete dust and twisting metal, but when the last bolt pulled free, he would plunge to the nightclub floor and die.

Khan shimmied along the curtain rod. The singer was not far away, but he still had no way to reach him. Where were the damn club employees? How did the mirror drive away the jiangshi if they tracked people by sound and their breath? The basic irrationality of the supernatural was a damned irritating thing.

Tristan cried out as the ladder jolted from the wall. That was it. It couldn't take many more jolts like that.

Khan took hold of one of the curtain ropes. He couldn't see what it was attached to or how it was anchored and there wasn't time to check. "Hey!" he shouted, as he kicked away from the ceiling.

CHAPTER SIXTEEN

At first the rope seemed to spool out as though it wasn't anchored at all and the Professor thought he'd doomed them both. Then something caught and he began to swing outward as well as down.

Tristan's ladder tore free from the wall and he began to lean away from the wall. For a moment, Khan was sure he had mistimed everything, but the singer reached out as Khan reached down, and they caught hold of each other, wrist to wrist.

The ladder crashed to the floor with a tremendous noise, while Khan continued to swing out over the club. The rope slowly spooled out, which meant they would be within reach of the creatures on their backswing. Khan lifted the singer up so he could wrap his arms around the Professor's neck. He smelled pleasantly of lilacs and rose water.

Then they began to swing back toward the stage, too low, too low. Most of the jiangshi had leapt into the pit after them, but there was one on the stage. Khan shouted, raising his right leg and struck the dead man with all his weight and strength just as it hopped toward him, knocking it high through the air and slamming it against the wall.

"HAH!" The shout echoed through the room. It was the voice of many men but it did not sound like a cheer for the Professor's mighty, bone-jarring kick.

Out on the nightclub floor, the employees had formed an orderly square, the front rank holding trash can lids as shields and the rear ranks holding long, crudely-sharpened spears over their shoulders.

The phalanx advanced down the center of the club. The Professor clamped his hand over Tristan's nose and mouth and they crouched together at the edge of the stage.

The jiangshi advanced on the employees, but strong as they were they had no chance at all against that formation.

After, in the parking lot, Professor Khan sought out Bertie. Jameson and Sylvia were with him. "Detective Cross took his car back," Bertie said. "He just got in and drove off without a word."

"Better than arresting us, I guess."

"Rather!"

Bill emerged from the side of the club, with Tristan and a few others close behind. Professor Khan nodded to him. "That was an impressive phalanx you organized in there."

"Thanks," he answered coolly. "The ancient Greeks have long been an interest of mine."

"Ah," Khan said. "Quite."

"Listen here, Mr. Ape. Did you create those things? Or bring them down on my place?"

"No!" Bertie and Sylvia exclaimed almost in unison. Their genuine surprise seemed to convince Bill, but the Professor still added: "No, sir, I did not."

Bill nodded and stuck out his hand. Khan shook it. "Then get out of here before the cops show."

"We will, thank you. Er, if you please, don't damage those dead men more than they have to be." They both glanced at Jameson, who seemed almost in a trance. "It's not their fault they were raised up, and they have families."

"I was just getting their bodies ready," Jameson said, as though talking to a ghost beside him. "That arrow struck the lock off the kennel and Sir Barks got loose. He started chasing this pregnant black cat, who jumped over the table and... and..."

"Sssshhhh," Sylvia said. "It's over now."

Bill rubbed his chin. "All right. I'll see to it. Mr. Ape, any time you come into one of my clubs, the drinks are on me."

Bill waved at Jameson as though he was a spill that needed cleaning. Two men took hold of him and led him into the club.

Tristan laid a hand on Professor Khan's forearm, and the expression on his face was intense. "Thank you," he said quietly, then ran back into the club.

Sylvia began to fuss at her hair in the side view mirror of the nearest car. "Well," she said without looking at them, "you two sure know how to spice up a girl's life."

CHAPTER SEVENTEEN

Professor Khan and Bertie followed Sylvia through an alley, up a flight of stairs, across a darkened back yard and into the side yard of her house. Mrs. Flewellyn's house was fully ablaze by now, as was the oak that Khan had climbed onto the roof of her back porch, but they could hear sirens approaching. Better to get farther away while they still could.

Detective Cross had parked his car to block theirs in, and he waited for them on the front steps. It was a tense few moments, but Sylvia convinced everyone the best thing would be to go to her father's house where they could clean up and talk for real. Cross agreed.

If the homicide detective was sore about being dragged out of his car, he was saving his payback for later.

Dr. Leveque's home was way out in Malibu, situated at the end of a rocky spit of land. They parked in a concrete shelter that shielded the vehicles from the spray of the waves.

The house itself was octagonal and made mostly of glass. By the security lights, they could see the walls had been painted the color of pink cake frosting, and the roof was slanted like the lid of a hatbox that wasn't on all the way.

There were two cars already parked in the enclosure. One was a rather fancy black Bentley. The other was a modest white coupe with a middle-aged man in a fedora behind the wheel. He stared through the windscreen at nothing while Sylvia and the others milled around him, showing no reaction to anyone else's presence. Only the occasional blink of the eyes proved he had any life in him at all.

Sylvia frowned at him, then stalked to the house. The front door was ajar, and she breezed inside. Khan kept close to her, just in case, but there was no reason to worry for her safety. The only person they found in the house was a curvaceous young woman who couldn't have been more than twenty-two, her lips painted bright red and her hair fixed into tight platinum curls.

Upon seeing Sylvia, she looked uncomfortable enough to jump out of her skin. "I only came by to get my things."

Sylvia just stared at her without answering. The woman draped a fox stole over her arm, snatched her purse from the top of the bar and, as she spun toward the door, a heavy gold cigarette lighter fell out of it onto the floor.

They stared down at it in silence. The young woman wrung her purse in both hands as though trying to strangle her embarrassment. "Antsy said I could keep that," she said. "It was a gift, but last time I was here I forgot—"

"Take it and go," Sylvia snapped. "Leave the key."

The young woman stooped and stuffed the lighter into her purse. As she hurried to the door, she set a tiny key ring on the telephone table. She turned her head as though she was about to look over her shoulder, but didn't dare. "I'm real sorry," she said. Her heels tapped against the tile floor as she retreated through the door.

Bertie followed her and shut the door, watching her through the window. A few moments later, the coupe roared away from the house.

"I say," Bertie murmured. "What an enticing creature."

"Come in and sit down," Sylvia ordered. They did, even Cross. The center of the room was dominated by two semicircular couches and a glass disk that passed for a coffee table. Sylvia went to the bar while they tried to make themselves comfortable. "Drinks?"

"Bourbon," Cross said.

"I say," Bertie said, sounding more enthused than he should have. "A gin and tonic would be gorgeous right now. With a twist of lime."

Sylvia looked at him with an utterly flat expression. "There are no old ladies living here, so there's no gin."

Professor Khan cleared his throat. "I'll have whatever you're having."

"Quite," Bertie agreed.

She brought them sour mash whiskey on ice. Khan took a polite sip and set his down, while Bertie seemed unwilling even to touch his glass to his lips.

Sylvia sat across from Detective Cross, the two of them clashed their glasses together and took sizable gulps.

"God," Sylvia said, pressing the cold glass to her forehead. "I don't even know where to start."

"We start with the local civic authority," Khan said. "Detective Cross, do you plan to charge us with a crime or imprison us?"

The fat little detective swirled the contents of his glass, then gulped down the remainder. "Not at this particular time, no."

Sylvia stood. "That answer earns you a refill."

"But you will have to talk to all of us in an official capacity once the authorities discover the damaged fence in Mrs. Flewellyn's back yard, the broken windows in Sylvia's home, and your partner's body."

"There is no body in Sylvia Leveque's home." Cross accepted a refilled glass. "Detective Waters's current location is unknown and will remain that way. For now."

Sylvia dropped into her chair. "I assume that will cost me."

Cross looked around the room. "Yes. But not as much as you think. I wouldn't have these gray hairs if I didn't have a light touch."

"So then," Professor Khan said, "someone shot an arrow with a message tied to it to bring me here, and someone shot an arrow that raised the dead— or caused a chain of events that raised them—and those dead men nearly killed us. Both arrows, on superficial examination, appear to be the same."

"They are," Sylvia answered.

"Did your father create them?" Khan asked. Sylvia stared down into her drink without answering. "I assume there's a bow, somewhere, yes? Is there more than one?"

"No," Sylvia said. "Just the one."

"And you don't have it."

"No, I don't. It was stolen the night my father committed... The night he shot himself."

Detective Cross spoke up. "You think someone forced your father to off himself."

"No." Sylvia still wouldn't look at them. "Yes. Yes, I do think that."

Professor Khan rubbed his face. "The so-called sharpie in a red suit! And Mrs. Flewellyn snapped a picture of him, too. If only she had given it to us before the fire started."

"I don't need any damn picture," Sylvia said. "A sharpie in a red suit? I know exactly who that is."

CHAPTER EIGHTEEN

201 YEARS EARLIER

Enshu Kiku had never imagined the wind could sound like this. Windstorms had ripped through his valley many times, tearing down trees and destroying crops, but on the open ocean, with nothing to deflect it but the towering waves, it sounded like the whole world was *screaming*.

He gripped the railing and struggled toward the back of the boat. *Aft*. That's what it was called. The waves, rain, and wind threatened to pitch him into the ink dark waters, but he kept his feet on the rolling deck and his swords snug against his hips. Enshu might have been a samurai, descended from a long line of warriors renowned for their faithful service, but these were modern times. He was nothing more than a bureaucrat. Still, he must not falter.

The captain was little more than a silhouette against a slightly darker storm. "We must turn toward land!" Enshu shouted.

"Thank you for your expert opinion!" Captain Higoshi shouted back. "For the moment, I will keep the bow pointed into the waves. I can not..."

Whatever else he said was carried away by the screaming wind. Enshu was certain he was better off not hearing it. He wasn't really in the mood for sarcasm. "Of course we must do as you think best, but I would feel better if we could be closer to dry land."

"We're safer here at sea!" Higoshi roared. "We'll be blown a little off course, but it's easy to find yourself after you get lost. Much harder to revive yourself after you've drowned. Don't worry about your rice cargo!" Enshu almost struck the man; he didn't care one bit about the rice. His wife and daughters were below. The captain's shouts didn't give him a chance to speak. "This is a good ship! She's been through worse storms than this—not many, but some. As long as the sails are tied—"

His next words were suddenly cut off. Along with the screaming of the wind, there was a new sound, like the flapping wings of a huge and terrible bird. Terror made Enshu's whole body freeze up—what monstrous beast lived inside this storm?—when a flash of lightning lit up the ship.

There was no giant bird. The sail had come loose, and the wind was tearing at it.

He was seized by a sudden panic. This could capsize the ship. Sailors began to shout to each other as they moved along the deck, and as Enshu stepped toward the captain, he heard a man shout that the lines had been cut.

The samurai leaned out and took hold of the wheel, feeling the rope looped around one of the spokes. Why hadn't the captain responded to the loosed sail? He'd never known the man to be shy about shouting orders.

There was another flash of lightning and Enshu, holding onto the shuddering wheel, found himself a hand-width's away from the captain's dead face. For one absurd moment, it seemed that Higoshi had decided to play a prank on him, sticking out his tongue and making his eyes bulge at the exact moment of the flash. But no, he was dead. Jutting from the center of his chest was a metal shaft.

Enshu grabbed hold of the weapon, and a sudden wave made the entire ship rock. He felt the captain fall away from the weapon and by the dim light—what was that light? Lightning had set the crow's nest above them aflame—he could see the wheel straining at the ropes that held it in place.

The first mate rushed out of the darkness, taking hold of the wheel and correcting their course so they met the next wave head on. His expression was wild and terrified.

Doom. They were all doomed.

Metal shaft in his hand, Enshu made his way back to midship. His wife and five daughters had been given a small space beside the crew's quarters, and he kicked open the hatch and practically fell down the rolling ladder. The fire in the crow's nest, far from being doused by the rain, seemed to have grown in intensity.

A lit oil lantern swung wildly from the ceiling. It was foolish to keep it lit in these seas, but he couldn't deny that he was grateful for the light. His wife clutched at his arms and helped him to his knees. "What is happening?" she demanded. He had never heard her sound so frightened in her life, but she still sounded a thousand times braver than he felt.

"The captain has been killed, the sails are—"

A wave struck the port side of the ship, throwing them all off their feet. His daughters screamed in terror. The youngest was only six, the oldest thirteen—none of them had had the decency to be born sons, but his love for them was more fearsome than any storm in the world.

"Listen to me!" he shouted. "Listen! We will all survive this night. Do you hear? You will all grow up, and you will marry honorable men! I will personally present these three hundred year old swords to one of your sons! This I promise you!"

"We tied ourselves together, father," his eldest said, and he saw that it was true. They'd knotted a long coil of rope around all of their waists.

He grabbed the end of the rope hanging from the knot around his wife's torso. "Yes!" he cried. "All of us together!"

But before he could loop it around himself, a jagged black rock burst through the starboard side of the ship, battering him with broken planks. The oil lamp went out, plunging them all into darkness.

The whole world seemed to roll over and tear itself apart, and Enshu felt the icy waters engulf him.

CHAPTER NINETEEN

"Come on, before I get too drunk."

Sylvia stood and led them through a sturdy metal door. The gleaming steel stairs were cold against Professor Khan's feet, but they weren't the cause of his goosebumps. He was about to see Anselme Leveque's private laboratory.

"Don't touch anything," was the first thing Sylvia said. She flipped a switch as they came through the basement doorway, filling the room with bright, but indirect, light. She gestured toward the half-dozen work benches lined up like schoolroom desks; they were covered with odd equipment, most in a state of disrepair. "I don't say that because I'm afraid you'll damage something or ruin an experiment. Some of this equipment has live current running through it and some has fragile shielding over radioactive elements."

Detective Cross stopped in the middle of the room. "This don't sound safe for regular folks."

"It's a work room for my father and myself," Sylvia responded. "It wasn't designed for tour groups."

Professor Khan caught Bertie by the wrist just as he was about to push a large green button, then guided the young man's hand into his own pocket. "What have you brought us here to see?"

"This way." Sylvia led them to two rows of movie theater seats. As they settled in—Khan took command of a loveseat against the wall that would accommodate his frame—she pulled down the screen and began to set up a projector. "Father wanted to demonstrate this invention in Geneva next October, but his health... His doctors didn't want him to risk a long journey. So he prepared this presentation."

She flipped on the projector, and a brief countdown, Anselme Leveque appeared on the screen.

He looked much like Khan remembered him: trim, white-haired, with a pointed little beard. The film was black and white, of course, but his suit was so dark it could only be black. He had dark circles under his eyes that had not been there before, and he didn't have the same chipper energy that had made him so charismatic back in Salzburg.

"Gentlemen!" Leveque said. "I am sorry I can not make this presentation in person, but I—and my invention—do not travel well. Therefore, I am forced to make this presentation far removed from my respected peers and colleagues. Well, let's not waste time. As I promised some years ago, my research into thought radiation suggested practical applications that even I had not anticipated. I present to you the Improbability Bow."

Professor Khan leaned forward to peer at the screen. Leveque stepped aside to reveal his invention: it was tall—taller than he was—a piece of metal curved like an English longbow. The bottom was mounted immovably onto a broad gleaming base shaped like the oversized shoe of a clown. The lower limb of the bow was connected by bundles of cables and braces to a box of flashing lights on the front part of the base. Set into the front of the bow was some sort of crystal.

"As you can see," Leveque said, "the bow itself is made of steel and the string is a piece of steel cable, yet is still flexible enough for an old man like me to draw and fire."

Shoot, Khan corrected mentally. Guns are fired, but bows are shot. Not that it mattered. He stared at his friend's image as he described the various parts of the bow. Why had he killed himself? Had his health diminished to the point that he couldn't go on, or had he been forced to pull the trigger?

He glanced at Sylvia, but she was standing behind the projector outside the beam of light. Whatever emotions she experienced were for herself alone.

On screen, Leveque had begun to explain the design of the arrows, which were identical to the one that had delivered the note to Khan. "Each carries a bafflium core to interpret and preserve the intent of the archer. They're shielded by layers of tin and aluminum foil, which prevents the ambient thought radiation of the universe from striking the bafflium and confusing the intent."

Anselme turned toward the camera with a self-satisfied smile. "What does this mean? Gentlemen, I have created a bow that *can not miss its target*."

"That's incredible!" Bertie exclaimed.

"Shaddup," Cross snapped, "or I'll break you in half."

Professor Khan looked at Sylvia again, but she had turned her back.

Leveque had zoomed the camera out to show more of the space they were in. Khan recognized it as Sylvia's back yard. "As you can see," Leveque said. "I place the target here." He laid an archery target flat on its back behind the bow. "Then I put on the headset..." From the bundle of cables and braces, he removed a circle of metal that he placed on his brow like a crown. The lights on the device began to flash rhythmically and the crystal on the front began to glow. "Then I nock the arrow. Before I shoot, I must concentrate on the target." He shut his eyes, thinking hard. Then pulled back the arrow.

The bow bent. Not too much, but enough. When Leveque released the arrow, it shot forward at great force, away from the archery target behind him.

Then a black disc appeared in the air, like a hole in the universe. The arrow vanished into it. A scant second later, another hole appeared behind Leveque, but turned ninety degrees. The arrow shot straight down out of it and struck the bullseye.

CHAPTER TWENTY

Leveque hung his headset on the bow with a great, self-satisfied grin on his face. He lifted the edge of the archery target to display for the camera that he had struck a bullseye.

"This is no trick, gentlemen. Of that I assure you. If I can think of a target, this bow can strike it. It is the quintessence of thought made reality. Thank you."

Anselme Leveque grinned like a proud father, then the screen went white as the film ran out.

"My God," Cross said. "I could kill anyone in the world."

"You're thinking too small," Khan said. He turned to Sylvia. She switched on the lights, and he could see her expression was hooded. "Isn't that right?"

"Let me show you this."

They followed her down the stairs into an underground vault. Cross stopped just before they entered and bent low to examine the door latch. "Someone tried to break in here."

"They succeeded," Sylvia said. "For all the good it did them. Nothing was taken. They didn't even try to steal Father's notes. Come on."

Bertie scratched the top of his head. "Aren't we supposed to be finding out about this bloke in the red suit or something?"

Professor Khan waved at him to be patient. Sylvia was explaining this, and they had to let her do it in her way.

One side of the vault was given over to a huge vacuum tube array. The wall beside it was hung with a gigantic map of the California shoreline. In the middle of the floor was another display base. Khan turned to Sylvia. "This is where you kept the first prototype of the Improbability Bow, isn't it?"

Sylvia shook her head, absent-mindedly resting her hand on a gray vacuum tube. "This is the prototype. Most of it, anyway. We moved it here when Father bought the place. You see, the film only *hints* at what the bow can do. If the operator thought *I want to hit a target that will make me rich,* that's what it will do."

"I say," Bertie interrupted. "But what if 'making one rich' meant assassinating a beloved family member or two?"

"The bow hits the easiest target. If you choose one carelessly, the consequences could be terrible."

Professor Khan walked toward the map of the California shoreline. "It's a bit like the old story of the genie that grants wishes, hm? Or making a deal with the devil. You have to phrase your wish... I mean, the target you want to hit, very carefully."

"Exactly."

Khan places his finger in a tiny puncture mark in the map. "Buried treasure, my dear?"

Sylvia's expression was still stoic, but her face had gone pale. "My father was a good man, but he wasn't a saint."

Detective Cross spun toward her. "You're the one! I thought I recognized your name because you were one of Jim's chippies, but it was your pop that found Blackfoot Le May's buried treasure!"

"It was worth eight million dollars, but we sold it to the Royal Museum for half that. That was Father's target, a buried treasure we could claim for ourselves."

Khan nodded. "The Anselme Leveque I met in Salzburg couldn't have afforded the house you live in, let alone this one."

"A substantial portion of that money is out there on those workbenches. Science and inventions are expensive, Professor. We could never have done this work without those gold coins."

"Inventions?"

CHAPTER TWENTY-ONE

She didn't need much prodding. "A sonic neural stimulator, a whistle pitched to attract insect life, an instant recharger, a shrinking beam, a gyro-balanced set of ultra-stilts, an endothermic mine, a—"

"My dear, did you say 'shrinking beam'?"

As she spoke, she began to show a spark of life for the first time since Khan had met her. "Imagine if you could reduce the contents of a ship's hold so that it could carry enough cargo for a hundred ships. Food could be carried to famine-struck parts of the world for pennies. Unfortunately, it costs two thousand dollars each time it's fired, and the effects barely last an hour. But someday..."

"How many pirate treasures did you dig up?" Cross's eyes gleamed. Clearly, advances in container shipping didn't interest him.

Sylvia shook her head. Her spark dimmed. "The bow isn't just a cable and a flexible frame. It has to do calculations of its own."

"Like a difference engine," Khan said.

"Something like that," Sylvia answered. "That's what the vacuum tube array was for, to calculate the shot. You see the arrow that we shot into the map? The one that pinpointed pirate treasure? That shot took six years to calculate. Six years from the time it passed through the hole into the Universal Thought Space and the time it emerged again."

Bertie exhaled as though it was the most ridiculous thing he'd ever heard. Professor Khan shot him a poisoned look. "Still, even with one shot every six years..."

"Father didn't have six years, not after his heart attack. Maybe he would have, if he'd taken things easy, but he had money so he had to have girls and cars and... I can't blame him. He was so lonely when Mother died. But he wasn't patient enough to wait for an experiment that might not finish in this lifetime. That's why we needed something more advanced than the array."

"The crystal," Professor Khan said, realization dawning as the words came out of him.

"The Calicos Jewel," Sylvia corrected him. "It's well known, in some circles. It's supposed to be cursed. I... acquired it, with quite an unpleasant commotion, from an archaeologist who had just removed it from a tomb somewhere south of the border. Rough-looking fellow, carried a bullwhip. We were supposed to negotiate for it, but he was under the impression that I represented a museum. There was gunfire. And explosions. It was all completely horrifying, but I did manage to get away with the Calicos in my purse. Anyway, it has an extraordinary and unique structure. With the proper inputs, the jewel could do the same calculations as ten trillion of my vacuum tube arrays. As you can see, the shot is nearly instantaneous now."

Cross put his wrinkled hand on Sylvia's elbow. "And it could find more pirate's treasure?"

"If it was out there to be found."

"My dear," Khan said. "I assume that this bow could also shoot an arrow at the other side of the world? Or back in time?"

"Professor, one of these arrows could pierce God's earlobe in the moment before the Big Bang."

"So," Cross said. "Someone shot an arrow that created those vampires what were supposed to off Sylvia?"

"No," Khan said. "My dear constable, no." Everyone, including Sylvia, was poised to argue with him. "The arrow that Jameson Lee gave to us was not shot to kill Sylvia Leveque. If it had been, she would be dead, correct? The bow never misses."

Sylvia suddenly understood. "Mrs. Flewellyn!"

"And her photograph. Someone wanted to destroy them both."

"But hold on," Cross said. "Wouldn't it have been easier to shoot at the gas line or something?"

"Yes," Sylvia answered, "if the shooter had said 'I want to hit a target that will burn down Mrs. Flewellyn's house with her inside it.' But we don't know if that's what he said."

Khan said: "Perhaps he asked the bow to prompt a complete stranger to kill her. Or perhaps he asked it to destroy all evidence of his theft."

Cross nodded, looking thoughtful and troubled.

Bertie crossed his arms petulantly. "That's all fine, but we still haven't established who the bloke in the red suit is."

"Well," Khan said, "Miss Leveque did not say so explicitly, but I infer he's the fellow who arranged for her to meet the man with the bullwhip and acquire the Calicos Jewel."

She nodded. "Max Devlin."

When he heard that name, Detective Cross spat out a particularly foul word.

CHAPTER TWENTY-TWO

Despite the size of the house, there were few places to take their night's rest. Sylvia took the master bedroom of course, and Detective Cross claimed the guest bed. Bertie and Khan were forced to bunk on the ridiculously plump semicircular couches.

But it wasn't just Bertie's snores that kept the Professor awake. He was thinking about that bow. The Improbability Bow. It could hit any target at all... it was effectively a wishing machine.

And Khan had one of the arrows rolled up in his jacket beside him. All he had to do was find the bow, put on the headset, and shoot that arrow. Then he could have anything he wanted.

He could undo the biggest mistake of his life. He could be reunited with his queen, the woman he loved.

If he were suddenly faced with the chance to abandon everything, would he do it? Leave Oxford, say goodbye to the Centurions, never eat bangers and mash again? For love?

He damned well would and he knew it. Truthfully, he should never have left her side in the first place. For his queen, and the chance of a life with her—just a chance!—he would leave it all behind, propriety be damned.

The next morning, they piled into Sylvia's father's car—it was large enough that the Professor could sit low in the backseat where he would attract as little attention as possible. Detective Cross insisted on driving; he refused to be driven anywhere by a woman, and he had somehow come to the conclusion that Bertie and Khan would be unable to drive on the correct side of the road.

"My God, look at that!" Bertie, who was sitting behind Cross, had his face pressed hard against the window. They had stopped at a red light at a busy intersection. "Professor, can you see? These people, walking to and fro, yes? Going about their business?"

Professor Khan tried to look through the same window, but Bertie's large frame blocked his view. Were there more jiangshi? "What is it, Bertie?"

"The men, sir. Many of them are walking around on the street *without hats*. My word, it's indecent! And I suspect several of those women aren't even wearing stockings."

"Ah," the Professor said. "Well, when in Rome, Bertie."

The young man fidgeted with his hat. "Oh, sir, I don't think so. I just couldn't."

The light changed and they moved on.

On the way, Cross explained that Max Devlin was a local deal maker. In fact, he was THE deal maker. The big crime bosses back east had declared L.A. an open city: anyone could operate there and no one would go to war for territory. As a result, the city had attracted more than its share of small-time hustlers, pimps, stick-up crews, and confidence men. When Devlin first blew into town, the Keystone Cops were still big. He was a nobody. But in no time at all, he became a somebody.

He made his rep by creating movie stars. With his help, Manhattan tennis players became hard as nails private investigators, Iowa farm girls who still smelled of a chicken coop became French aristocracy, gravely-voiced Kansas City barmen became jazz singers. It didn't matter if they had talent or not; if they could make the deal, they were in pictures. And they always had to pay a price.

Bertie squirmed in his seat uncomfortably. "He sounds almost like the devil."

"He ain't," Cross said. "He's a man, but some people, they ain't like regular folks. They have a kind of a spark or a shadow to them. It's like a fuel that makes them seem bigger than other folks, but they ain't no devils."

"Not everyone is so perceptive, Detective," Khan said.

Cross scowled into the rear-view mirror. "I'm wearing the badge, ain't I?"

"Devlin operates beyond the picture business, though," Sylvia said, turning the conversation back on track. "He's known in scientific circles, too, for being able to get his hands on obscure materials and instruments, even something like the Calicos Jewel. If you don't care too much where it comes from and can meet the price."

"What did he demand of you?" Cross asked. "Money?"

"No. I had to give him a prototype father was working on, a rejuva-ray. It never worked as well as we'd hoped, but Max thought he could make use of the remaining charges it held. But it was worth it."

Bertie couldn't let that pass. "It worked too well, wot? Once you had this Devlin person's attention, he realized you had made him out of date. Why make a deal to achieve one's dreams when one need only shoot an arrow."

Sylvia gave Bertie a level look. "So you're convinced he took it?"

"I'll say! I'd wager he did something unfortunate to your daddy before hauling the thing off."

Cross shook his head. "The bow looked heavy."

"It is," Sylvia confirmed. "And it's large. There'd be no way to move something like that unseen."

"Still," Bertie insisted. "A device that could get you anything you want? A lot of blokes would risk all for that prize."

The vague unease that had haunted Professor Khan all morning flared suddenly, but he still wasn't sure what was wrong. He had the feeling he was missing something, but what? "Sylvia, my dear, how many arrows did your father make?"

"If you're asking how many arrows the thief, whoever it is, still has, I honestly can't say."

"One less, I'm thinking," Cross said. "I put a call in to a pal at the station this morning. Last night, a film director by the name of Lindenholm got himself hurt in a car crash. Tire blowout. He'll recover in time, but he won't be making no pictures for a while. Cause of the blowout—"

"A metal arrow," Khan said.

"Right the first time. I'm gonna check it out later. Meanwhile, we're here." Cross turned toward a massive iron gate. The sign above it read 'MAMMOTH PICTURES.' "Devlin has a couple offices around town, but scuttlebutt is that this is the place to find him."

They paused at the security booth. A guard leaned out and said: "Identification?"

Cross held up his badge. "This is all the ID I need. Open the gate."

The guard looked them over as though dealing with a carload of people driving a gorilla onto the lot was something he did every day. His response was scrupulously polite. "Officer, this is private property. Unless you have a warrant or an appointment—"

"Sonny," Cross interrupted, "I ain't no *officer*. This is an LAPD *detective's* badge, and that gives me the authority to open anything in this city, including your thick wooden skull. Now push that button and say: 'Park anyplace at all, *Detective*,' before I climb out of this car and beat you to death."

Professor Khan couldn't see the guard's eyes, but he could see the way he frowned. Sylvia stared out the passenger window as though averting her eyes from someone else's shame. Bertie's eyes were wide and shining.

"Park anywhere at all, Detective." A buzzer sounded and the gates swung open. Khan could see enough of Cross's face to recognize the smug grin there.

They needed to rid themselves of this detective, if they could.

As they glided to a stop in the parking lot, Sylvia said: "That was a disgusting display."

Cross responded: "But effective."

The first person they stopped, a pot-bellied carpenter with a belt full of tools, knew exactly where Devlin's office could be found. They began making their way through the morning crowds in the growing July heat, passing through the alleys between the studio buildings.

Many of the people they passed were workmen of the type seen on construction sites everywhere. Surprisingly, making movies involved a lot of blue-collar tradesmen. But it also involved vikings, cowboys, be-wigged courtesans in jeweled gowns, gangsters in double-breasted suits, men wearing buckskin and eagle feather headdresses who talked in rapid fire Yiddish, young men in silver jump suits with a huge V down the front, women in coconut bikini tops... In short, they passed through crowds of artificial people.

"By Jove, Professor! What do you think!" Bertie pointed to a small group of... Good Lord, they were people in gorilla suits, loitering near a stack of ladders, drinking coffee through a straw and stuffing lit cigarettes deep into their plastic mouths.

Khan gave Bertie a baleful look, then pulled the brim of his hat over his eyes so he would not have to see.

Six "blocks" later, Cross said: "This is it." The building he pointed toward was not like the huge, impersonal warehouses behind them. This was a bungalow in a long row of them—there were even trees and shrubs to break up the heat with a little greenery. Even better, it was within sight of a small gated side exit. If things went badly they'd be able to make a quick retreat.

Cross marched up to the front door and threw it open as if he owned the place.

CHAPTER TWENTY-THREE

The two men waiting in the lobby leaped to their feet. They held their hats in both hands, wringing the brim, and both were clearly disappointed that Cross was not the man they were waiting for.

Professor Khan followed the detective toward the receptionist's desk. "I wanna see Devlin," Cross barked. "Now."

"Hold on there, fella," one of the waiting men said. He was a little guy with a rough voice and a gigantic nose. "No offense, but I gotta talk to Max about a radio deal. See, there's a line of waiting clients here."

"Absolutely," the other fellow said. He was a genial but goofy-looking man with the widest mouth Khan had ever seen. He smiled like it was a nervous habit. "And I'm at the front of it."

Cross squared off against them. "Look at you both, standing here like dogs waiting to have your ears scritched. Shove off." He flashed his badge.

That stymied them. They turned to the receptionist, who sighed as though humoring people was the most tiresome part of her job. "Mr. Brown, Mr. Durante, I really think you should take Mr. Devlin's advice and do a bit of charity work. Mr. Devlin likes that. He'll call you when he's free. Honest."

They shuffled out of the bungalow. Khan turned to the receptionist—she was a young woman with fashionably short black hair and a splash of bright red lipstick on a ghost white face. "Excuse me, young lady..."

But Cross wasn't going to ask permission. He marched around her desk and, ignoring her pleas, threw open the office door.

Khan didn't want to barge into the room, but he couldn't let Cross be the only one to confront Mr. Devlin, so he trailed behind with the angry receptionist.

It was a large office, with an imposing oak desk, a high-backed chair and a crisp leather couch below a window blocked by venetian blinds. The desk blotter had nothing on it but a telephone. There was a huge closet with folding doors along one wall. A gleaming chrome padlock held it shut.

Devlin wasn't there.

Cross turned to the receptionist and jerked his thumb at the huge closet. "What's in there?"

She folded her arms across her breasts and glared down at him. "Equipment." When she saw that answer wasn't going to satisfy him, she elaborated. "Film equipment. You know? Cameras? Lights? This is a studio lot."

Cross's voice dropped to an angry growl. "Where is he?"

The receptionist stood sideways in the doorway as though hoping he would take the hint and leave. "Out on the lot. Somewhere. When Mr. Devlin tours productions, he can be impossible to reach. By choice."

"I don't believe that for a dirty second," Cross snapped. "I don't care if he's sleeping with the mayor's wife; you tell me where he is right now, or you're going to come—"

"Come with you down to the station," she finished. "This is one show tune that never goes out of style. With a certain class of people."

"If you're that familiar with the way the world operates..." Cross said. He barreled by her and snatched her purse off the corner of her desk. After a quick search, he found a five-dollar bill and slipped it into his hip pocket.

"Yeah," the secretary said, "I know how the world works. And I suppose if I don't cooperate, you'll be bringing in my boyfriend or my mother next."

Cross stepped close and narrowed his eyes up at her. "I don't even waste time on boyfriends. I'll bring in your landlord."

The receptionist sighed. "At this time of the morning, he's probably in studio 16C. It's a private sound stage he leases. But if he isn't there, it's not on me. He doesn't always let me know where he is."

"If he ain't there," Cross said. "I'll be back here, and our conversation won't be so pleasant."

Cross marched out of the office, with Bertie practically skipping along behind him. Professor Khan and Sylvia glanced at each other, then she followed. The Professor felt a powerful urge to apologize, but he knew it would not be welcome. Instead, he strode out into the blazing desert sun.

"See here, Detective!" he called.

Cross spun around, his flabby jaw set forward. "You got something to say to me?"

Khan had to be careful. He was in a foreign country and Cross represented the local authority. What's more, he was armed and capable; Khan wouldn't soon forget the ruthless speed with which he had knocked Bertie senseless. "We're going about this all wrong. We can't strong-arm everyone we see."

"He's right," Sylvia said.

"No, he ain't," Cross snapped at her. "I was busting hoods before you were born, sweetheart, so don't tell me how to run an investigation." He turned his attention to Khan. "And you. You ain't in charge here."

"I'm not trying to be, Detective."

"That ain't how it appears to me. Because if you think I'm scared of you—"

"Detective, if we keep charging about like a bull in a china shop we're going to alert Devlin to our plan."

"That's what I want," Cross snarled. "I'm shaking his tree to make him panic. Panicky hoods make mistakes. When he screws up, I'll grab him."

"Unless he has the bow," Sylvia said.

"This is my point," Khan said gently. He wanted to address the money Cross had stolen from that young girl, but he couldn't see a safe way to come at the subject. "If he has the Improbability Bow, he can kill all of us as easily as wishing. We need to get the bow before he realizes we suspect him of having it."

Cross rubbed his smooth-shaven chin. "We could just snatch Devlin right now."

"One of his confederates might know about the bow," Khan said. "That receptionist, some of the workers here, even the second silhouette that Mrs. Flewellyn saw on the night Dr. Leveque died. That person could effect Devlin's rescue with a wish."

Cross gritted his teeth, then swept his fedora off his head and mopped the sweat from his thinning gray hair. "Dammit, this is how police work is done, LAPD-style. You thump heads until you thump the right one."

Khan turned toward Sylvia. "I have a different idea."

CHAPTER TWENTY-FOUR

Studio 16C was situated almost in the center of the complex, where the crowds of tradesmen and costumed actors were thick and moved like tides. Still, Devlin's private studio had its own entrance, separate from the rest of the building.

They entered through the side door into an empty little entrance hall, presumably designed to prevent sunlight from reaching the main room. There were sounds of sawing and hammering echoing out toward them. Detective Cross gave Khan a look that said *Go right ahead, make your play*. Khan marched down the hall.

"By Jove!" Bertie said. "Would you look at that!"

The studio was not a small room—it was two hundred feet square, and the ceiling was at least forty feet above them—but most of it was filled with small-scale replicas of the buildings of Manhattan. Battery Park lay just before them, and beyond were other streets, other buildings.

New York had never been the Professor's city—he had visited, of course, but he had never loved it the way Sally Slick loved it—so he could not identify every building by sight, but he quickly recognized the most famous.

The smaller buildings, perhaps ten or twelve stories tall, came almost up to the Professor's chin. Other, taller buildings towered above him. The street appeared barely wide enough for him to squeeze through, although it would be a tight fight.

Sylvia moved up beside him. "It's a miniature replica of Manhattan."

"Not quite," Khan said. "The Empire State Building is too far south. Do you see? It ought to be in midtown."

"Correct!" came another voice, moving through the crowd of workmen at the "north" end of the set. He was a man of average height, with neatly-combed black hair and a dark red double-breasted suit over a black shirt and tie. He had the same thin, stylish mustache as Bill the nightclub owner, and he extended his hand confidently as he approached Professor Khan. "We moved the Queen of the Manhattan skyline down into the center of the other tall buildings. This is Los Angeles, sir; when reality is inconvenient, we refashion it to suit ourselves. I'm Max Devlin."

They shook hands. "My name is Professor Khan."

Max stared intently into Khan's face. "My God. You are the real thing, aren't you?"

Sylvia interrupted. "Hello, Max."

As if a switch had been thrown, Max turned all of his attention to her. "Sylvia, I heard. I am so sorry for your loss. I couldn't attend the service; my face at your father's funeral—it would have hurt his reputation. Still, what a brilliant man. It was a loss to the world."

"Thank you for sending the flowers."

"You recognized them."

Sylvia nodded. "I knew who they were from."

"If you need anything, even if it's just to get out of the house and have a night on the town, you give Max a call, okay, babe?"

In playing the role of the concerned friend, Max's tone and body language were perfect, but the Professor didn't miss the way his gaze moved up and down Sylvia's body, and the tiny flick of his tongue to his lip. Sylvia's answer was neutral. "Thank you for the offer, Max."

A second figure—a pale, colorless man in a blue pinstripe suit—stood nearby. He was close enough to listen but not so close that anyone felt like engaging him. Max's bodyguard? His wide-brimmed fedora cast a shadow over a face as cold and still as porcelain.

Max turned to Detective Cross, who was standing behind them. "We haven't been introduced," Max said. "But I know who you are. Detective Emil Cross." Cross just lifted his chin in response. "Well, you won't find any pimps or hookers to shake down in here."

Max turned his back on the cop and glanced at Bertie. It was a brief look, a mere second's appraisal, but he turned away. There was nothing about Bertie that interested him.

"Professor," he said, lowering his voice, "I wonder if I could interest you—"

A side door to the studio banged open, catching the attention of the work-crew. Everyone turned to the portly blond man who was hustling toward Max.

"Max, have you heard?"

Max rolled his eyes. "Alan, look, this is a bad time."

"No, it can't wait! That director I told you about cracked up his Bentley last night! There might be an opening with whoever they hire next!"

"Alan, I already know who they're going to hire next." Max put his arm around the blond man's shoulders and turned him around. "I put a call in. About you, pal. Does Max keep up his end of the deal? Now go home and keep close to the phone."

"Okay, Max. Will do."

"And lay off the barley juice, would you? A little bit of chub is fine but too much and you're dropped."

"Will do, Max," the man said. "And thank you."

"Oh, Max!"

Khan was sure he saw Max tense up at this new voice. He practically shoved Alan toward the exit. The actor took the hint; he didn't leave at a run, but he was close to it.

The voice who had called Max's name made him step back and wring his hands together. The blood drained out of his face, and he took a handkerchief from his back pocket to mop his brow.

"Hey, there, kiddo. How do you like the way things are going so far?"

A little girl of no more than six skipped into view. She was dressed in a little pink dress and wore shiny black saddle shoes. Her hair had been carefully curled into ringlets. "I love the way my doll city—Oh my gosh!"

She had just caught sight of Professor Khan. She advanced toward him reverently, with an amazed expression on her face. "Are you a real gorilla?"

Khan glanced at a pretty young woman in a modest brown dress who hovered nearby. The girl's mother? If so, she didn't seem concerned about her safety, as so many parents were around him. "That I am, young lady."

"Oh, that's silly. Gorillas can't talk!"

"We can if little girls ask as politely as you just did. My name is Khan."

"My name is Shirley Temple. I'm in the movies."

Khan nodded soberly. "That must be very hard work."

Her expression became very serious. "Oh it is, but everyone is so nice to me! Look! I asked Max to build me a doll house, and he's building me a whole doll city instead! Would you like to see?"

She took the Professor's hand and led him across Battery Park toward one of the streets. She fit neatly between them, but Khan quickly realized that the space was narrower than he'd first thought. Even turned sideways, his belly and shoulders would scrape against the faux-stone buildings.

In fact, several carpenters had stopped work to crane their necks at him. He suddenly felt very self-conscious. "Shirley, my dear, I don't think I can fit through without damaging your toys, and I wouldn't want to do that."

"Oh well," she said. "That's okay, Mr. Khan. I guess there isn't much for a big ol' gorilla to do here anyway. Did you bring your dinosaurs with you?"

The Professor felt a sudden chill. Did the child remember more than she should have? "What did you say, my dear?"

"Dinosaurs, silly! I swear I saw a whole bunch of gorillas just like you teamed up with dinosaurs. They were march, march, marching through the streets like the angriest parade. Do you have a dinosaur with you? Max says that I must have seen a movie set but I don't think so."

"I don't know about Max, young lady, but there are no dinosaurs here today."

"Goodie! They had scary teeth. What do you think of my New Yorkers?" The little girl waved toward the streets of the fake Manhattan.

The pedestrians were comprised of dolls of every sort and the cars were a mismatch of styles and sizes. Clearly, they had been bought from a toy store, not constructed like the other props.

"Shirley, honey," Max interrupted, "why don't you go over to your mother. The friendly gorilla-man and I have a few things to discuss."

She gave him a salute. "You betcha!" then scampered toward the woman in brown.

"Adorable, isn't she?" Max said. "She's going to be big. Huge! I'm not kidding."

"And yet you're as white as a sheet," Khan said.

Max shrugged and smiled, looking a little embarrassed. "Kids make me very nervous. Always have. Babies especially, but kids, too. They're so unpredictable. I'm always thinking they're going to set something on fire or something. I'll bet that sounds crazy, huh?"

Professor Khan shook his head. He glanced at Bertie to make sure he was out of earshot. "I make my living as a schoolteacher, Mr. Devlin, I spend most of my working life around people who despise children."

Max laughed. "You're okay, Professor. It's hard to believe, but you are. And call me Max. So listen, hey? Because I have an offer to make you." He looked around the room to make sure no one could overhear. "How would you like to be a movie star?"

CHAPTER TWENTY-FIVE

"Is that what you do?" Khan asked. "Turn random people into film stars?"

Max laughed again. His color and confidence were returning quickly. "Absolutely. It's easier than you think, and the more average the schmoe who makes it big, the better it is for me."

"Really? How so?"

"Moving pictures are the pre-eminent art form of the twentieth century. Don't argue with me, Professor; it's true now and will be even more true in the coming decades. At the moment, nothing is more popular than the picture shows. The stars are our modern royalty, and Hollywood is our Versailles.

"Except in the good old U.S. of A., you can become a prince no matter who your mommy and daddy are, so ambitious daydreamers from all over the country flood into L.A. the way rain runs off a mountain toward the sea. And all they think they need is the one thing that will get them to that coronation: the Lucky Break.

"Sure, there are real talents in this business. Actors who can do a hundred voices. Actresses who can break your heart with nothing more than a look. Singers who can shatter a wine glass with a note. But there are others, too: regular folk who look like they stumbled into a movie the way John or Jane Smith might stumble into a diner. When audiences see those schmoes up on the screen, their first thought is always *I could do that*.

Max leaned in close and lowered his voice. His grin was conspiratorial. "*I could do that* is going to be the engine of this town. It's going to be the machine that turns Los Angeles from a desert outpost with a few factories into a world-class city. It's gonna fill this burg with every dissatisfied car hop and soda jerk in America. What's more, once that little angel you just met starts tap dancing across the screen, every fame-hungry young parent is going to load their adorable little moppets into the backseat of their jalopies and speed westward.

"And out of all those people, some small fraction of them will have something special to offer. Those are the ones who will have to come to me."

Professor Khan fought back a smile. He knew that humans didn't much care to see his fangs. "And am I one of your average schmoes?"

"Absolutely not," Max said with conviction. "You, sir, have something else. You are unique. That makes you valuable. I've been wanting to see a movie made about that thing in New York, the invasion. What if—"

"Impossible," Khan snapped. He glanced over at Max's pale companion. He had not moved at all, not even to twitch his nose.

"I don't mean as the heavy," Max said, talking over the Professor's objections. "We could write you a role as a hero, helping the humans defend against the invaders. Okay, scratch that. What about the part of the mentor in a picture I'm putting together about a jungle boy. You would be the gorilla who raised him!"

"It wouldn't work," Khan said, "because—"

"Of course! We don't want a jungle setting. You're a man of intelligence. You want something in the modern world. How about a circus picture? It could be a comedy. Or not. I know!" Max turned and waved at the miniature skyline behind him. "We'll take our inspiration from a recent blockbuster. What do you say to a starring role in KING KHAN?"

The Professor glared at Max, his mouth screwed up on one side. It was a look he'd used to silence students many times, and he was secretly surprised to see it work here.

"First of all," Khan said sharply, "I suspect you are unaware that 'King Khan' translates as a *tautology*." Max furrowed his brow; he clearly didn't recognize the term, but the disgust in the Professor's voice made it clear it was A Bad Thing.

"Second of all, you can not put me in a jungle or circus movie, because while I may not be a man, I am most certainly a male. When you put clothing on a man in a gorilla suit, you do so for comic effect. When I dress, I do so out of modesty." Max's expression lit up with realization, but the Professor wasn't finished talking. "Perhaps now you would understand the reasons if I told you I walked out of that particular gigantic ape movie."

"Well, sure, professor," Max said. His smile faltered but like salesmen the world over, he wasn't ready to give up. "But this is a land of special effects trickery. I'm sure the gals in the costume department could whip up a pair of camouflaging trunks for you."

Khan lowered his voice. "Tell me, old boy: if you were asked to appear naked before a camera, would you consent to wear a pair of flesh-tone shorts that made you look smooth between your legs?"

To his credit, Max laughed long and loud over that one. "No. No, I most definitely would not. But I have the phone numbers of about fifty guys who would jump at the chance."

Professor Khan sighed. Of course he did. "You must understand, Max, I have ambitions—large and powerful ambitions—but none of them involve playacting for an audience. And that's certainly not why I came here to see you today."

"Fair enough," Max said. He looked around at the carpenters and other work crews, and everyone suddenly became less interested in their conversation and went back to work. "What did you come to see me about?"

"This fellow who provided you with the Calicos Jewel..."

Max stepped back and folded his arms across his chest, but he was intrigued enough to finish Khan's sentence. "Dr. Jones?"

"Is that his name? The chap with the bullwhip? I heard there was a bit of commotion involved in the exchange."

Max looked bemused. "You could say that."

"Have you heard anything from him? Or about the jewel? You see, it seems that someone has stolen a piece of equipment from Sylvia's father's lab, and we suspect it might be this bullwhip-wielding fellow. This Dr. Jones."

Max glanced at his pale companion and smiled. "You think he might have snuck back to reclaim his gem, eh? Last I heard he was in French Indochina, but these young guys bounce around quite a bit."

"I was hoping you heard something, or maybe heard from him directly. You see, there's something this Dr. Jones doesn't know about the device he's stolen: It's extraordinarily unstable."

The comfortable, knowing smile on Max's face faded. "How so, Professor?"

"Well, Max, you see, the way the device works is this: it opens a hole in the universe—I know it sounds utterly unbelievable, but I assure you it's true."

"Sure, Professor," Max said impatiently. "I trust you."

"Excellent. But it's only a prototype. It's meant to be used under carefully-controlled conditions. According to Dr. Leveque's notes, there's a chance of catastrophic failure every time it's used, and the chance grows each time."

"Wow." Max rubbed his chin and looked around the room. "That's... That's a dangerous toy for Leveque to be playing with."

Khan kept his voice low and his tone urgent. "Precisely. Anselme was always a man with many secrets, from his friends, his own daughter... But his state of mind before he took his own life... I shouldn't speculate. So to be clear, Max, the reason I... *we* came to you is that we are hoping you can arrange a deal with this Dr. Jones to return the prototype. No questions asked. Of course Sylvia would be willing to make it worth your while. And his." Sylvia had already agreed to write a check, if she had to.

Max's face had gone pale and he had a sheen of sweat on his forehead. "I don't know, Professor. This isn't the first time someone's asked me to recover some stolen property for them. It's a messy business."

"Nothing would be messier than a malfunction of this device!"

Max glanced worriedly at his companion. "Catastrophic failure, you say?"

Khan nodded his head. Max had bought in. The bow would soon be in Sylvia's possession again. Now all that was left were details. But he had to be careful not to appear overeager. "In my considerable experience, the more powerful the device, the more devastating the failure."

Max dabbed at his forehead with his handkerchief. "These studios are always too stuffy. I hate being stuck inside. Okay, Professor. I can't promise anything, of course, but I'll put out a few feelers."

"We are incredibly grateful," Khan said, then he gently clapped Max on the shoulder. "Thank you, my friend."

"This device," Max said, as he and Professor Khan started toward Sylvia and the detective, "have you ever seen it in action?"

"Of a sort," he admitted. He turned casually toward Max and unbuttoned his coat. "I received a message tied to one of these." Then he opened his jacket to show the metal arrow jutting out of his inside pocket.

Max's eyes suddenly went wide, his mouth fell open greedily, and he lunged forward as if to snatch it away. Khan stepped back, closing his jacket. It had only been one step, and Max had only let his expression slip for half a second, but it was enough."

Max smiled and took a deep breath. "Gave myself away there, didn't I?"

"Indeed you did," Professor Khan said.

"So much for my poker face." Max looked over at his companion, and the man unbuttoned his jacket. "But you gave yourself away, too."

CHAPTER TWENTY-SIX

"Max—" Khan said, feeling the situation slip out of his control.

Max waved him to silence. "Forget it. When I slipped up, you should have pretended to be shocked. That was the right play, and you blew it."

The Professor shrugged. "What can I say? I knew I'd made a mistake as soon as I showed you the arrow. I lost my own poker face in a fit of self-recrimination. But Max, I was not fooling when I talked about catastrophic malfunction."

"I said forget it," Max straightened his tie and smoothed his lapels. "No sale. I asked Leveque if his machine had any problems, and he said it was fine."

"He was protecting his daughter," Khan said, but they both knew Max didn't believe him.

"It's funny," Max said, his expression thoughtful. He laid a toothpick into the side of his mouth. "I've always heard that the easiest mark in the world is another scammer, but I never thought I could be taken myself. But you were good, Professor. You showed the real thing here. Talent, just like I was yapping about before. I'm impressed. Truly."

"Thank you."

"I want that arrow."

"Tell your man," Khan said coolly, as the pale man in the dark suit slid his hand under his jacket, "that if he draws a weapon on me, I will tear his arms off."

Max raised his eyebrows. "And here you sounded so civilized."

"I'm English, sir. We did not plant the Union Jack in a ring around the planet by shying from violence." The pale man still had his hand under his jacket. Khan tensed his whole body, ready to pounce on him, roaring. Maybe, if he was frightening enough, he might ruin the man's aim and save himself a bullet in the gut. "I'm not playing."

Max waved the pale man off. "Mr. Wisp, see to the car, would you?"

Wisp buttoned his jacket and faded back into the cityscape, his slender form moving between the buildings like a ghost.

Shirley, the little girl, stood just outside the replica of Battery Park. She stared at them with wide, frightened eyes.

Max pressed his lips together. "We can come to an understanding. What do you want for that arrow in your pocket?"

Professor Khan gave him an even look. "The Improbability Bow. That's my final offer."

Max laughed and shook his head, as though watching a chess player make a move that would cost him the match. "You were doing so well before. I have other arrows, you know, and I'm getting better at using them."

"Maybe so, but will you risk losing another one to rid yourself of me? And risk a malfunction, too?"

Max grinned at him. "If I have to."

Khan backed toward the entrance. "I pray, for the safety of this city, that you do not. Come along, Sylvia. Detective, Bertie."

Max Devlin stood like a giant at the edge of the fake skyline, watching them with a confident smile. As much as Khan hated to admit it, Max's self-assurance seemed to steal his own.

They emerged into the burning noon sun of Los Angeles. The baked asphalt burned the Professor's bare feet, and he hurried through the crowd until he found a scant bit of shade on the western edge of a building. Beside him, a half-dozen British red coats stood out of the sun to catch a smoke.

"You blew it!" Cross's flabby face was flushed red. He moved to just a few inches from Khan's face and shouted at him. Bertie's eyes went wide and nervous but like Max, Cross didn't even notice him. "We had one chance and you missed it!"

"No, he didn't," Sylvia said. "And I'll thank you not to scream about my private business in a crowd of strangers."

Cross took a deep breath. "We're looking for the gadget, ain't we? He blew our chance to get it."

"But thanks to him, we know who has it," Sylvia turned her cool gaze toward the Professor. "I never thought anyone could play an operator like Max Devlin, and yet here you are. I heard every astonishing word." She removed a very small device from her ear.

"And yet the detective is correct," Khan said. "If not for my misstep at the end, we could have made a deal for the bow."

The nearest redcoat leaned out in front of the Professor, his mouth hanging open. "My god. That's the most amazing mask I've ever seen."

Khan nodded at him. "Thank you. I grew it myself."

The fellow didn't seem to know what to say to that. He looked a bit disconcerted as he backed toward his fellow actors.

Sylvia folded her arms across her chest. "You're right, Professor. It's less than ideal. However, Max is a powerful figure and a lot of people owe him favors. If we'd tried the little detective's methods—"

Cross sneered. "Watch it, girly."

"If we'd tried it his way," Sylvia pressed on, "Max would have denied everything. He may still set his friends on us, but at least he won't feel as threatened."

Khan nodded and rubbed his chin. "Plus, we've confirmed that he's our thief. Thank you, my dear. I shall not recriminate myself so ferociously."

"Amateurs," Cross spat. "I'm taking advice from amateurs. Well, I know what to do."

"What's that?" Khan asked as Cross marched off into the crowd. The mob of cavemen, knights in armor, and female robots parted for him like mice scampering out of the way of a charging mastiff. Sylvia, Bertie, and the Professor hurried after him.

"We gotta strike now," Cross said over his shoulder, "before he has a chance to prepare. I'm going to toss his office, and we'll see what the so-called 'film equipment' in his closet really is. And if it ain't there, I might find some paperwork or something that would give us a new place to look."

The tarmac was hot against Khan's feet, but he endured. "Don't you need some sort of legal authorization to do that?"

"Yes," Sylvia said, trailing close behind. "A warrant."

"You two talk like you just stepped off the bus from Naive, Iowa. We can arrange a back-dated warrant later, if we have to. Welcome to Los Angeles."

Khan and Sylvia exchanged a wary glance, but they followed along, passing through groups of actors in costume that flowed around them like waves. Once, they lost sight of Cross amid a group of a dozen or so faux-baseball players, but Khan caught sight of him just as he rounded a corner.

They ran to catch up and nearly collided with him. He had stopped just within sight of Max Devlin's bungalow.

Through the thinning crowds of people, they saw the entrance to Max's office was guarded by four burly private security guards.

CHAPTER TWENTY-SEVEN

"Back!" Cross hissed. "Outta sight."

Just a few paces away was an open door. They ducked inside. The air was stifling, but the concrete floor was cool. Bertie stood in the middle of the corridor like someone's lost pet. Cross pulled Khan away from the entrance against a rolling rack of clothing. "Can you take them?"

"In a fight?" Khan responded, then immediately felt foolish. Of course Cross's first thought was to beat them up. "If they are unarmed, yes, almost certainly. But I won't do it."

A pair of guards ran by the open door. Sylvia turned to them. "Wait here." She went back into the sunlight "Oh!" she cried, then laid her hand nervously on her cheek. "Oh, Mr. Security Guard! Has something awful happened?"

One of the guards, a strapping young man with scarred knuckles, stopped long enough to look her up and down. He liked what he saw. "There's somebody on the lot pretending to be a cop. Fake badge and everything. He's threatened to kill one of the producers, I guess, so we're looking out for him."

"Oh, my," she said, "Be careful."

But the guard wasn't done with her. He took her chin in his hand and said: "Doll, meet me by the main gate at six. You won't regret it." Then he hurried away.

When Sylvia came back in, she had become her reserved self again. Khan bowed slightly her. "That was quite a performance, my dear."

"Apparently, this place is inspirational. I think it's time we left."

"You can bury that idea," Cross snapped. He glanced at Bertie, then turned to the Professor. "How many can you take?"

"It doesn't matter," Khan said. "Against so many men I would have to inflict serious injuries, and I won't do it. They're just doing their jobs."

Bertie turned leaned down to Cross, lowering his voice to a whisper. "Don't you have your revolver, old boy? You—"

"What if they're carrying heat, too?" Cross snapped. "If they start shooting at me, how am I supposed to shoot back with no bullets? I used up all my shells on those dead men, and I haven't been back to the station or my place since to pick up more."

"No guns," Sylvia said. "That would be awful."

"I agree," the Professor said. "Besides, I have a better idea."

"Pfft!" Cross waved him off. "You and your ideas."

Bertie spoke up. "What is it, Professor?"

Khan waved vaguely toward the bungalow. "This is a stalling action and we all know it. Max can't keep a half-dozen guards stationed outside his bungalow full time and he knows that his office isn't a safe place to hide stolen items, especially if Detective Cross returns with a dozen uniformed constables."

"Officers," Cross corrected.

"Quite. My apologies. If he's keeping the Improbability Bow in his office, he's going to want to move it soon. What's more, the front door of his bungalow is within clear view of the street, through that wrought iron gate."

Cross rubbed his chin. "You want to set up a stake out."

"I do. But we'll have to get off the lot safely first. If we're apprehended, Max will have time to move the bow while we're in custody."

"I like it," Sylvia said.

"So do I," Cross admitted. "But we should split up and meet at the car. Anyone not there in, say, twenty minutes will be left behind. Except me. If I don't make it there, you call the Hollywood Division and ask to talk to Mackie. Tell him where I am. Got it?"

"I do," Khan said.

Sylvia had already taken a long black wig off the costume rack. "We'll have to do this the smart way," she said. Khan was startled by the change in her appearance with just the wig.

For him, she grabbed a long black cloak and hood. After he put it on, she handed him a scythe to carry. Bertie didn't get a costume; Sylvia hung his green hat and jacket on a hanger, then turned to Cross.

"Forget it," Cross said. "I'm not wearing any kind of costume. I'm going to be exactly who I am."

He turned and bustled out into the blazing sun. Khan, Sylvia, and Bertie looked at each other and shrugged. Sylvia offered her arm to Bertie and they strolled out together. Professor Khan counted to ten and followed.

He'd originally hoped to keep them in sight in case they were grabbed by security. While Sylvia had proven herself quite capable, poor Bertie had been more than a little sheltered. It wasn't fair to put the complete burden of looking after him on Sylvia's shoulders.

Unfortunately, it was impossible to move quickly with his scythe in one hand and his floppy hood dangling over his face. He lost track of them almost immediately. Ah well. There was little to worry about even if he were to be captured; the most awful thing he could do would be to confess their plans, and Khan was not afraid of that.

So he made sure to walk in the shady part of the road, and he was careful not to hurry too much. That ensured he was the last person to reach the car.

All three of the others looked at him warily. Cross cleared his throat. "You know how you and I are getting out of here, don't you?"

"On my way over here," Khan said, "I realized I'd probably be safest in the trunk."

Bertie opened it for him. A blast of hot air washed over them. "It'll be beastly, sir, I'm sorry to say."

"Suitable for a beast then?" Khan said, but his joke didn't go over. The back of the vehicle sagged as he settled his four hundred pounds into it. Cross hopped in and squeezed in beside him. "Let us out again as soon as possible, please."

Bertie slammed the lid, The trunk was as dark and stifling as the inside of an oven.

CHAPTER TWENTY-EIGHT

It was dark when the three remaining guards outside Max's office were finally relieved of their duties. After Max's assistant/bodyguard, Mr. Wisp, waved them off, he went into the bungalow alone.

It had been a long day. Khan had been woozy from the heat of the trunk, even though he'd only been inside for fifteen minutes—long enough to get through the queue at the gate and to find a pumping station where they could fill the tank and the portable container in the wheel well. Sylvia had run into a cafe for a large glass of water for him, and he needed quite a few minutes in the shade of the backseat, with all the windows down, to recover.

It hadn't just been the trunk, it had also been the hot tarmac, the blazing sun, and the unbearable crowds. Gorillas were built for the heat, it was true, but they were not accustomed to deserts.

Still, he would not permit them to dawdle over him. Cross found a parking space on the street where they could watch Max's front door through the wrought iron. Bertie began to complain of boredom after twenty minutes, but fell silent when the detective described stake outs that had lasted weeks at a time.

Sylvia brought them meals, although she appeared to resent it. Of course the Professor could not walk into a cafe and walk out with a bagged lunch, and Cross refused to talk about it except to say he didn't want anything with rice in it. Bertie kept trying to insist he wanted more "Jewish food," since he'd been so impressed by his morning meal with Sally Slick, and could scarcely credit it when Sylvia and Cross insisted he wasn't in New York anymore. No one thought him capable, so it was Sylvia who brought them bags of something called a "burrito."

Professor Khan had seen his share of the world and knew the value of a nice wrap—these were especially delicious—but Bertie was enraptured by them. He wanted to eat them for every meal and began to make plans to invest in a "burrito shop" back in Oxfordshire.

The long day dragged on, and they took turns catching naps.

So they were well-rested, hydrated, and fed by the time Mr. Wisp entered the bungalow.

"I don't think that's a good sign," Cross said.

"I am forced to agree," Khan answered. "If he were moving the bow to a safe location, he would hardly be entering alone. "

Wisp re-emerged, this time carrying a narrow leather pouch nearly two feet long. He quickly finished wrapping it in newspaper, then stuffed a long strap into one end.

"I say," Bertie murmured. "That looked an awful lot like a quiver."

"Damn," Cross said, and slid the key into the ignition.

Wisp got behind the wheel of a yellow coupe and waited patiently while the guard rolled the gate open. He pulled into the street and turned right.

Everyone in Leveque's car had hunkered down low to not be seen, but Wisp didn't even glance in their direction. Cross turned the key and did a quick u-turn to fall in behind him.

Sylvia leaned forward. "Lucky for us that his right tail light is damaged but not out. It's very distinctive."

"Damn," Cross said. He craned his neck to see above the dash and ground his teeth. "Damn damn damn."

Professor Khan cleared his throat. "Detective Cross, I'm getting subtle hints that you think this situation is more complicated than it appears."

"That's Wisp we're following. I shoulda figured this for Devlin's next play, but Wisp is so damn slippery I can't even catch a thought about him."

Professor Khan had a sudden sinking feeling. "Tell me about him."

"His full name is Wilson Oswald Wisp. He's supposed to have come from your part of the world, Wales—"

"Welsh?" Bertie blurted out. "With a name like Wilson?"

"I ain't the one who christened him!" Cross snapped. "I don't even know how much of this is true. He has no fixed address, and damn few temporary ones. No family, no girlfriend, no friends. Just employers."

Khan's voice was quiet. "What does he do?"

"He's a mule. If you want something delivered, he delivers it. We've pulled him over a few times, but whatever he's carrying seems to disappear. No trace, no evidence. Later on, we get word that the stuff he's supposed to be transporting has arrived at the location. Get me? He's got a kind of genius for this. Worse, he's gotten people killed." Cross paused.

"I'm intrigued by the way you constructed that sentence, Detective," Khan said.

"Eh?"

"You didn't say he killed people, or even that he hired killers. You said he'd gotten people killed. That needs explication."

Cross scowled into the rear view mirror, but before the Professor could rephrase in more common language, he explained. "It ain't that he does anything to people. That's clear. We've tailed him, and usually nothing comes of it: we catch him with nothing or he gives us the slip. But sometimes bad things happen to the people on his tail. Two flatfoots in Century City were hit by a dump truck while crossing the street. Two others down in Crenshaw were torn apart by half a dozen junkyard dogs. One of those guys... I knew him. Combine that with other stories, and I know Wisp is somebody you don't mess with lightly. He can lead people into trouble."

"But he hasn't even glanced about," Bertie said. "Not to look in the rear view mirror or anything. And that yellow car with the broken light—it's so easily followed! He doesn't seem like a master smuggler to me."

No one responded to that. Cross only gripped the steering wheel with white knuckles.

Wisp drove eastward. The neighborhoods turned residential, then thinned out even more. Soon there were more scrub lots than homes. They began to pass airfields and orchards. Everything was utterly flat, like driving across the bottom of a gigantic bowl.

Wisp, his head silhouetted in the lights of his dash, never turned his head once.

CHAPTER TWENTY-NINE

"We just crossed into Maravilla," the detective said. "We're out of my jurisdiction. Again."

They kept going, puttering down a long straight road through orange and peach orchards, passing small clusters of buildings that had sprung up around gas stations.

Finally, Wisp pulled off the road into a long, wide gravel parking lot. At the near end was a wide, squat building with a blinking neon sign above it that read "The Sombrero," but there were several other buildings there: the ubiquitous auto filling station/repair shop, a bodega, and other large, dark structures with no explicit purpose.

Parked near the entrance to the club were four or five dozen cars, although none as fancy as Leveque's. Wisp found an empty space close to a nondescript building beside the club and picked up his newspaper package.

Cross parked close to the road. The four of them watched Wisp duck into the alley beside the club.

"So," Sylvia said. "A trap?"

"Yeah," Cross said. "It sure looks like one."

"I should go alone," Khan said. "I will be in no danger."

"Sir?" Bertie said. "How do you figure that?"

"I just do, my boy. Trust me when I say that, of all of us in this car, I'm the one who will emerge from a trap with my life. It's a certainty." He opened the door.

"We're all going," Sylvia said. She climbed out too.

Cross cursed under his breath. Bertie muttered: "I know how you feel, old boy." But they both got out of the car.

"I mean it," the Professor said as they followed him across the parking lot. "I'm in no danger here. You should withdraw."

"I know you're a smart fellow, Professor," Sylvia said, "but you aren't invincible. We're in this together."

Cross muttered another curse as they reached the mouth of the alley.

It was dark. Very dark. The side of the alley that bordered the club was lined with trash cans and crates. Khan lifted the nearest one and saw it was full of old beer bottles, chicken bones, and corn husks. Bertie took a deep breath and started to plunge forward into the darkness, but Khan held out both of his hands to keep him back. He was going to lead the way.

The gravel was painful on his feet, but he was grateful that there was no broken glass. In no time at all they had left the faint glow of the lights above the door of the club. They were far from the city, but there was no moon and the stars still seemed to be dim. Air pollution, no doubt.

No, the Professor scolded himself. He had to focus on the danger before him, not the trivialities of his situation. He advanced some dozen paces without coming upon anything unusual. He glanced behind him and saw Bertie, Sylvia, and Cross in silhouette against the lighted parking lot. When he looked in the other direction, he saw nothing but inky darkness. If only he'd thought to bring a torch.

He kept moving forward, feeling his way carefully. Mr. Wisp had no more than a three-minute headstart, but if he lurked in the darkness with a weapon, ready to pounce on them...

It felt wrong. The whole thing felt wrong. Following Wisp felt like his confrontation with Max—he was going up against someone more powerful than himself, someone like the Centurions, except this time Khan didn't have the edge that comes from being underestimated. Professor Khan wanted the others to turn back and let him go forward alone, but they thought that was cowardice.

Wisp didn't jump out at them. Khan's hands, reaching forward in the darkness, touched wooden planks. He felt carefully along it, eventually touching the brick walls on either side. The fence went higher than he could reach, and there were no latches or hinges.

Cross flicked a lighter, casting a dim light. The fence reached twelve feet above them. A side door led into the club, but when Bertie pushed against it, he found it locked.

There was no sign of Wisp. He had disappeared.

"Hey, pachucos!" came a cry from the entrance to the alley. They turned as one and saw their way blocked by a great many shadowy figures.

CHAPTER THIRTY

Two of the figures switched on torches, shining them into Khan's eyes as they advanced.

"Pardon me," the Professor said. "We were following a fellow and he went into this alley, but now he seems—"

"Hey, you should shut up, you know?" the man spoke with a Spanish accent.

Cross drew his revolver from beneath his jacket. "No damn body tells me to shut up."

The men in the alley gasped and drew back, the torch beams focusing on Cross's revolver. Bertie looked down at it and blurted: "Oh, good show! Here I thought you said you had run out of bullets!"

Cross gritted his teeth and, after a moment's hesitation, the silhouettes at the end of the alley began to laugh. The alley filled with the clicks of gravity knives releasing their blades.

"I don't care what anyone says," Cross said stubbornly. "I ain't taking orders from no Mexicans."

"How about giving in to this, then?" One of the torch beams was redirected toward the hand of the lead man. His sleeve was of a beautiful burgundy color, and he was aiming a gleaming chrome revolver at them. "Now drop yours, señor."

The group of men was almost upon them. "I won't," Cross spat.

"Oh just do it!" Sylvia shouted, then she wrenched it out of his hand. He let her. Sylvia set the gun on a trash can lid beside them.

"Gracias," the man in the burgundy said. "Now maybe you can explain why you're sneaking around on the side of our club?"

"As I was trying to explain," the Professor said. "We were trailing a man. He had robbed this woman, and we hoped he would lead us back to her property. He parked out front and came into this alley, but seems to have disappeared."

"What kind of car was he driving?"

Sylvia spoke up. "A yellow coupe."

"Hey hey!" the man called. "You see a yellow coupe out in the lot?"

A voice from the mouth of the alley called back. "No! Nada."

"He doubled back," Cross said bitterly. "He doubled back and left us here."

"That was muy clever of him," the man in the burgundy jacket said. "If he exists."

The men, now close enough for the bounced torch light to illuminate them, looked rather young. They were all dark-eyed and dark-skinned, although the similarities ended there. They also wore wide-brimmed hats, over-sized double-breasted jackets with padded shoulders and huge lapels. Zoot suits.

Khan tried to put on his most reasonable tone. "I assure you, sir—"

One of the men picked Cross's gun off the trash can lid beside him. Then he noticed a long bundle wrapped in newspaper. As he lifted the corner, Sylvia blurted out: "That's mine!"

"Is it now?" the gunman said. He tore the newspaper away, revealing six bundled sticks of dynamite attached to a ticking time piece.

CHAPTER THIRTY-ONE

Vehicular transport: standby mode.

Incursion event: perimeter phase commenced.

Security guard: solo station/distracted by textual entertainment/ armed with metallic projectile weapon.

Chance for successful stealth bypass: 21%

Stealth advance

Stealth bypass: failure.

Security guard host suitability: Gender: Male, Age: Approx 50 local revolutions, Wealth/cultural anti-violence ranking: low.

Preliminary host suitability: 9%

Host suitability assessment aborted.

Guard aggression rating: 0.2%

Guard inquiring about host body's well-being.

Deploy info beam.

Guard neutralized.

Incursion event: building phase commenced.

Current population of laboratory building, this level only: five persons.

Population within range of immediate sensory apparatus: zero persons.

Host suitability assessment routine suspended.

Items in range of immediate sensory apparatus: clean water dispensary, extinguishing equipment for combustible materials, manually operated combustion alert system, axe.

Items of immediate use: zero.

Prize material located at edge of secondary sensory apparatus.

Advance.

Advance.

Advance.

Entrance to laboratory containing prize material identified.

Incursion event: laboratory phase commenced.

Population within range of immediate sensory apparatus: one persons.

Interrogative call from within laboratory.

Advisability of host response: 11%

Response not sent.

Stealth advance.

Stealth advance.

Laboratory population identified: lab technician/graduate student. Likelihood 87%

Student host suitability assessment: Gender: Male. Age: Approx 20 local revolutions. Wealth/cultural anti-violence ranking: low.

Preliminary host suitability: 14%

Host suitability assessment aborted.

Additional interrogative call: Threat to summon local militia/security force.

Likelihood that threat is a tactical feint: 9%

Advisability of host response: 97%

Stealth mode cancelled.

Advance.

Host response: tactical feint: assert inability to locate caregivers.

Prize material located and identified with primary sensory apparatus.

Risk of student interference in successful procurement: 100%

Likelihood of successful procurement: 0.3%

Student interrogative: Location of host caregivers.

Supplemental interrogative inclusion: reference to Christian place of punishment in the afterlife.

Likelihood that student will successfully send host to Christian place of punishment in the afterlife: 0.4%.

Deploy info beam.

Incursion event: procurement phase commenced.

Advance.

Procure prize material.

Incursion event: withdrawal phase commenced.

Advance.

Advance.

Advance.

Advance.

Withdrawal phase completed.

Vehicular transport: standby mode cancelled.

Procurement mission completed.

CHAPTER THIRTY-TWO

The lights inside the clubhouse were a welcome change from the darkness of the alley. The zoot-suited gangsters still shoved and shouted at them, their voices joining into a cacophony that would have been incoherent even if Khan understood their language. But he did not need Spanish lessons to decode the way they were gesturing with their knives.

The one advantage of being in a lighted room was that he would see the knife thrust coming.

The room itself looked like a mix between a warehouse and a boy's clubhouse. There were couches, second-hand coffee tables, dart boards, and pool tables mixed with rough crates stamped with brand labels for tequila, beer, and several brands of whiskey, at least three separate drum kits, and tools of every kind.

"Oh my God, sir," Bertie blubbered. His eyes brimmed with tears. Sylvia twitched like a spring under tension and Cross crouched low like an animal caught in a trap.

Professor Khan pushed them all behind him. The shouting crowd of young men, their knives, the leader's handgun—it all seemed so distant. Whatever else may happen, he knew he would not die here. Well, he was pretty sure of it. He didn't like the idea of gambling on his hunches, but the others needed his protection.

They backed across the room while the young men shouted at them and pointed with their knives. They really were wild with anger, and Khan couldn't blame them.

"It's a set up," Khan said as calmly as he could. He didn't even try to raise his voice. No one could hear him, but he kept his gaze on the man in the burgundy suit and repeated himself.

The man waved at his companions to silence them. He still held the pistol in his hand, and it was directed toward Khan's belly. Then he aimed it at Cross. "Who do you work for?"

Cross bared his teeth. "I'm LAPD, you dumb..." But he wasn't willing to finish that sentence, not while staring down the barrel of a gun.

The man turned to two others beside him, both wearing dark blue pinstripes. "Check him." The men slapped Cross's black fedora off his head, then opened his jacket to take his badge from his inside pocket.

"He ain't lying, Jorje," one of the men said as he handed over the folded leather. Cross's thin gray hair stuck up from his sweaty scalp, and without his hat his ears stuck out and his cheeks seemed especially plump and veined through with red. He might have seemed comical but for the look in his eyes.

Jorje wasn't impressed. He looked the badge over, then smirked at Cross. "You're outside your jurisdiction, Detective Abuela."

Cross flushed scarlet from his scalp to his collar. Khan put a hand on his shoulder and said: "We were set up."

Jorje turned to him almost reluctantly. "Who do *you* work for, Mr. Monkey-Suit?"

Khan kept his gaze steady on the leader. "I'm going to answer your question literally: The University of Oxford."

"So why would some university want to *blow up my club*?"

"See here!" Bertie interjected, apparently jumping to the defense of his school.

Khan interrupted him. "They don't, of course. None of us do."

A slender young man in a light green pinstripe pointed an accusing finger over Jorje's shoulder. "She said the bomb was hers!"

There was a chorus of shouts at this, and the zoot-suited men surged forward, almost pushing Jorje into them.

"If you give me a chance to explain," Khan began, but they weren't interested.

"Drag them out to the orchard!" one of the men shouted. "We can chain them to their own bomb."

"You think this is a game?" Jorje said. "You think this is fun and games? We built this place ourselves. We stock the bar. We book the bands. We protect it from every other tough guy who tries to muscle in. You think you impress me, with your white faces and your L.A. badges?

"I am descended of the Gabrielinos, who were living on this land before your people ever *heard* of Plymouth Rock. When Los Angeles was first founded, my ancestors were living there, while yours were still shooting at red coats."

"Actually—" Bertie objected, but Sylvia and Khan silenced him with elbows to the gut.

"I spent most of my life," Jorje continued, growing angrier with each word, "up in Los Angeles or out here in Maravilla. Do you think I'm some dumb spic you can bully? Do you think I'm a child? Do you think this is the first time I've ever seen *a gringo in an ape suit and a dress?*"

The man's anger was so palpable that Professor Khan felt a chill prickle the many hairs down his back. It occurred to him that he might have miscalculated his personal risk here.

Jorje wasn't finished. "I'm not thrown off my game because of you. Now you are going to tell me who is moving against my club, or my boys are going to get those axe handles over there in the corner and they are going to beat you like piñatas until candy falls out."

Before Khan could frame his answer, the door to the clubhouse swung open with a crash. The zoot-suited men spun in surprise at the sudden noise, then bent low. Was this a second attack?

A young woman strode through the doorway. She couldn't have been older than 17, but she carried herself with the regal bearing of a queen. Her skin was a gorgeous dark reddish brown, her glossy hair held back by a golden head dress decorated with a fan of long white feathers. Her dress was a robe of fine cloth, its design so complex it was almost hypnotic to look at, with golden bangles to hold it in place.

The young gangsters gasped as one, astonished by her beauty. Bertie, Sylvia, and Cross all edged forward to see her as though drawn by a magnet. "Isn't she cracking," Bertie muttered.

A young man in a mustard-colored suit broke away from the others and approached. The Princess—Khan couldn't think of any other name that made sense for her—glanced at him briefly, then turned her attention back to the crowd. She seemed to be searching for someone.

The bold young man had a smile on his face as he murmured gentle words in Spanish, but when the Princess tried to step around him he blocked her way, then he did it again. He wanted her attention, and he wasn't going to let her walk away from him. Bad show.

The Princess turned toward him, her expression still utterly impassive. Khan noticed something strange—as her head turned, her features seemed to lag behind slightly, as though her beauty was a mistimed projection.

"Move away!" Khan shouted. "Move away from her now!"

The young man turned to grin scornfully at him, as did several others, including Jorje. The man in the mustard-colored suit turned back toward the young Princess and laid his hand on her shoulder.

Immediately upon touch, her flesh turned to smoke, rising up from her as if she were a bonfire. Revealed beneath was the dried, shriveled, hairless corpse of a mummy.

CHAPTER THIRTY-THREE

If the young men were loud in their rage, they were positively deafening in their terror. Khan immediately felt someone fall against him in the chaotic jumble of bodies. Detective Cross sank a hard left hook into the stomach of the nearest gangster, then knocked another to the floor as he sprinted toward the back door.

The man in the mustard-colored suit was screaming, his voice standing out from the others because it was higher and more urgent. The mummy—the Princess—jammed her left hand into his stomach. The man's whole body jerked then sagged backward. Blood splashed onto the floor as he collapsed.

Everyone gaped at the mummy, his still-beating heart in her hand. Her mouth fell open like a serpent unhinging its jaw, and she gulped it down whole.

Men screamed. They fell to their knees in prayer. They threw their arms around each other in abject terror. One very small man in charcoal leaped forward and plunged his knife into the Princess's heart, for all the good it did him.

Khan spun toward Sylvia and Bertie. "Back door." Bertie's legs convulsed as if anxious to take advantage of their newfound permission to run, but he turned to Sylvia and made an "after you" gesture. They fled together.

In the center of the room, the Princess had caught hold of the knife-wielder's jacket, but he had squirmed half free of it. Jorje stepped forward and held the gun no more than a foot away from her, then started squeezing off shots. The gun's retorts were sharp in the big, echoing room, but just as in Sylvia's living room, bullets were ineffective.

"Everyone out!" Khan roared. The men in their beautiful suits suddenly jolted away from him, moving in a tide toward the back door.

The small man was still squirming madly, trying to escape the oversized jacket in the Princess's grip. Jorje snatched a pool cue off the table behind him and brought it down on both of her forearms with all his considerable strength.

The cue shattered, shards of wood flying in every direction, but not only did the blow fail to break the mummy's grip, the Princess's arms didn't move at all. It was as though Jorje had attacked the top of a concrete wall.

"Out!" Khan yelled, over and over. It wasn't necessary, but it made him feel better.

The small man slid out of his jacket and flopped onto the floor, hatless. In just his white shirt and high-waisted pants, he looked vulnerable and terrified. My God, he was little more than a boy.

Jorje grabbed him to drag him away, but the Princess caught hold of the gang leader's cuff.

"No!" Khan shouted. As the Princess drew her arm back to plunge it into Jorje's torso, the Professor leaped.

He caught hold of her elbow with both hands. His weight threw all of them off balance, knocking the mummy to her knees and Jorje onto his back. The Princess strained against him and he exerted his entire strength, bringing the full might of a mountain gorilla to bear in a single heave.

But he could only slow her down, not control her. It was his full might pitched against only her left arm, but he could do nothing more than delay her attack. She was too much for him.

A delay was all that Jorje needed. With a quick slash, he cut through the sleeve of his jacket, then tore the rest away as he leaped to his feet. Then he was on his feet, turning toward the door to follow his fellows.

Then he stopped and turned back. The Professor needed only a glance at the man's expression to see what he intended: he did not want to abandon someone who had come to his aid.

"Go!" Khan shouted at him.

Jorje did, reluctantly, as the Princess turned toward the Professor. Her gripping hand tore his tweed jacket and popped the buttons of his shirt. Then she drew back her left hand.

CHAPTER THIRTY-FOUR

Bertie was wildly relieved to see that the back lot behind the building was lit, even if it was only by a single flood light. There was so much desert here, so much wilderness... A chap could vanish forever in this sort of darkness.

There wasn't much safety in the light, either. By heaven, ever since he'd arrived in this mad desert city, he'd been caught up in a whirlwind of trouble. He'd heard more gunshots over the last two days than in his entire life.

The men in their gaudy suits streamed through the back door, spilling all over each other in their panic to escape. Bertie and Sylvia glanced at each other; she was panting from fear more than the exertion of running a few dozen yards, but their flight was stymied by a huge wooden fence quite like the one that blocked the alleyway. This one started at the back of a nondescript building then ran some thirty yards into the darkness. They could either climb that, somehow, or run into the dark and forbidding orange groves.

Sylvia turned to him. "The car! We should go around and have the car ready for the Professor. Except Cross—"

There was a blare of a car horn out in the lot, playing the tune of The Brabant Song.

Sylvia continued in a sinking voice. "Except Cross has the keys."

"I say, was that your Daddy's car horn?"

It sounded again, but this time farther away. "I'm afraid so."

"Good heavens!" Bertie fumed. "What is on with that chap? He's..."

Sylvia finished his thought for him. "... Only out for himself."

Bertie stamped his foot in agreement. "It's extraordinarily frustrating."

The gang leader stumbled through the exit, looking rather roughed up. Bertie couldn't help but admire that suit. Could Bertie pull off a look like that back in London? With his frame? In tangerine or perhaps plum?

Probably not, but it would be a dash to see the expressions on the old gang's faces if he tried. Assuming he survived this accursed mission with Professor Khan.

Speaking of, where was the Professor? "I say!" Bertie called. The fellow who seemed to be the leader—Jorje?—hurried toward him. His jacket was missing half a sleeve for some reason. "Where is the Professor?"

"The gorilla?" Jorje glanced back at the darkened door in a way that did not inspire any confidence at all. "He..."

"No," Sylvia whispered harshly. She bolted toward the building. Bertie would have stopped her himself, but gosh, people can be so sudden. It was Jorje who caught hold of her and held her back. "He saved my life!" Sylvia cried.

"He saved my life, too, señora," Jorje's voice was low and reassuring. "And he may prevail yet."

They turned back toward the clubhouse.

The Mummy Princess stepped through the door, her left hand soaked in blood.

CHAPTER THIRTY-FIVE

101 YEARS EARLIER

Abdallah al-Othman was a strong swimmer. Once the rumors reached him that his father planned to send him on a sea voyage, he'd set aside time to learn. It was only after he'd gotten on board the ship that he'd been shocked to discover that the sailors—men of the sea to the last—did not themselves have the skill.

There was no reason to learn, they explained. If the ship were to sink, swimming would only prolong the inevitable.

Abdallah had replied that it was his intention to prolong the inevitable for as long as possible.

Unfortunately, his plan was put to the test when the West African crew grew weary of their Portuguese captain's heavy hand with the lash. They turned their knives against the Europeans first, then on the only paying passenger. Abdallah would have to swim to Batavia if he intended to make use of his reservation at the Hotel de Provence. In the face of all that bared steel, he leapt the rail holding a life preserver as close as a blood brother, leaving behind his fine silk clothes, his books, his oud, and worst of all, the letter to the bank his uncle had written for him.

He drifted for two days and one night, caught in a powerful easterly current. As the sun beat down unmercifully upon him, and his mouth became parched and his lips split from salt water he could not drink, those sailors' attitudes began to make sense. Instead of dying sensibly in a few seconds, he was dragging it out. The temptation to push the life preserver away was strong, but he thought of his mother and held on.

Two hours before sunset, he saw a dark shape against the horizon. At first he thought it was a ship, but as he got closer he recognized a lone volcano against the horizon, bright green foliage ringing the base.

Life! The current was going to carry him by the island, but he kicked with all his fading strength, and well after dark he clung to the preserver while white caps drove him toward a ring of black rocks that surrounded the beaches.

He awoke on sand. Sweet, precious sand. His head was pounding and his mouth was parched, but he was alive.

And caged. Someone had put him into a wooden cage like a wild animal.

A hooded figure in a kimono approached and set a halved coconut full of water just outside the cage. Abdallah scrambled toward it.

"Nyet! Nyet!" The cracked old voice surprised Abdallah, and he turned around to see a second cage beside his. Inside was an old man with wild grey hair and beard. He'd been a big fellow once, but now he looked half-starved, his weathered brown skin stretched over tendons and bones.

The old fellow mimed lifting a bowl to his lips and made a tiny sipping sound, then again, then again. He wanted Abdallah to drink slowly. Was the water in the bowl poisoned? Or was it dangerous for a thirsty man to drink too quickly?

Either way, the old fellow was in a cage, too, so Abdallah decided to trust him. He pressed his mouth through the wooden poles and sipped the water, slowly. It took great exertion of his will, but he did it. After, the hooded figures brought him a second bowl and a platter of charred fruit and fish. Abdallah ate and drank, then collapsed into a deep slumber.

It was daylight when he woke next, and the sun was low on the horizon. He laid his hand on the sand near the cage so his shadow barely touched it. If the shadow grew over the wood, night was coming and he would make his first escape attempt. If the shadow retreated, he would stay where he was for now. It retreated.

The old fellow in the next cage woke sometime later, and they quickly established that they shared a common language: French. The old man was ecstatic. "You do not know how long I wait for someone to talk at," he said in his abominable accent. "Too many men have come and gone."

That piqued Abdallah's curiosity. "How many have there been?"

"A dozen. Maybe more. Most of them were from Africa or China, and we could not parley. I had no way to warn them about the tests."

Abdallah perked up at that. He liked taking tests. He was good at them. "What sort of tests?"

"Behavior tests," the old fellow said. "And if you fail, you die. That cage is the first one. It wouldn't be too difficult to break out, but you're being watched. You're always being watched, and if you try to break out," he drew his pinky across his throat. "HHHKK!"

"Thank you for telling me this," Abdallah said, bowing as well as he could in the confines of the cage. So much for his planned escape attempt. "What is your name, please?"

The old fellow looked sad. "I can no longer remember it. You can call me Piotr. Can you tell me what year it is?"

"We are near the end of 1248."

"That is not—I mean the Christian calendar. Never mind. I should have known the first man I could speak to in decades would be a Turk."

Abdallah was no Turk, but he saw no reason to correct the fellow. They were given water and fed again; the Russian refused to talk in the presence of their jailers. Abdallah tried to see if the hooded figure serving him today was the same as yesterday, but it was impossible to tell. He made note of the color and shape of the dirty hand holding the bowls, and of the narrowness of the eyes peering through the tiny gap in the hood. If the old man were any judge, he would have plenty of time to study them.

Mid-afternoon, he was released from his cage to dig for clams. It was difficult work, but as Piotr suggested, he did it diligently and without complaint. A hooded figure with a crude spear stood guard over him, but he surreptitiously noted two more standing in the tree line with bows.

"What do they want with us?" Abdallah asked that evening, after eating a share of the horrid clams. "Manual labor?"

"They need men," Piotr said, smiling. "Do you understand? Men."

"Men to dig clams?"

That made the old Russian laugh. "I have never heard it called that before!" Then he laughed some more. "You can't tell, can you? They may be wearing men's clothes, but those are women! Mademoiselles! That why they need men! To *make daughters.*"

The old man's gap-toothed leer was off-putting, but still. Abdallah was a civilized man with sophisticated tastes. Wild native women in men's clothing? How intriguing. "Only daughters?"

Piotr shrugged. "That's how it seems. They've been trapped here for a few generations, but they only seem to have daughters. Not sure how many there are, even. Ten? Twenty? They do not gossip at me."

Abdallah looked down at his fire-roasted fruit. He'd sampled the wares of markets all over the civilized world, but he'd never tasted its like before. Could this be the reason they bore only daughters? "What can you tell me?"

"It is simple," Piotr said. "From what I hear, there is only one source of sweet water on this island, and they know where it is. Supposedly, they have some sort of shrine there—to enter is to die. And you get to live for as long as you behave yourself."

"I must admit," Abdallah said after much thought. "Everything you've told me fires my curiosity."

"Feh," the Russian answered. "Curiosity is for women."

Women and educated men, Abdallah thought, but there was no reason to say it aloud. His companion was clearly an unlettered man of the sea—not a bad sort, but nothing special, either.

In contrast, Abdallah was a poet, scholar, and scientist from a culture famous for all three. Once his curiosity was piqued, it had to be satisfied. Over the next several weeks, he was given numerous tasks. He did them all in a friendly and obedient manner, and only showed his displeasure—mildly—when he was returned to his cage. He wanted them to give the impression he was a willing worker who hoped for better conditions.

After nearly a month and a half, four armed figures released him from his cage after dark. Abdallah knew what was going to happen next, and he begged for—and received—permission to wash himself in the surf before he was brought into the woods. He had a reputation to protect, after all.

He cheerfully allowed them to tie him spread-eagle to stakes in the ground. When he was well-restrained, three of the women left, and one remained with him. Being tied up was not a new experience for him, but the wild woman—who never took off her hood—did not know what she was missing by restraining his hands.

She did speak to him, though, in Japanese. Unfortunately, he had never studied it. At least he knew the kimonos were not an affectation.

Eventually, he developed a good idea where this forbidden place had to be. When he collected fruit or coconuts or hunted for eggs in the trees, he made careful note of where the mademoiselles did not want him to go. Surely this secret, forbidden place, whatever it was, would be there.

Three days after his first night in the jungle, they stopped wearing their hoods around him. For women who had descended from a single line, there was a great deal of variety in their skin tones and the shape of their faces. It was to be expected, of course.

After six nights tied to the stakes, Abdallah despaired of ever being permitted out at night on his own. He'd hoped that Piotr was kept in his cage because he had broken some law, but no. Good behavior meant life in a cage. Misbehavior meant death.

Unacceptable. Abdallah did not intend to spend the rest of his life digging clams and siring daughters who would barely speak to him. Without books. Without music. Without scholarly conversation.

And really, to be lorded over by a bunch of women! It would make an amusing entry in his biography, as long as his stay was respectably short.

On the next night of the full moon, he waited for Piotr to fall asleep. The old fellow had made a habit of obedience and Abdallah couldn't risk that he would sound the alarm. The first step was to unlash the corners of his cage; he'd spent the last few nights loosening the knots.

With luck, the secret shrine would provide him some way of escaping the island—a sea worthy craft, perhaps, or an easily-repaired dirigible. Barring that, he would return with provisions and lash the walls of his cage into a raft.

It wasn't a heroic plan, but it was the best he had.

He'd thought the sprint from the beach to the jungle would be the most dangerous part of his escape—it was the most exposed, after all—but he'd underestimated the amount of noise he would make once he entered the underbrush. It was a flaw every intelligent man struggles with: the tendency to assume you know all you need to know. At least he had correctly judged that the women had relaxed their guard: no one shot an arrow into him from the darkness of the jungle.

He quickly made his way to one of the many paths that criss-crossed the island and hurried along them by the light of the moon. Yes, it was possible to run into one of the mademoiselles on a path, but crashing about in the jungle would alert the entire family.

His luck held. He came to a trickling freshwater stream and followed it back to its source. A slender lake hugged the curve of the volcano, and Abdallah took the opportunity to drink his fill.

There. The moon was bright enough that he could see a clearing on a flattish part of the hill. He moved along the shoreline, gritting his teeth every time his foot slipped and splashed in the water. Each time it seemed as loud as a British sergeant shouting "Alarm!" but no one challenged him.

The clearing, once he reached it, surprised him. The well-tended ground was decorated by rows of rough-hewn planks, and it took him a short while to realize what they were. Grave markers.

This could not be their secret, could it? Unless this was ancestor worship. He'd thought the Japanese were more civilized than that.

One plank was larger than the others. It was set in a high place well back from the water, and something metal gleamed in the pale light. He rushed toward it and snatched it up. This marker had been built with a little shelf, and someone had set an arrow on it.

It was made entirely of metal, and the shaft was much too thick. Ornamental. No one would attempt to hunt or fight with this. Still, it was very strange. What significance could it hold?

As delightfully curious as his find was, it wasn't a boat or dirigible, and it wouldn't help him get off the island. He had a long night in front of him gathering fresh water—in something—and lashing his cage into a raft.

His hand fell on a rough part of the arrow. In the back, near the false feathers, there was a tiny plate with some sort of writing stamped onto it. The light was too dim to read by, but he could certainly bring it along with him and satisfy his curiosity when the sun rose on the open sea.

From behind him, Abdallah heard a sword being drawn from a sheath. He did not live long enough to hear another sound.

CHAPTER THIRTY-SIX

Professor Khan was not much of a climber. Yes, he was better than most humans and he'd done it before—just yesterday, in fact—but he wasn't a monkey. Climbing wasn't easy or comfortable.

It was especially awkward with half a dozen sticks of dynamite tucked under one arm.

Still, needs must as the devil drives, and all that. Khan stacked one trash can atop the other, then bounded up to catch the top of the alley fence with his right hand. A moment later, he was over. The worst part, as he expected, was the long drop to the ground below.

"Ye Gods!" he cried, as one of his bare feet struck a stone. He did his best to tuck into a roll to ease the impact. As soon as he returned to London, he was going to engage a glover to gin up some protection for his feet. Why had he not thought of that before?

Bertie, Sylvia, and Jorje heard his exclamation and raced toward him. "Professor!" Bertie shouted, his face split wide with a relieved smile and his arms wide for an embrace.

"Careful!" Khan said, extending his arm. "I'm holding the bomb."

All three came to a halt. The Professor glanced at the doorway to the clubhouse. Men were scattering in every direction, and the Princess was momentarily confused. She took faltering steps in one direction, then in another, as though she wanted to chase them all at once.

Khan realized they were in an untenable position and moved along the fence away from the buildings. "Jorje, my dear fellow, I know nothing about explosives. Do you—"

Jorje snatched the bomb out of Khan's hand, turned the dial on the timer slightly, then threw it with a forceful grunt. It arced high toward the clubhouse and the mummy, then exploded in front of her just a foot off the ground.

Jorje had already moved beside Sylvia, shielding her body with his own. Professor Khan realized too late that he should have done the same for Bertie, but when the shock wave struck them, lifting them off the ground and slamming them against the wooden fence, Khan knew he would have crushed the lad like a sack of balsa wood model planes.

The blast wave was hot and raw, tearing through their clothes and scraping their skin with hard-blown dust. The others fell hard against the fence, but no one struck as powerfully as Khan did. Wood splintered. The fence bowed backward. Their ears rang.

For a second, Khan thought he'd been struck blind and deaf, but then the dust began to settle over him and he could hear Sylvia and Bertie's choking coughs. They looked dazed—no surprise there, he felt a little wobbly himself—but otherwise unhurt. The wooden fence had bowed over, cushioning their flying bodies.

Jorje pulled a handkerchief from his pocket and pressed it over Sylvia's mouth and nose. She accepted it gratefully, and he looked back toward the source of the explosion. Khan struggled to his feet as well.

They were all dressed in torn rags—the force of the explosion had ruined their clothes. Jorje's expression betrayed a moment of grief, but only a moment.

The light above the back door of the clubhouse flickered unevenly. The explosion had damaged it but hadn't destroyed it.

Surely a blast that powerful would be enough to destroy a desiccated corpse?

But no. When the air cleared, they saw the Princess stalking toward them. The slender white feathers of her headdress remained intact. She wasn't even dusty.

The other zoot-suited gangsters had long since fled into the darkness of the orchard, but the Princess ignored them. She stalked toward Khan and the others. Whatever she was searching for, one of them had it.

"You must flee," Jorje said. "I thank you, Señor Simio, for saving my life after I treated you as an enemy. Still, it is clear. This dead thing has come to kill me, and you must be far away when it happens."

Then he turned away from them and clenched his fists, preparing for a fight he knew he could not win.

Just then, a figure darted by them, coming from atop the fence of the alley. The man sprinted toward the mummy, leapt high into the air, then landed on her shoulders.

His legs locked around her and his momentum carried them both backwards. He landed on his hands, pulling the Princess off her feet and hurling her back several feet. As she sprawled in the dirt, the man neatly rolled over onto one knee, his head bowed and his arms spread wide as though apologizing for offending royalty. He wore an impeccable charcoal grey suit with a navy tie, and his whole head was covered with a bright blue mask. He pleaded in a language unlike any Khan had heard before.

The Professor scratched at his chin. A masked man. Of course. If there was one thing this adventure lacked, it was a masked man.

CHAPTER THIRTY-SEVEN

The mummy pushed up onto her hands and knees. When she looked at them, her eyes were hidden in inky shadow.

The masked man's prayer-like pleading faltered, and he backed away smoothly toward Khan, Jorje, and the others. "I do not think my prayers will appease her this time," he called over his shoulder to them.

"She's changing!" Sylvia exclaimed. Khan looked back toward the Princess and saw that she had become a shadow, and that shadow was changing its shape while they watched.

Moments later, a jaguar with fur so dark it seemed to devour the flickering electric light, advanced toward them. Its eyes and teeth glowed like stars.

Jorje's hand began to tremble. "It has become..."

The masked man had reached them. He was almost as short as Cross, but the tailoring of his jacket suggested the physique of a Greek Hero. His voice was very low. "Angry. She has become angry."

Bertie was the first to flee, clambering over the collapsed fence in a clatter of elbows and knees. Sylvia followed, then the masked man. Khan grabbed hold of Jorje's elbow and shouted: "Come!"

He did. Together, Khan and Jorje ran across the wobbling fence onto the bare dirt beyond. A light switched on far to the left, and in the dim light they could see Sylvia and the masked man fleeing to the right, away from the buildings and the light, toward the tall wooden fence.

"Hey-ya!" Jorje shouted, as though trying to scare away an animal. "HEY-YA!"

But he wasn't shouting back toward the jaguar. He was shouting toward Bertie, who had stopped running all together.

Bertie? Not running from danger? The Professor realized he was missing something and slowed. There. Directly opposite Bertie was a huge—

My God, it was an ostrich. They had broken into some sort of ostrich farm.

The large bird had its wings outstretched and its head lowered as it advanced toward the lad. It was trying to intimidate him, to drive him back, and it would have worked splendidly if the boy hadn't been fleeing a transformed mummy.

"Professor?" Bertie called uncertainly.

"Hey-ya!' Jorje shouted again, but instead of driving the ostrich back, it only enraged it.

It stalked forward. Professor Khan, who had been so civilized, so carefully subdued to avoid alarming his companions, finally cut loose. He roared, letting his gorilla nature emerge.

Bertie was so startled that he stumbled sideways, which saved him from a crippling kick to the leg. The ostrich had struck out at him, dealing him a glancing blow to his thigh.

Then the bird backed away and circled him. Khan charged forward and lifted Bertie off the ground. "Get your legs under you, my boy. Quickly."

Bertie did as he was told, just as the jaguar screamed. It had come to the top of the collapsed fence, moving with all the deliberate care of a hunter moments before the kill.

The ostrich turned toward the big cat and honked, spreading and shaking its wings to make itself look even larger than it was.

That was all the distraction they needed. The masked man had already hurled Sylvia upward to the top of the fence. Then he took a running start and jumped. Khan envied the fluid ease with which he topped the fence. Khan himself lifted Bertie to the top then left him to struggle.

"Your turn, my good man," Khan said, then without waiting for permission, he lifted Jorje to the top of the fence.

The gang leader folded his body over and reached back toward Khan. "Take my hand!"

Khan ignored the offer. From above, he heard Bertie whisper: "He weighs 400 pounds," but there still had to be a way out.

He hoped. The Princess had already proven she had little interest in his gorilla's heart, but would she, as a big cat, tear into him with her teeth and claws? There was something primal in the terror he felt, even though logic assured him he would not be killed. Not here and not yet.

But logic said nothing about being horrifically mauled.

A well-shod foot broke through the wooden fence, splintering one of the planks. To Khan, that seemed a capital idea. He grabbed the plank next to it and tore it out of the frame, then did the same to a third.

The gap was wide enough for him, so he threw the broken wood at the narrowing space between the jaguar and ostrich. The plank fluttered like a wind sock and bounced hard off the dirt, but it was enough to startle the ostrich into fleeing, finally. It was just an animal, but Khan didn't want to see even so lowly a creature murdered just to give him time to get away.

He squeezed through the gap in the fence. There was a distressing sound of even more tearing cloth, but he made it through. "Let's go!"

They ran into the orchard. Great heavens, it was dark out here. The distant, flickering clubhouse lights were so dim it was nearly impossible to avoid tree trunks or low-hanging branches.

Someone hissed—it must have been Jorje—and somehow they had all changed direction, running to the left along the path of the fence. Khan could hear voices farther out in the darkness as men shouted to each other in Spanish.

Suddenly, one of those voices screamed. Jorje rushed into the darkness toward the sound of the cry, and the masked man followed him. The Professor pointed to Sylvia and Bertie. "Get him to safety!" he hissed urgently, then raced after the two men.

Behind him, he heard Bertie's awkward voice. "Don't you mean 'Get *her* to safety?' Sir?"

Another voice screamed in the darkness, then another. Jorje kept changing direction to race toward them; the masked man and Khan did their best to keep up, but the farther they moved into the darkness the more slowly they had to move to avoid braining themselves against a tree.

Then the masked man cried out and threw himself to the side. A shadow flashed by him. The big cat was right here. Khan's adrenaline seemed to roar in his ears as the creature turned its attention toward Jorje.

The gang leader saw the big cat turn toward him. He backed against a tree and lost his balance, sprawling over tree roots. The creature growled and crouched for its attack.

Before it could pounce, Khan did.

CHAPTER THIRTY-EIGHT

The Professor landed on the big cat's back, heavily. The jaguar had all of the mummy's uncanny strength, but it could still be pulled off balance with the proper application of weight and leverage. Khan rolled it onto its side. He snaked his long arms under its shoulders and knitted his fingers behind its head. He wrapped his legs around its waist, pulling it down.

No, he wasn't stronger than it was, but he didn't need superior strength to hold a full nelson.

Jorje started toward him. "Don't touch me!" Khan snapped, but the gang leader drew a knife from his tattered pocket and plunged it into the big cat's heart several times. For a moment, the Professor dared to hope that the creature would be more vulnerable in its animal form, but that was futility itself.

"Go!" Khan ordered. "I will hold it as long as I can, but you must go now, and quickly."

"I won't!" Jorje said. "I won't abandon you."

"It would not do any good," the masked man said. "Once she hunts you, she will never stop until she gets what she wants."

"Who are you?" Jorje said. "Did you bring this thing onto my people?"

"No!" The masked man seemed no larger than a boy in the darkness. "I have followed her, not led her. I am merely trying to keep her from punishing indiscriminately. And you both are treating her with disrespect."

"She murdered one of my boys!" Jorje shouted, and the two men began to argue in Spanish.

"What is she and what does she want?" Sylvia asked, her sharp tone silencing them. As annoyed that the Professor was that she had not fled when he asked her to, he was grateful that someone was asking sensible questions.

"She has no name," the masked man said. "It has been lost to history. She is simply 'The Princess.'"

"By Jove, I am insightful sometimes," the Professor muttered.

"... And she is searching for something that was stolen from her tomb."

"Oh no." Sylvia said. "A jewel?"

"The Calicos Jewel," the masked man answered. "It was stolen from her resting place by a grave robber. She can sense the ethereal residue it leaves behind, but has not been able to find it yet."

The big cat struggled, but Khan held on. Barely. "While it's lovely to stand around and chat as though this is high tea—"

Sylvia stepped forward and knelt beside the jaguar, almost within reach of its claws. My word, didn't any of these people know how to run for their lives? Americans! "Oh, Professor," Sylvia said. "She's not hunting any of these men. She's looking for me."

Sylvia looked directly into the jaguar's eyes. "I don't have your jewel, but I have touched it. Can you sense that? Can you sense that the jewel passed through my hands to someone else?"

Sylvia moved her hand close to the big cat's mouth. The glow from the creature's eyes and teeth shone on her outstretched palm. Khan could see Sylvia tremble slightly, but she did not shy away.

He expected the big cat to start thrashing suddenly, but it didn't. Instead, it stopped struggling and stared at her.

Khan could not see the creature's face, only the back of its head and ear. Sylvia was looking deep into its eyes. "Wow," she said, with a tone that suggested reverence. "Wow."

The jaguar vanished. One moment Khan was straining to hold her, muscles aching, and the next she was simply gone, transformed into a billowing mist.

The mist swirled above them and drifted westward, moving very slowly against the wind.

"Is it over?" Bertie asked.

Sylvia nodded. "I think she's moved on."

The Professor sighed and rolled onto his back. He felt as though he could sleep for a whole year, although he'd also have a lifetime's worth of nightmares.

"This is intolerable," the masked man said. "Intolerable! Do you know how difficult she is to track in that form?"

Then he collapsed onto his face.

Professor Khan and Jorje both hurried to him, but Sylvia was closest. "He struck his head."

"It was probably when the big cat leapt at him. We should get him into the light and clean him up."

Men in zoot suits edged toward them, and Jorje spoke to them in Spanish, arranging for the masked man to be carried away. Sylvia went with them.

Jorje took one of the Professor's hands and Bertie took the other. Although both men leaned far back, Khan still pulled them to their knees when they tried to help him to his feet. Bertie seemed embarrassed, but Jorje only laughed. "Your friend was right. You are even heavier than you look, and you do not look tiny. Come with me and we will get you cleaned up."

"I'm afraid we can't accept your gracious offer," Professor Khan said. "Mr. Wisp is almost certainly heading back toward the city, and I would like to see if we can—"

"Forgive me, Señor Simio," Jorje said. He lifted the lapels of his shredded jacket; even in this dim light, Khan could see that his clothes were ruined.

It was only when the Professor realized how cold and breezy he felt that he realized how damaged his clothes were, too. "Er..." Whether it had been the explosion or the tear he'd heard passing through the gap in the fence, the Professor's kilt had been reduced to something that would not even have served as a loincloth in a jungle man movie.

"Come, Señor Simio. I thought you came here as an enemy, but you have saved my life. Twice! You must tell me what brought you to me, and I will find something for you to cover yourself. Perhaps you will think it flattering."

CHAPTER THIRTY-NINE

Bertie could not find a comfortable place to settle. It wasn't just that his clothes were stiff with dry California dirt. It wasn't just that his pants were torn and the ice pack on his leg did little to reduce the growing black and blue mark. (My word, but who thought an ostrich could be so blamed terrifying! In pictures they appeared so amusing, but if that great brute had caught him full on with that kick, it would have broken his leg!)

It was then he realized how useless he had been. The Professor had battled the living dead, had saved lives, had uncovered clues, but what had he done? Frighten the customers of a homophile nightclub into flight?

It was hardly the sort of thing to bring honor to the Blinkersly name.

He looked around the room. The back wall had buckled under the force of the explosion, and two enterprising fellows had stripped off their jackets to work on shoring up that part of the roof. Bertie had never been much use at trade, so his help would only interfere with their work and embarrass him.

A few of the crates at that end of the room had broken, and some delightfully scented whiskies were leaking out. Unfortunately, the men salvaging undamaged bottles gave him dark looks if he so much as licked his lips. Better to keep far back.

Of course, the whole point of the trip was to be an assistant to Professor Khan. It couldn't hurt one's unfortunately average grade, but the Professor was nowhere to be seen at the moment. The handsome fellow who ran the show had taken him into a room on the side of the building, from which emanated the sound of whirring sewing machines.

Then there was Sylvia and the fellow with the mask. Bertie had been shocked to see men going hatless in public, but this was another extreme entirely.

Stranger still, he missed Detective Cross. It was so... reassuring to have him on their side. The fellow's absence made Bertie feel vulnerable. Blast it, if the others could make do, so could he.

Resolved, he limped toward Sylvia and her charge. He had learned the fellow was a *luchador*, which made him some sort of masked fighting man from across the southern border. Bertie tried to imagine a regiment of rifle-bearing men calling themselves "Blue Hornet" as this man did, and wearing masks with bug-wing designs over his eye holes, but the whole thing seemed equally absurd, mysterious, and alarming.

When they returned from their battle in the orchard, three women— wearing much the same clothes as the men, including the long watch chain— tended to his injury without removing his mask. No one thought his covering the least bit odd. Had everyone heard of these commando blokes but him?

Sylvia stood beside the Blue Hornet with a steel flask in her hands. As he came close, Bertie heard her say: "It will stop the bleeding and swelling."

Hornet waved her off. "I am sorry, señora, but I treat my body as if it were a church. No sin must take place within, especially not the sin of drinking. I have my career to consider."

"I'm not sure why you won't believe me, but I swear to you that there is no alcohol in this."

"But I have seen this style of flask before many times, and I feel slightly dizzy, nothing more."

Sylvia held it up. "Yes. It's durable and non-reactive. The liquid inside it will arrest any bleeding you might have beneath your skull, and considering we have no idea how far the nearest hospital is, it could prevent permanent brain damage."

"I say," Bertie chimed in, "I haven't known the young lady for very long, but she's absolutely tops. As reliable as Welsh weather."

The masked man looked at Bertie for a moment, then said: "I do not know what that means, but..." He took the flask from Sylvia. "And what will this do?"

"Cure light wounds."

Hornet shrugged and tipped it back, draining the flask. When he'd finished, he grimaced. "That is not delicious." He screwed the cap on, then his expression slowly changed. "The pain in my head... I can feel my injury healing. This doesn't simply deaden pain, no?"

"No," Sylvia said. "You'll still have a bump, but at least you won't stroke out."

Bertie stared down at the flask in Hornet's hand. Might there be a few drops left for him and his leg? "Thank you, Señora," Hornet said.

"You're welcome. Can you see how many fingers I'm holding up?"

"Tres."

"Fine. Feeling any sudden pains in your neck or groin area? Any sudden loss of bladder or bowel control? Sudden deafness? Uncontrollable rages? Teeth falling out? Frozen joints? Skin sloughing off? Have a sudden urge to consume human flesh?"

Hornet and Bertie were very still. The luchador cleared his throat. "Er, no?"

Sylvia took the flask. "Ah. Good." She patted his shoulder. "Nothing to worry about then."

Bertie took that as his cue to back away... until he came upon the dead man. He was lying with a sheet over him now, and although nothing had been said, he was certain the authorities would never be notified. The fellow had died in a warehouse full of illegal liquor and while he certainly had a place among his confederates, it didn't appear that they liked him very much.

Nor did they think much of Bertie. The Professor had earned their trust, but Bertie did not care for the way they kept changing sides and his blank, watchful stare broadcast his distrust. A fellow who was helping them now had wanted to murder them barely an hour earlier. A police detective who had koshed Bertie quite vigorously had become their ally, then had run out on them. He'd always found inconstancy maddening. The whole thing left him in a whirl.

Perhaps that was the point. Professor Khan was his teacher, after all. Perhaps this constant adaptability was his first lesson.

He looked down at the blood-spattered sheet on the floor beside him. Lesson number two: do not step in the way of a woman who wants to walk around you.

While Bertie did his best to come up with a third lesson, a door opened behind him. He turned to see a figure step into the room in a powder blue zoot suit: a hat with a brim wider than Bertie's own hand, padded shoulders, lapels big enough to wrap fish and chips in, and a long chain that dangled almost to the floor tucked into high-waisted pants.

Bertie gasped. He was *definitely* going to show off that style to the fellows back in London.

Then the figure lifted his head so the brim of his hat no longer concealed his face. Good heavens! It was Professor Khan!

CHAPTER FORTY

"Well!" Sylvia said. "Don't you look smashing."

"Thank you, my dear," the Professor said. "Bertie, you're going to catch a fly in that mouth. Jorje, I am grateful that you and your friends have taken the trouble, not least because I had always believed pants would not fit my frame."

"What you needed," Jorje said as he straightened Khan's tie, "was a seamstress as talented as my Graciela." They both nodded to a young woman with heavy eyeliner and a maroon zoot suit of her own as she emerged through the door behind them. "And suspenders."

Sylvia stepped forward. "There's a problem, Professor. The car is gone."

Khan sagged. "Cross?"

Sylvia nodded. Blue Hornet leaped from the couch where he had been convalescing. "Do not fear! Are you returning to Los Angeles? Because I am heading there myself and will be happy to transport you."

"Accepted with thanks," Khan said. He turned to Jorje and extended his hand. "I'm frightfully sorry for the trouble."

Jorje shook his hand heartily. "Never apologize for wrongs committed by other men," he said, "but thank you nonetheless. If you ever want to dance to the best Samba music on the wrong side of the border, the drinks will be on me."

Professor Khan helped Bertie into the parking lot, where Blue Hornet was leading them to a huge blue phaeton Ford Model B. They all piled inside, the luchador behind the wheel, Sylvia beside him, and Bertie once again joining Khan in the back seat.

The Professor had hoped that the luchador would remove his mask when he drove, but no. Apparently, he never took it off, even when the back of his head was being stitched up. The fabric had been cut, though, and was now held together by a knot.

"You are of course intrigued by me," Hornet announced as he drove. "It is only natural. Masks are an irresistible pique to the curiosity." He turned toward them, his bright smile showing through the mouth hole. "My English is quite good, yes?"

"Indeed it is," the Professor said.

"I will tell you my story first, to ease your minds. Then you will tell me yours. Agreed? So! I am the Blue Hornet, a tecnico in the lucha libre scene in Mexico City. I am not the top of the bill—yet—but I am no longer at the bottom, either, if you understand my meaning. I am going places I could never have managed back in the little town where I grew up.

"I will not tell you where that is, for reasons soon to become clear. My father—who is a saint of a man, truly—arrived at the gymnasium one day to tell me that an American had stolen the centerpiece of the Princess's treasure, a jewel of unique design and value. The Princess, in her anger, strode out into the countryside in search of it, and many innocent people were harmed. My father needed me to follow her, to protect the guiltless from her wrath, and to assist her if I could."

"Why did your father come to you?" The Professor asked.

"Because she was already making her way northward, and he knew me, his youngest child, as a man who could see a job to the end! I have trained my body and my mind to be the strongest and the best, to exemplify the ethos of a virtuous man. A tecnico." Blue Hornet jabbed a finger toward the heavens to emphasize his point. "Also, I have a reliable automobile. My father's village is a poor one."

Sylvia sighed. "I had no idea that acquiring the Calicos Jewel would cause so much trouble."

"Neither did the man who took it, I'm sure. He is not the first to try, but he got farther than most."

"What can you tell us about this jewel?"

Hornet, for once, kept his gaze on the darkened road ahead. "Little. It is tied up with the story of the Princess, which I will tell to you now. Long ago, before the conquistadors set sail out of the east, the Aztec emperor found himself under attack from a demon. This demon could possess innocent people, hiding within them, waiting unseen for the moment to strike. They say it drove men mad with a single look, and it could make a man like a newborn child."

"Newborn...?" Khan scratched his chin. "What does 'like a newborn child' mean?"

"You know?" Hornet responded, "I can not say. That is how the story is always told: como un recién nacido. I was never clear on what it meant either, and I have heard this story my whole life."

"I apologize for interrupting."

"No need!" Hornet said grandly. "You ask insightful questions. To continue: This demon very much wanted to inhabit the emperor himself, but the royal palace had been sealed off. No one could get in, and no one was allowed to leave. For many days, the demon stalked outside the wall in one form after another, sometimes masquerading as a general with important news, sometimes as a beggar seeking shelter. However, no one would open the gates.

"Finally, a captain in the emperor's elite slingers appeared at the gate. He had found the demon's altar in a clearing in the jungle, he claimed, and on the altar he had found a jewel that could capture it. At first the emperor's court was convinced it was one of the demon's tricks, but the emperor's eldest daughter knew the man, and insisted the captain was still himself.

"You see, she loved him, and he loved her, but of course there could be nothing between them. The princess convinced her father to accept the jewel. A basket was lowered, and as the jewel was placed inside, the demon discovered what was happening and attacked. The jewel was brought into the palace, but the brave, handsome captain, he was killed.

"Heart-broken, the Princess offered herself as the vessel to entrap the demon, and her father, a man equal parts cruel and desperate, agreed. She was permitted to run through the gates to the body of her great love, and there, the demon found her. Greedy to take control of a form no one would dare to harm, it entered her body and mind, unaware that beneath her robes she wore the mysterious jewel. Together, they were trapped, and helpless.

"The emperor ordered a secret tomb be built, and she was buried within, neither dead nor alive. Centuries have passed, but whenever an opportunistic thief breaks into her resting place to steal the gem and release the demon, she walks once more, roaming the land until she reclaims them both."

CHAPTER FORTY-ONE

"Demon, eh?" Professor Khan had no idea what to make of Hornet's tale. "How much of this story do you think is true?"

Hornet turned both palms toward the sky. "It is difficult to say. It is a very old story, and such things tend to become embellished over time, as men of learning must surely know. Still! There is a Calicos Jewel. I have been inside the tomb myself to see it. And there is a princess who walks the night, as we have all seen."

"Is Calicos the name of the demon?" Sylvia asked.

"Did I leave that out?" Hornet asked. "Because it is so. Now it is your turn to tell me your story, yes? Somehow you have come in contact with this cursed jewel; I would know how."

Professor Khan rubbed his jaw, unsure what to say. This masked wrestler seemed like a decent fellow, if a little egotistical, but did they dare the risks of sharing the true nature—

"We're searching for a magic wishing bow and arrow," Bertie blurted out. "A man named Max Devlin took it but we don't know where he hid it."

Sylvia turned and scowled at him, obviously thinking the same thing as Professor Khan. Bertie seemed oblivious to their disapproval.

For his part, Blue Hornet took the announcement in stride. "A bow and arrow that grants wishes! This world is truly full of wonders. I would like to help you recover it so I might make a wish of my own. I would desire to become the most beloved tecnico in the lucha libre world."

Bertie sighed. "I would wish for someone I could spend my life with."

Khan looked at him, surprised. Had he forgotten Petunia so quickly?

Hornet turned to Sylvia, sitting beside him. "How about you, señora?"

"I would wish to have my father back," Sylvia said bitterly.

"He has recently passed?" Hornet said, his tone softened. "You have my sympathies, señora."

"And how about you, Professor Simio?"

"Khan," the Professor said absently. "My name is Professor Khan." His thoughts whirled; he could remember vividly the moment the queen asked him to stay with her as her consort. It had thrilled him, of course, because he cared for her so deeply, but he had felt the gaze of his companions on him, and he had been embarrassed by the forthrightness of her proposition.

A bolder fellow—a more experienced fellow—would have simply accepted. It was what his heart wanted, after all. Sadly, when it came to the fairer sex he was neither of those things. He'd been so shocked that he had blurted out the wrong answer.

Now he was back in the human world, where he was hated or feared by those who did not believe he was some sort of circus trick. He had friends among humans, yes, but despite the kindness they showed him, they were a different species. The gulf that created between them—that terrible loneliness—could never be bridged.

The world held other intelligent gorillas, of course, but they were cruel and warlike. He had confirmed his status as an outcast when he helped thwart their invasion of New York. He could never find community there, even if he had felt moved to seek it.

But to stand beside the woman he loved atop the towers of a distant world?

Khan's hand rested on his left breast, where he could feel the bafflium-core arrow beneath his jacket. The others were waiting for his answer. "I have seen war," he said, "and fought terrifying enemies, but if I could have any wish at all, I would undo a foolish moment of cowardice."

There was silence then, broken only by the rumble of the car's engine. The dark road was a lonely one, with few lights in sight.

"I should not have been surprised," Hornet finally announced, "that a discussion of wishes would be suffused with regret."

"What next?" Sylvia asked. She turned to look at the Professor. "Cross is gone. Wisp must know his attempt to kill us failed. Devlin could shoot the bow at any time, if he feels threatened."

"Assuming he has any more arrows," Bertie said.

"We must assume he does," Khan answered. "But that he will hold them dear."

All this talk about wishes had kindled a fire in Khan's belly. He ached to nock the arrow in his pocket against Leveque's bow, draw it back, and make his wish. He was restless with it and impatient to have it done.

Concern for propriety had stayed his hand for too long.

"I have had enough," Khan said. "We have to move against Max as soon as possible. I'm willing to gamble that he has hidden the bow in that office closet."

Sylvia nodded. "So am I."

"No more games," Khan announced. "I'll tear that padlock out of the wood myself. I say we gather the resources we need to kick down the door to his office, and then we'll take what we want."

CHAPTER FORTY-TWO

LAPD Homicide Detective Delbert Gustav liked everything about his job except the corpses. There was something unnatural about the way people looked when they died. The moving pictures made it seem like a fella just laid back and closed his eyes, but the truth was so much worse, especially when there were pieces.

Somehow word had gotten around that he had a weak stomach, which was ridiculous. It wasn't that he couldn't take it. He could. He just didn't *want* to take it. Big difference.

But tonight's job was the best sort: a young woman of no specific occupation and questionable morals had been found strangled in a motel room. It was nasty business, but his cut of her cash and jewels would be worth almost fifty bucks. Even more promising, the desk clerk had turned over the name of her pimp along with a five-spot and a heavy revolver he shouldn't have had. The pimp would be worth at least a c-note and, with luck, the name of the john who did her, too. As he stepped into the motel parking lot, he thought his night was turning out pretty sweet.

"Hey, Gus."

Delbert nearly jumped out of his skin. His foot struck a planter as he turned around and he fell onto his backside right there on the concrete. "Jesus! Emil, you shouldn't startle a guy like that. What if I'd shot you?"

Detective Cross glared at him. "You'd have to remember you're carrying to do that." It was true. A truly tough operator—and Cross might have been the toughest—would have grabbed their piece on reflex. Delbert never did. "Speaking of which, I need one. A piece."

"You lost your piece? Christ, Emil—"

"Shut up, Gus. I'm working a blue folder and I don't have time to horse around. Now give up the gut blaster you took from that desk clerk."

Delbert took the gun from his pocket and handed it to Cross. It hurt to think of the dough he could have scored by hocking it, but nobody crossed Cross, not even fellow cops. "A blue folder? Is that why you and Jim weren't at roll call this morning? Hey, where is Jim?"

"Where's your partner?" Cross snapped. "Tipping a few back, as usual? Don't give me that look. I ain't some paper doll to start crying about a Dracula flying off with my number one suspect."

Delbert flinched. Eleven years earlier, he'd filed a report saying exactly that, but the captain had laughed in his face and refused to acknowledge he had a blue folder case. Still, he knew what he'd seen—fangs, glowing eyes, the whole deal.

But if Emil Cross said he had a blue folder, no one would question it. No one would dare. "Is your blue folder related to the Baby Face Attacks?"

"Maybe. Spill."

Delbert spilled, telling him about the scientists who had been attacked in their homes and laboratories, drugged into comas and shaved. Every part of them had been shaved.

Cross frowned. "Any idea who did it?"

"No clue. None of the victims have come around so there's no one to give a statement. There's no sign of forced entry, either."

Cross grunted. "Huh. Anything taken from the house?"

CHAPTER FORTY-THREE

The car Detective Cross took—Khan wasn't ready to use the word "stole" in reference to the police, no matter the circumstances—was sitting in Leveque's car park beside Cross's own vehicle. The hood was warm.

The detective himself waited for them in Leveque's living room, car keys and a tumbler of scotch on the table before him. Sylvia marched across the room and snatched up the keys. "Make yourself comfortable, why don't you?"

"Already did," Cross growled. "Where did you pick up this one?"

Blue Hornet was about to respond, but Khan laid a hand on his shoulder to silence him. "Why are you still here? What use could you possibly be to us at this point?"

Cross picked up the tumbler and clinked the ice before taking a sip. "You got this backwards, gorilla. You're my operatives and I'll make use of you any way I like. I ain't done with you yet."

"No," Sylvia said. "You stranded us with that mummy. I don't work for cowards."

"Call me what you like, sister," Cross snarled as he stood. "I look after myself first and only. Right now I have a score to settle with Max Devlin over the death of my partner, and a prize to take from him."

"You can't have the bow," Sylvia said. "Bad enough that Max stole it. I won't have you taking it, too."

"I don't want your bow," Cross said. "All I want is a shot. I just want to take one shot."

"To do what?" Bertie interjected. His eyes were shining. "What would you wish for?"

Cross glared at him. "That's my business."

Sylvia shook her head. "I still say no."

Before Cross could respond, Hornet stepped forward and put his hand on Cross's shoulder. "The señora has given you her answer, friend. Perhaps you should heed it." Hornet and Cross were both of a height, but where the luchador was all easy, languid athleticism, the old detective was as tense as a coiled serpent.

"Take that hand offa me," Cross said, "or I'll bite it off."

"My friend, I invite you to show the proper respect to—"

But Cross wasn't going to listen to any more. He slapped Hornet's hand from his shoulder, and Hornet, in one smooth motion, caught hold of Cross's elbow.

What happened next was too quick for Khan to follow closely, but somehow Hornet had taken control of Cross's arm and was bearing him to the floor. Cross, who was no taller than Hornet but much heavier, moved his weight backward and then forward again, partially freeing himself from the hold.

They fell to the floor together, rolling away. Khan started toward them, but they were both too skilled at fighting to be interrupted so readily. Hornet adjusted his position, grappling for better position. Cross sank a hard, fast right into Hornet's crotch.

The luchador gasped but did not stop fighting. The blow was powerful enough for Cross to create a bit of space between them and he slipped his hand beneath his jacket.

Khan fell upon them both just as the detective drew his revolver. He yanked the barrel away from the luchador and a shot rang out. A bottle full of cloudy yellow liquid not twelve inches from Bertie's head shattered.

The whole world suddenly seemed tinged with red. Khan ripped the gun out of Cross's hand and roared into his face. He lifted the little cop above his head like a rag doll, bared his fangs at him, and struggled with the animal urge to hurl him through the picture window onto the rocks outside.

Instead, he shook the detective, then tossed him contemptuously onto the nearest sofa. Then, because that wasn't enough to ease the rage growing inside him, he did the same to Hornet. Still, his fury could not be quenched. He went down on all fours and roared again.

Cross fell against the sofa cushions, then tumbled to the floor. His hat fell off, buttons popped from his jacket, and his gray hair went in every direction at once. Hornet fell with no more dignity.

Cross's eyes were wide and focused, his stained teeth bared, but his voice was utterly calm. "All right, then," he said. "You're in charge."

Blue Hornet struggled onto one knee. "I would call you a rudos," he said to the detective, outraged, "but you do not even have that much honor!"

Khan spun on him and bared his fangs. "Enough."

Hornet raised his hands and bowed his head. "Enough, then. I am a soldier; you are the general."

"No," the Professor said, trying not to sound as though he might break into a rage again at any moment. "No, it's Sylvia's property we are trying to recover. She will be in charge."

CHAPTER FORTY-FOUR

Sylvia opened her mouth to speak, then shut it again. Professor Khan turned to Bertie, who was standing perfectly still, his face a ghostly white.

"Bertie, my lad, are you hurt?"

"No, sir." Bertie's voice trembled.

Sylvia laid her hand on Bertie's elbow. "There's an ice bag behind the bar. My father used to use it for his hangovers. Please fill it for the luchador, then take him to the guest room on the side of the house."

Hornet waved his hand. "I do not need—" The Professor's look silenced him. "Of course. The general has issued orders, and I obey."

Bertie filled an ice bag from the chill chest behind the bar, then helped Hornet out of the room.

Cross smoothed his thin hair and put his hat back on. Khan wanted to tell him it was rude to wear it inside, but it wasn't his home.

"You still need me," Cross said, his voice urgent. "You know it. What's more, I owe Devlin for what happened to Jim Waters. I can live without a wish, but I can't live without paying Devlin for what he did to my partner."

Sylvia looked down at the little detective with her chilliest stare. "I owe him for Jim, too."

"And there's more," Cross said. "Somebody has been robbing scientists all over the Southland."

"What are they taking?" Khan asked.

Cross's answer surprised them all. "Bafflium." Khan absent-mindedly touched his jacket where the arrow was kept. Cross nodded and looked at Sylvia. "I know you have one, too. But that's not all. The thief is taking something else, too: hair. He's shaving the scientists and putting them into comas."

The Professor was baffled. "I suspect you have the order reversed. I assume this is an ongoing investigation."

"It is," Cross confirmed. "They're calling them the Baby Face Attacks. I can't go back to the precinct yet—I can't go home, either, not without this thing with my partner settled, but a pal gave me the scoop."

"And more bullets for your gun."

"A new gun, if you ain't noticed," Cross said.

Khan turned to Sylvia. "Do you think Devlin could be making more arrows on his own?"

"No," Sylvia said firmly. "Each arrow is a technical marvel. Believe me."

"Quite. Could he have made a deal with someone else to make copies of an arrow in his possession?"

She didn't want to answer that one.

"He could," Cross said. "If there's a way to make a deal, Devlin can do it." He looked up at Sylvia "You ain't safe."

She didn't react. "That isn't breaking news, detective."

"Except I know you took one of these arrows from Lee, and you're probably carrying it right in that big purse. Devlin knows not to mess with me. I can be useful to you."

"Until the next dangerous situation," Sylvia said, "when you show us the soles of your shoes again."

Cross didn't flinch. "What do I have to do to earn that wish?"

Khan had the sudden urge to pick up the little detective and shake him some more, but Sylvia just waved him off. "We'll talk about it later. Can you make us something to eat?"

Cross scowled. "I don't cook," he said. Then his expression softened. "Sandwiches?"

"That would be perfect. You'll find chicken timbales, beer, lettuce, jellied oranges, preserved kumquats, bread and more in the crisper."

Cross nodded and started toward the kitchen. Khan said: "Wash your hands first," to his retreating back.

Sylvia glanced nervously at the gun in Khan's hand. He dropped it into his jacket pocket. "I don't want to be in charge," Sylvia said. "I'm not sure what we should do next. Honestly, I don't see how we can get the bow back without getting killed. I don't think even you could carry it off the lot, not without being stopped by studio security."

"Very true, my dear," Khan said. "I would much rather carry it out in my pocket. You still have that shrink ray, don't you?"

CHAPTER FORTY-FIVE

Khan and Sylvia did their best to bring order to Leveque's workshop, but it was a lost cause. They had to content themselves with clearing a workbench and stacking the functional gadgets they discovered onto it, to be sorted out later.

"What do you think of these ultra-stilts?" Sylvia asked.

They looked very much like metal pants. "Why do you want them?"

Sylvia caressed a node built into the outside of the ankle, where the telescoping stilt must have been kept. "The gyroscope makes them very easy to use. In fact, it's harder to fall over in them than it is to stand straight. A person on stilts can move quite fast. I've clocked thirty-five miles an hour at a steady stride."

"I would be concerned with power lines."

She had to concede that point. "What about this bowel-loosening grenade? It releases a pulse that causes everyone within thirty feet to—oh, let's just forget about this one."

"I agree."

"And this is... Well, my father called it a death ray."

Professor Khan looked down at the long chrome tube with the red crystal set in one end. It looked very much like a wizard's wand, except for the cables that attached to a backpack battery. "Death ray?"

Sylvia's voice was uncharacteristically hushed. "It fires an electrical pulse that interferes with nerve and heart function. Instant cardiac arrest. It turns out that making devices to kill people is one of the easiest things in the world."

Khan moved it off the table. "My dear, Mr. Devlin has certainly cost several people their lives, but I am not ready to assume the role of his executioner. I want nothing to do with a death ray."

"I already got a death ray," Cross said as he descended the stairs. "It ought to be right here in my holster."

He set the metal tray of food on top of a pile of equipment before Sylvia could warn him not to. Luckily, there was no live current to strike him dead. Cross took a little plate with a sandwich off the tray, along with a bottle of beer, both of which he handed to Sylvia. "Chicken with lettuce, just like you said. Your father had good taste in suds."

When the Professor received his sandwich and beer, he was shocked to discover that Cross's idea of "good taste in suds" was a German pilsner. Philistine.

Cross looked down at the equipment they were selecting, but when he opened his mouth to speak, Sylvia spoke first. "Have you brought food to the others?"

The little detective scowled. "Not yet," he said bitterly, then carried the tray upstairs.

When the door slammed behind him, Sylvia collapsed onto a stool. "Oh, Professor. These men..."

Khan moved a stool beside hers and sat. "What is it, my dear?"

"Who are these crazy people who are helping me? Bertie is a sweet boy, but please don't take offense when I say he's not the hero type."

The Professor raised his hand. "You won't hear a complaint from me on that score."

"Cross is a vile human being—I half expect him to take cover behind me whenever trouble starts."

"Only half?"

"And this luchador, whatever his name is, struts around like a peacock. Is there anyone I could trust less? You're the only one I feel I can rely on, and you're not even a human being!"

"That's true enough," Khan said.

"Oh, I'm sorry, Professor. I didn't mean to be awful, not to you. You've been perfectly wonderful."

"Sylvia, I've traveled all over the world, and I can assure you I speak with great authority when I say that there are very few genuinely courageous human beings in the world." She laughed. "And you are one of them. The way you approached the Princess and the way you risked your life for your neighbor were entirely heroic."

"I've tried," she said, as though admitting to a crime. "But I've felt so detached..."

"Sylvia, you just lost your father under the most trying of circumstances. Of course you feel detached from this madness. You're grieving. Nothing could be more natural."

"I just don't think I can rely on those others," she admitted, "and I don't think I can do this alone. Maybe a month ago, before Father did what he did, but not now. It's too much."

"The others will be useful; I'll see to it. Meanwhile, you and I will look after each other, for your father's sake."

She sighed. "Endothermic mine."

Professor Khan looked down at it. It was as big as a dinner platter and nearly a foot tall, with a red indicator light on the top. "Of course," he said. "Why not? But how will we carry it?"

Sylvia patted a gadget that looked like a cross between a camera and a phonograph. "Remember the shrinking beam? What we decide to bring with us gets shrunk down, along with the shrinker itself. They'll all fit into this purse of mine, along with..." From a shelf on the wall she removed a bulky flashlight almost as long as her forearm. The bulb was made of purple-tinted glass. "The shrink beam wears off in an hour, but we can erase the effects completely with just a few seconds of exposure to this infrapurple light."

"Infrapurple, you say?"

"Instant gadget," Sylvia said, trying to smile. "Just add light."

They returned to the pile of gadgets on the table.

CHAPTER FORTY-SIX

It felt strange to stand in Anselme Leveque's office. Professor Khan's letters had almost certainly been opened at this desk, beside that window, with the waves crashing against the rocks late at night. He tried to imagine the man hunched over to write a reply.

He felt a profound sense of absence that made him weary and sorrowful. How many brilliant minds had the world lost? It didn't have any to spare.

He laid Anselme's fountain pen on the blotter beside a stack of excellent stationery. The paper had a lavender tint to it.

How could he have failed to recognize this paper right away?

There was a knock at the door. "Enter," Khan said as though this was his office back at university.

It was Bertie, and he looked haunted. "Professor..."

He couldn't finish what he had to say. Khan cleared his throat. "Bertie, I'm going to send you home. Today."

"What?" The young man took several steps toward him, and Khan had the feeling he might suddenly grab hold of his lapels. "Sir, you can't!"

"I can and will," Khan answered. "It was kind of you to accompany me on this journey and you have helped me immensely, but I should never have put you in so much danger."

"You're in as much danger as I am, sir."

The Professor slid the paper around on the desk, then set his pen on it. "No, not really."

"Professor, you might be stronger and faster than a silly fellow like me," Bertie insisted, "but you've been incredibly brave, too."

"That's just not so, Bertie."

The young man looked about to argue, but he clamped his mouth shut instead. He walked the darkened window, wringing his hands in a frustrated way. "This is an unusual sort of place, don't you think, sir?"

There was only impenetrable darkness on the other side of the glass; Professor Khan had no idea what Bertie was staring at. "In what way?"

"I imagine that any big city is a place where a chap could start over, become a new man. You hear about it all the time, don't you? Some cowherd's daughter in Breconshire moves to London to pursue a career on the stage. Sometimes a story like that will even have a happy ending. But it feels different here. It almost seems as though the normal rules have all been suspended. Men walking down the sidewalk without hats, as it were."

"Bertie, are you thinking of staying in Los Angeles after we wrap all this up?"

For a moment, Khan was sure the young man was going to say *yes*. "Oh, no, sir. My family, my name and inheritance, the manor... Leave *England*, sir? I could never. But I don't think I will return as the same person who left."

The Professor kept silent. Bertie would continue when he was ready to. "The one thing Daddy—" He stopped himself as though he hadn't meant to use that word, but it had come out like a bad habit. "—Never wanted to talk about was The War. My Uncle Rupert, though, he did. An awful lot of it comes down to luck, doesn't it, sir? You can have the training and the stratagems, you can take the high ground or some other thing, but the other fellows are going to shoot at you, and it's a matter of luck whether the shot hits you or your best bloke beside you."

For a moment, Khan was back on that distant planet again, his fellows dying all around him. It seemed profoundly unfair that they should have fallen that day and he did not. "There's an element of luck in everything we do, my boy. Battle, business, love... You're thinking about the gunshot, aren't you?"

Bertie didn't turn away from the pitch dark window pane. "It missed me by inches, sir. Does it seem strange that a single bullet has affected me so? I was so shocked to see those hopping corpses, and that mummy chilled me to the core. That ostrich—well, it could have kicked the life out of me. And those Mexican fellows were so angry when they saw that dynamite. Sir, their anger was implacable. I had no idea how to turn them away from the idea of murder. But that single gunshot from someone who was supposed to be on our side, nearly erased me."

"Bertie, that was my fault. I was careless—"

He turned toward Khan. "No, sir. That's not true and I won't hear it."

"You must hear it," Khan answered. "I have been secure in my own safety, but I have been careless with yours. How could I ever face your mother and father if the worst happened to you, my boy? How could I face Petunia?"

"I choose to stay with you, sir. We can't leave something as dangerous as the Improbability Bow in the hands of a creature like Max Devlin. I won't flee while you risk your life, sir. But my parents..."

"Why don't you write to them? And Petunia, too."

"Yes, sir." He stepped to the desk and took the second fountain pen from the blotter. "Of course you're right." He picked up a sheet of stationery, then stared at it a moment. "I say, Professor. This looks awfully familiar."

Khan held up the sheet he'd been about to write upon. "Indeed it does, my boy. Remember when I said the note tied to the arrow was a forgery? Well, I realized quite a while ago that wasn't true." He took the note from the pocket of his jacket. It was creased and crumpled, but the stationery was the same as the paper on Leveque's desk. "You called me brave, Bertie, but I haven't been. Not yet. You see, once I realized that the note wasn't a forgery—that it had actually been written by me and sent back in time to strike the boards between my knees, I knew that I was in no real danger. Pain or injury, perhaps, but not death."

The young man snapped his fingers. "Because you hadn't sent the note to yourself yet. But sir, isn't it possible that we could send back the same note you brought all the way from England? Sort of a genie's loop, I should say?"

Khan handed him the crumpled note. "The note I received wasn't as tattered as this one, and the ink hadn't been smeared by ocean spray. No, my boy, I have to write it myself. However, we don't know who shoots the arrow that draws me all the way around the world. Perhaps you do. Perhaps it is Max Devlin."

"It could be anyone," Bertie said.

"But only I could write it. Since I knew I would have to write it at some point, I knew I would survive at least until I did."

Bertie handed back the crumpled note. "You could alter the message, sir. It's a shabby amount of information for our old selves to go on."

"Best not, Bertie. Tempting fate and all that."

Khan laid out the note he received and, after taking a deep breath, copied it neatly onto the clean sheet of paper. He rolled the new one tight and slipped it into his pocket, then threw the old one away.

He stood. "Write your letters, Bertie. It's nearly time for all of us to be brave."

CHAPTER FORTY-SEVEN

The desert sky took on a peculiar color before dawn. The English sky at morning—when it wasn't gray and overcast—was a beautiful rich blue. Here the sky looked slightly yellowed, as though the night wasn't long enough to shed the desert heat.

The sun had not yet risen by the time they parked their cars on the street beside the studio. The plan was to slip in before dawn and be out with the bow before Max had a chance to finish his breakfast. If there was trouble, they had already parked several cars around the neighborhood with the key under the passenger floor mat.

Assuming it was there in his office, locked in the closet. If it wasn't, they had no idea where to turn, nor did they have a way to protecting themselves from the next arrow Max shot.

The Professor and Bertie were the first to arrive at the cafe where they planned to regroup. As Khan entered in his zoot suit, the man behind the counter pointed at him. "We don't serve no Mexi food here."

Khan looked at him, the wide brim of his hat moving high enough to show his face. The counterman was stymied for a moment, then shook his head and went back to collecting dirty plates.

No one came to take their order while they waited in a corner booth, but by the time Sylvia, Cross, and Blue Hornet arrived, the counterman was staring daggers at them. He seemed positively grateful when they left without ordering.

They walked to the end of the block and crossed the street to the guard station at the East Gate. Khan was alarmed to see that, even at this early hour, there were one or two people arriving for work. Not too many though. Not yet.

Hornet took the lead, and the Professor was careful to walk with his head down. In his blue zoot suit, with the brim shielding his face, the two guards at the gate would see what they expected to see. Cross and Bertie stayed close.

Besides, Hornet had Sylvia beside him. No one would be looking away from the two of them, not in the time it took to cross the street.

A young couple were turned away at the gate, absolutely shocked that tourists were not allowed to wander the studio lot. As they walked back down the ramp toward the sidewalk, Blue Hornet gave them a broad, friendly hello.

Then, in one smooth motion, he rushed the guard station and leaped onto the nearest guard. Before he could react, the guard was on the ground with a forearm across his throat.

Cross charged into the booth and koshed the second guard. Sylvia leaned through the window and, after a brief search, threw a switch. The gate began to rattle open. It sounded as loud as a roller coaster, but no one came to investigate.

Khan picked up the guard that Cross had knocked out and slung him over his shoulder. The man in Hornet's grip was struggling feebly, his eyelids fluttering. When he sagged, Khan lifted him under his arm. Sylvia threw the switch the other way.

Khan carried the guards inside and the rest of the group hurried through the closing gate. The tourist couple slipped through just before the lock clanged shut. They were grinning broadly—Khan thought they looked a bit tipsy—and gave him a thumbs up before rushing off into the lot.

Max Devlin's bungalow was the fourth on the left, and it was dark. All the bungalows were dark, although they could hear hammering and see lights moving out among the studio buildings. Cross rushed ahead, his fat little legs bustling like a beetle's. With a twist of his wrist, he confirmed that the door was locked. He slid the shim already in his right hand into place and burst the door inward.

Bertie handed the crowbar to Sylvia as they all rushed through the doorway. Khan had decided that she would be the one to break open the padlocked closet. The Improbability Bow belonged to her, after all, and he trusted her more than anyone else in their group, including himself.

They moved quickly through the darkened lobby, around the empty reception desk and to Devlin's office door. Bertie fell behind so Professor Khan could be as close to Detective Cross and Blue Hornet as possible— both had sworn to follow the plan but Khan did not trust either of them. He didn't know Hornet very well and Cross, he knew all too well.

Devlin's office was not locked. Cross threw open the door and let Sylvia enter. The detective and the luchador were close behind, and Khan was near enough to grab either of them. Of course, Cross had his revolver, and Hornet might have picked up—

All three of them stood inside the office. Hornet rubbed his hand nervously. "Does it seem that the plan is going too well?"

Cross answered in a hushed voice. "Sometimes it's like this. Be glad."

A streetlight shone through the partly-drawn curtains, making it barely possible to move without colliding with the furniture. Sylvia wedged the crowbar against the lock from above, then used her weight to burst the metal plates out of the wall.

Khan had an odd feeling about the room. It seemed so full. The bow must be here, he thought. He felt a flush of impatience as Sylvia fumbled with the crooked screws interfering with the closet door. He was moments away from shooting an arrow of his own. Only moments from being reunited with his queen!

Sylvia slid the door open. Immediately, a shadowy figure in the darkness of the closet moved toward her, and before any of them could react, the blade of a katana, gleaming even in this dim light, was at her throat.

Suddenly, the high-backed chair behind Max's desk spun around, and the desk lamp switched on.

Max Devlin.

Professor Khan felt a sudden flush of shame. Of course the room had felt full. He'd let his own greed override his caution and led them all into a trap.

CHAPTER FORTY-EIGHT

1 YEAR EARLIER

Admirals. There were few things in life as dangerous as an admiral.

Reginald Westcoat, loyal British subject, faithful public servant, and self-described ladies' man, had learned to hate admirals, and through them the Navy, boats, the ocean, the beach, sand, gulls, fish, and ropes with knots in them. Life used to be so good for Reggie. His cousin had set him up with a job working for the Crown in Hong Kong. He'd fattened his bank account with honorariums from Chinese businessmen currying favor with the queen. He'd fallen in with a circle of hilariously misbehaved fellow Brits. He'd even developed a taste for Eastern women.

By God, it was a good life. Then, one night in the club, he'd decided to make a move on a white woman, just for a change of pace. How was he to know she was mistress to some admiral or other? Was he supposed to turn a private investigator loose on every chippie he bought a drink for?

Suddenly, he'd been expelled from the club, the chaps in his circle seemed to forget his name, and his delightfully bribe-worthy assignment had been given to some other rotter. He wasn't even permitted to make excursions to Tokyo or Osaka on his pretend business trips anymore.

Now he was sitting in a sea plane, enduring the endless roar of its propeller, running down the most tenuous leads his new employer, the MPHD, could dig up for him.

Time travel? It was ridiculous. There were no "faint traces of anomalous temporal disruption" to be "investigated," and the smirk on his new supervisor's face when he'd given Reggie this assignment had confirmed it. This was just a way to separate him from civilization.

He glanced over at the pilot, a narrow-faced fellow with buck teeth and an Adam's apple that should rightfully be called an Adam's grapefruit. Their earphones made it difficult to talk, and Reggie was glad of it. The fellow was distressingly devoted to his assigned mission.

An island rose above the horizon in front of them. "That's not on any chart," the pilot said, his voice surprisingly deep for such a willowy fellow. Reggie didn't have anything to say, so he kept his mouth shut.

The plane set down in a lagoon, which was a hair-raising experience. As the engines shut down, the pilot took off his ear protection. "I stay with the plane," he said, as though he was reading Reggie's mind.

"What do you suppose happened to this place?" Reggie asked, pointing to the jungle. Downed and shattered trees littered the place.

The pilot shrugged. "Big storms blow through here all the time. Speaking of which, there's another due just after sunrise tomorrow. You get three hours on the island, but if you're not back before sunset, I'm taking off without you."

Reggie looked nervously at the dense green undergrowth. "What if I fall and break my leg or something? How do I signal for help? Fire a shot into the air?" He laid his hand on the revolver at his hip.

The pilot said: "I stay with the plane."

Brilliant. Reggie set out along the beach. There were no giant tiger tracks, no crocodile prints, and no well-stocked beach front bars with rows of gleaming whiskey bottles behind the bar and flirtatious waitresses. However, after about two hundred yards, he did come across a lattice of wood lashed together with jungle vines. It was too crude to have washed ashore from the civilized world, so it had to have been made here by a native population. Who were probably cannibals.

Still, it had been smashed pretty thoroughly. Reggie approached it as though it was a sleeping snake. The bush it rested on had grown through it, but not too much. He hadn't even glanced at a piece of greenery since the last time his mother had bored him with news of her garden, but this suggested, what? A month? A little more?

He found a path through the jungle and followed it, making sure his watch was fully wound. After a very short walk, he came upon a tumble of broken trees and rough lumber.

It had been a treehouse, a big one. In fact, it had been large enough to house some three-dozen people. The storm that tore through this island had toppled and crushed it entirely.

There were no bodies. There should have been, but there weren't. Clearly some of the natives had survived. Reggie unbuckled the strap over his revolver.

There was a broad path leading away from the treehouse site; Reggie was no wilderness tracker, but his blind Aunt Millie could have seen the way the grass had been crushed and flattened. Laying his hand on his weapon, he followed the trail through the jungle.

Eventually, he reached the shore of a small, narrow lake. The trail came through a stand of trees and ended at a clearing. A rough wooden skid lay on its side—Good Lord, there was dried blood on it.

Reggie stepped into the clearing, recognizing it instantly for what it was: a graveyard. There were forty new graves to go with perhaps sixty older ones, all marked with wooden markers.

Kneeling at the far end of the yard, back toward him, was a young woman. She was sweaty and filthy from hard labor, but Reggie liked the long curve of her neck.

"What ho, eh?" he called. "What happened?"

The woman stood and spun around in surprise. He realized she was wearing the daisho, the dual swords that Japanese officials sometimes affected. Also, her traditional Japanese robe had been torn and tattered in delightful ways.

She laid her hand on her weapons and stalked toward him, her face grim. Reggie instantly drew his revolver, but it didn't seem to deter her. "Intruder," she said in Japanese, "the price of entering this sacred place is your life."

Didn't she know what a gun could do? Perhaps it was time to educate her. "I think not," he said in Japanese and shot a grave marker beside her.

She jumped back in shock and dismay, then stared down at the broken plank. How odd. Guns were completely new to her. When she looked at him, she said: "You speak our language. A man who speaks our language."

"It's true," he told her. "Your country is far from here, but I have visited it many times. What happened to this place?"

She looked around. "A storm. A storm like no other. All of my sisters and cousins were lost. Only I survived."

"Are you alone here?"

She nodded. "You should not be here. No man is allowed here. It is my duty to slay you." She took another step forward.

"Here, now, I thought we'd settled that." He aimed his weapon at her, but once again it did not stop her. "Don't force me, please."

"I must," was all she said.

"Would you just wait a minute? There's plenty of time for slaying!"

She stopped advancing. "I must serve my lord."

"And who is that? How long have you been on this island?"

"Nineteen years."

"So long? How did you end up here?"

She seemed confused. "There was a shipwreck. Our lord sent us here, to wait for him and to serve. Ten generations of my family have been faithful."

"Good Lord! Do you mean you've lived your whole life on this island? Ten generations? That's..." Reggie tried to translate that into years but the numbers wouldn't come together. "That's a long time. Say, you wouldn't have seen an anomalous time whatsit around here, have you?"

She had no idea what he was talking about, which wasn't a surprise since he wasn't even making sense to himself. Still, the idea of leaving her here all alone broke his heart a little. Such a waste of a beautiful young woman. "I say, you're a gorgeous thing; if you promise not to try to slay me, I'd be happy to take you away from here."

She seemed stymied by that. "I—Your offer is generous, but I can not accept. I must remain here and wait for my lord to claim me."

"You mean a daimyo? Beautiful, no one even knows you're here. I'm not teasing; this island isn't on any chart... Ten generations? Darling, your lord, whoever he was, has to be long dead."

"I have a symbol. A promise from a powerful lord that... It is the reason my family is here, and we are to await our summons."

"A symbol, eh? May I see it?" Her face hardened and her hand went to her katana. "I will only look, I swear. No touch. Hey, what if I'm the messenger sent by your lord to call you home?"

Her look of disgust showed what she thought of that. "You may look, but I will kill you if you touch."

"Agr—Wait!" Once he was standing right beside her, his handgun would not protect him from her steel, not if she was any good. "Will you promise not to kill me for any reason except for touching this symbol from your lord? I don't want there to be a misunderstanding."

She nodded. "I swear on my honor."

Together they crossed the cemetery toward the highest part of the slope. Reggie quickly realized that all the markers were brand new. The storm must have destroyed them all, but each of them was marked with a name and a date... This poor girl must have had to remake every grave marker from memory.

At the highest point of the clearing was a marker slightly larger than the rest. "This is my ancestor, the only male of my family buried on this island. The five hundred year old swords I wear belonged to him. He is the one who said the arrow directed us here, although he died before he could explain properly."

The marker had a little shelf carved out of it, barely more than a notch, and laid across it was a battered metal arrow.

It had seen better days, that was certain. It was tarnished beyond belief, and the foil on the outside had begun to peel away. What was this thing? It was too short and fat to be shot from a bow, and—

"Hello, what is this?" He leaned closer to the peeling part, careful to keep his hands behind his back. The pretty young samurai had grown tense in a way that made him nervous. He bent low and peered around the curled foil at the inside.

Good Lord, there was some sort of machinery in there.

"And when did this show up on the island again?" Reggie blurted out.

"When my family did," the young woman said. "Ten generations ago."

Two hundred years.

He backed away and spun toward the jungle around them. "Is this a prank?" he shouted in English. "Is this a bloody prank you're playing on me?"

He expected the pilot to lead his circle of former friends—and maybe the admiral, too—out of the treeline, laughing.

But no one appeared. His voice echoed through the jungle, sounding terribly lonely. The young samurai looked up at him, puzzled. "Is this a—" he started to ask in Japanese, but he knew the answer already. No one was playing a joke on him. He'd been sent to find an anomalous time thingy, and here it was before him.

He bent down to examine it again and saw there was a tiny plate mounted on the back. Most of it was out of sight because the stamped letters were facing down, but he could see one word.

"*Return*" he read, translating it to Japanese. The temptation to turn the arrow a quarter rotation was intense but he knew he would lose his hand, and probably his life, if he tried it. "That right there reads *return*."

The young woman's eyes went wide with astonishment. "You can read it?"

"My gorgeous darling, I may have learned to speak your language—"

"Badly."

Women. So typical. "But those letters are in my native tongue, you beautiful devil. If you were willing to turn it for me, just a bit, I could read the whole inscription to you."

"I don't know..."

"Od's Blood, woman! I have to file a report on this to my new superiors, and they will be quite put out that I did something worthwhile. I... How about this then: You let me read this inscription to you. Whatever it says, I read it, fairsy squaresy. Then I will get you off this damn island, a deal that comes with a fine dinner and a bottle of sake, if you've a mind. In return, you'll answer some questions for my report. You won't get a better offer, darling, because you certainly can't survive here all by your lonesome."

"The arrow is mine," she said stubbornly.

"Of course. I would never steal from a gal."

"All right then. You will translate."

She rotated the arrow so the plate was fully visible. Reggie Westcoat, unwilling agent of the MPHD, bent down to read it. Then he began to laugh and laugh.

CHAPTER FORTY-NINE

Max Devlin smiled at them from behind his desk. He wore another red suit, but this one had pinstripes and a slightly darker hue. Khan could not help but wonder if it was the lateness of the hour that made him look so pale and worn, or if he had other stresses working on him.

Whatever the case, he was as smug as a well-fed cat beside a fire.

It was Sylvia who was in the greatest danger, though. Khan turned toward the figure who held the sword at Sylvia's throat, just below her left ear. It was impossible to tell where in the world she had come from: her skin was dark, her hair highlighted with red, and her eyes had the slight fold that suggested her ancestors—some of them, at least—had come from east Asia.

But if her person indicated she was of mixed race, her clothing was extraordinarily specific. She wore the kimono, sandals, and sash of a traditional samurai warrior.

And she looked to be about eleven months pregnant.

"Marvelous, isn't she?" Max said. He leaned back in his chair and knitted his hands behind his head. "I mean, the bow can do amazing things, but you can never really predict what will happen. Look at this." He leaned forward and took a newspaper off the blotter on his desk.

Beneath it lay another one of Leveque's arrows, but it was worn and pitted as if by long years. The aluminum outer covering had darkened and peeled away at the corners, and the metal "feathers" had broken off long ago. There was some sort of tiny plate on it but the text was too small for Khan to read without his glasses.

Max read it aloud to them: "*Return to Max Devlin, Mammoth Studios, Los Angeles, CA.* I shot this arrow not two hours ago, when I heard that Wisp had failed. I mean, if there was one thing I did not expect it was that Wisp would fail. The man is amazing when it comes to his particular area of expertise. But when I got the call that you had returned home, I knew I couldn't keep coddling you. I knew I would need an operative you would not be able to stop."

"Max," Khan said. "You do not want to hurt Sylvia, believe me."

"Two hundred years," Max said, as though Khan hadn't spoken. "That's how far back this arrow went. Ten or eleven generations of this pretty young woman's family were taken out of their original destiny, whatever it was, and directed towards me. All so that I could make use of her. Isn't that amazing? Who knows what those people went through! But my name and address were on the arrow, and now she treats me the way a samurai treats his lord—or her lord, in this case: with absolute devotion and obedience." The young woman's expression was stoic and unreadable. "She showed up at the security gate five minutes after I shot that arrow in my time, two hundred years in hers." He looked down at the blotter. "And here it is. Ruined. Another arrow lost to me."

Khan interrupted again. "Sylvia is the only person alive who can make more arrows."

Sylvia glanced over her shoulder at him in surprise. Max seemed genuinely startled.

Then he chuckled. "Oh, that's a good one, Professor. Under other circumstances, I think I would have liked to stake you in a couple of the big poker games around town. The way you bluff, you'd have cleaned the town out. Unfortunately for you, Sylvia here was not ready for your trick, and her surprised expression has given up the game. Nice suit, by the way. No, don't move." Max held up his hand. "No matter how fast you think you are, you're not as fast as my samurai here."

"She ain't faster than a bullet," Cross said, his revolver in hand.

Max didn't even have a chance to look alarmed. "No," Sylvia said. "No, I don't want you to harm this woman and her unborn child. Not even to save my own life."

"Put that away," Professor Khan said. They weren't going to shoot a pregnant woman.

"Now," Max said, "I know you have arrows of your own. At least two, yes? Show me."

Khan took the arrow from his inside pocket but didn't hand it over. Who was going to shoot the note to him in the past? Should he explain the importance to Max? Would he care?"

Max smiled. "Ah. I'm going to offer you a deal—"

"This is nonsense," Hornet cried. "I am a luchador! More, I am a tecnico! I can not stand idle while a woman's life is threatened!"

"Hornet—" Khan hissed.

"Professor, I can subdue her without harming her. Watch!"

He leaped forward, vaulting over Max's desk to land between Devlin and the samurai. Even as he moved toward her, as quick and graceful as the jaguar had been, the young woman was just as fast. She spun and, with an astonishing speed and economy, slashed at Hornet as he ducked low.

The katana sliced off the knot holding Blue Hornet's damaged mask in place. He cried out in surprise, his hands moving toward his face to hold the cloth in place.

Everyone was in motion. Sylvia had taken advantage of Hornet's attack to move away from the samurai, and Khan caught her arm to yank her back. Max dove for a drawer in his desk, obviously grabbing for a gun. Cross had already slipped out of the room. Bertie cried out: "She missed him!"

"No, she didn't," Khan answered as he reached into his jacket.

Max had a gun aimed at Blue Hornet as he crouched beside a filing cabinet. "Kill them!"

"Flee, my friends!" Hornet shouted at almost the same time.

The Professor yanked Sylvia behind him as the samurai came toward him. Her hands were as quick as striking serpents, but her heavy belly made her lumber a bit as she walked.

She swung her sword directly at the spot where Khan's neck and shoulder met.

CHAPTER FIFTY

Professor Khan anticipated her move. He raised the metal arrow.

The foil around the outer casing was as effective in blocking the finely-honed steel of a katana as a cigar wrapper, but bafflium was incredibly dense. In the moment before his parry struck, Khan imagined the sword slicing through the arrow like a carrot, then cutting off his own head.

It didn't happen. The sword struck with surprising power, but the arrow held.

The samurai stepped back, her eyes wide with shock. She looked at the end of her blade in horror.

There, about three-quarters of the way from the tang to the tip, was a tiny notch in the steel.

"Let's go!" Cross roared from somewhere behind them. Khan backed into the outer office and let Bertie slam the door shut. He grabbed the receptionist's desk and upended it against the door.

The samurai was held at bay, for now, but if Max started shooting through the door...

"We don't know where the bow is," Sylvia said, her voice full of grief. "We don't know where it is or what happened to it."

The Professor glanced down at the arrow in his hand. As he'd expected, the sword had cut an all-but-imperceptible notch in the protective foil. Another arrow ruined. He slipped it back into his pocket.

Bertie tripped over the unconscious guards on his way to the exit, falling to his knees by the door. He grabbed the knob and opened the door a crack. "Professor..."

"What is it, Bertie?"

"There are quite a few men in uniform in front of our escape route."

Cross pulled the door open all the way. Low-slanted golden sunlight shone onto a cluster of studio security guards standing against the gate. There must have been at least a dozen. "I count at least three scatterguns," Cross said. "The rest have pistols. Damn it. We'll have to reach the south gate. That's where I parked my ride."

As they slipped through the door, Sylvia grabbed Professor Khan's elbow. "There," she said. "There, I see it."

They all turned to follow her gaze. Wisp was driving a forklift along the path, heading south along an asphalt path. The forklift's payload was a huge crate, large enough to contain the Improbability Bow.

"He's moving it!" Cross blurted out, then lunged forward through the door. Sylvia was right beside him.

At the bottom of the little staircase, Khan caught hold of their shoulders and pulled them back. "No! We're not going to be led into another of Wisp's traps. If he's going south, we have to go north. Or west."

The security guards had noticed them beside the entrance to Max's bungalow. "Wherever we go," Bertie said. "We have to go now."

Max himself stuck his head out the window. "Help! I've been robbed!"

"You there!" a burly one shouted. "Stay where you are!"

"Like hell," Sylvia said. She bolted out of the doorway and ran across the walkway. The guards yelled for them to stop, then the chase was on.

CHAPTER FIFTY-ONE

Professor Khan followed Sylvia across the tarmac, raw fear clenching at his guts. The guards had guns, and she was leading them across open ground. They headed for the row of bungalows on the other side of the pavement, and Professor Khan suddenly realized Bertie was running beside him, interposing his body between his teacher and their guards.

"Capture them!" Max shouted, which gave Khan a glimmer of hope. He still wanted the remaining arrows more than he wanted them dead. They still had hope.

They passed between the bungalows and out of sight of the guards, but it was only a moment's safety. Sylvia and Cross ran along a worn path, cutting through a gap in the bushes.

"Inside!" Cross shouted, and they crossed out of the greenery toward the nearest of the warehouse buildings. Already, workmen moved tools and equipment around the perimeter of the studio buildings, weaving through actors in full costume. As Cross sprinted toward the open hangar doors, a wall of Roman shields parted for him as if he led a stampede of elephants.

"We're late for a call!" Bertie yelled as they pushed through the crowds of people, jumping over coiled cables and sprinting around massive racks of lights. People glanced back at them, irritated, but they got out of the way.

They sprinted down a set of wooden stairs painted to look like white marble. At the bottom was a long, wide swimming pool. It took Khan a moment to see that Cross was heading toward the lit "exit" sign at the far end of the cavernous room.

When the reached the narrow pathway along the pool, a group of barefoot young women in swimsuits and bathing caps appeared at the far exit, rushing through the door, bumping each other like ripples in a pond. Someone was pushing through that crowd. Khan knew exactly what that meant, but it was Sylvia who responded first.

"In here!" she snapped, shoving Bertie and Cross into the empty orchestra pit. Khan followed them, crouching out of sight. Sylvia whipped a long striped towel off the bandstand and wrapped it around herself.

A moment later, a group of ten security guards pushed through the swimmers and barged into the room. They stormed down the stairs.

Khan ducked all the way down. "That way!" Sylvia cried, pointing back behind them. "They went that way. They were wearing stolen security uniforms!"

Being well out of sight, the Professor didn't see the men as they ran by, but he did hear a chorus of "Thank you, ma'am," "Kindly, ma'am," "Grateful, ma'am," "You look lovely, ma'am," and "Hey, wait a minute."

Uh oh. Khan peeked over the edge of the orchestra pit. He saw one of the guards, a lean young man with a boxer's flattened features, looking Sylvia up and down. He alone had noticed that her feet were not bare.

The other guards had stopped and turned toward her, crowding forward in the narrow space. Sylvia shrugged. It had been a good try.

Khan leaped to the edge of the bandstand and roared. The men, mere feet away, were so startled that they stepped back as one and fell into the pool.

"Let's go!" Cross said unnecessarily. He vaulted over the front of the bandstand and ran up the stairs on the other side of the room. Swimmers cleared the path for him and the others following behind. As Khan came through the door last, a gunshot struck the doorjamb beside him.

They ran across the asphalt into the next building. Cross looked behind him, his flabby face livid. "Are those mooks shooting at us?"

"Keep going!" Sylvia yelled.

They piled into the next building, running across the darkened work area. Ahead, there was an old west saloon with chairs and tables overturned. Men ringed the set and two cowboys stood face to face, their hands near their holstered guns.

"Keep away from Miss Elizabeth," the handsome one said. "Or you'll regret it."

The other man looked like a giant. "I don't scare easy, Kid."

Then Cross, Sylvia, Khan, and Bertie barreled into the scene. At first, everyone stumbled back, too stunned to react—someone behind the camera cried out "What in Heaven's—?" When Cross drew his revolver and fired three shots back at their pursuers, the cowboys broke out screaming, leaping through windows and diving behind the bar. The giant shrieked and ran frantically around the saloon, waving a handkerchief over his head.

"Come on!" Khan shouted.

Cross started after them. "I only shot over their heads," and he followed them through the swinging doors into the backstage. The guards were still following, but not as closely.

As they crossed the alley into the next building, Sylvia called: "Professor!" She placed something tiny in his hands and shined the infrapurple beam on it while they ran. Suddenly, Khan found himself holding a device that looked like an oversized police whistle. The bug-summoner.

"Damn!" Sylvia said. "Wrong one!" She started rummaging through her oversized purse.

"Keep going," Khan urged. He pressed the whistle to his lips and began to blow as they ran through another stage. Why not?

A swarm of insects seemed to spring up from nowhere, billowing around them. They sprinted straight through another set, where a trio of actors pretended to hack at jungle vines with machetes. A flimsy "branch" smacked against the Professor's hand and the whistle bounced out of his grip into a jumble of fake vines.

As they ran out of the far end of the set, they left the actors slapping wildly at their necks and arms.

Khan glanced back as they ran out of the building. A few of the guards waved their arms wildly in front of them as the swarm forced them to shut their eyes and mouths. They collided with the set and the equipment—to the vocal dismay of the director—but it was only a few. Their pursuers were still coming strong.

CHAPTER FIFTY-TWO

At the entrance to the next building, Sylvia was waiting for him. "I found it!" She pressed something into Khan's hand as they ran inside together. She held the infrapurple beam over his palm, the light wavering unsteadily with every step. "It's heavy," she said at the last second, when the gadget suddenly became full size.

It was the endothermic mine, and by Jove she was very much right about it being heavy. Khan stumbled past the light stands and camera equipment onto a desert oasis. Two men in ragged clothes lay stretched out on the sand as though crawling toward the water.

"Not in the water!" Sylvia shouted, and with all of his strength he raised the mine to shoulder height as he plunged into the pool and staggered through to the other side.

"Is there a gorilla in this scene?" someone shouted from behind the camera. "Get me a script, because I want to know if we need a *gorilla in a wet zoot suit for my scene*!"

At the far edge of the water, Professor Khan let the mine fall heavily onto the sand. The clatter of footsteps approached from behind. So close, the guards were so close!

"Sorry!" Sylvia said as she yanked an empty canteen hanging around an actor's neck, snapping the worn leather, then tossed it toward the mine. She and the Professor were already sprinting up the faux-dune when the mine went off.

Hot air blew into their faces like an explosion in reverse then immediately afterward, a wave of terrible cold air washed over them. Snowflakes began to drift lazily toward the floor. Glancing back, the Professor saw the foremost guards slip on the icy surface of the water, falling and sliding across the set.

Cross and Bertie were waiting impatiently at the exit. "My dear," Khan said, "please hurry."

Sylvia was still hunting inside her purse, the infrapurple flashlight tucked under her arm. "All I need is—"

Cross yanked her arm through the door. She yelped—and the flashlight slipped from beneath her arm.

Khan lunged for it but he knew he was too far to reach, not before it shattered on the sidewalk.

Bertie's left foot shot forward and he caught it perfectly across the top of his foot, With a quick jerk of his knee, he lifted the torch into the air and caught it in his right hand like a fencer.

Professor Khan gaped at him, astonished. The lad shrugged. "Striker, sir."

"I have it!" Sylvia shouted, drawing something too tiny to see from her purse.

Inside the next building, the stage was set like the inside of a tenement. Two beautiful people in drab clothes stood around a stained kitchen sink, with a little old man hunched over the table.

"I'm slaving away at double shifts at that factory!" the man shouted in a clear, ringing voice, "all to buy your poppa's medicine! What more do you want from me?"

Cross ran through the scene, dragging Sylvia behind him. She broke away long enough to set something as small as a tie pin on the corner of the table. "Right there, Bertie!"

He raced in and shined the light on it. The Professor came in just behind him, glancing nervously back toward the way they came. Despite everything, the guards were gaining.

"No, no, no," said a voice from behind the camera. "My take! You ruined—"

Suddenly, the sonic neuro-stimulator appeared on the table. Bertie didn't need to be told to press the big red button.

The pulse of sound that came from it seemed to fill the Professor's very bones. It swelled within him, flowing through his muscles. He felt an unbearable urge to *croisé devant*. As he started toward the exit, he leapt, throwing his arm above his head and touching his heels.

Relief flooded through him, and he continued to prance as he crossed the room. If only he were still wearing his kilt, he might have done justice to the kicks. Bertie scooped Sylvia into his arms and waltzed her off the stage. The beautiful actors in their shabby clothes stepped toward each other and, hands around their hips, began to spin in a circle. The hunched old man sprang from his chair and cartwheeled across the threadbare rug.

From behind the camera, the director teetered awkwardly *en pointe* with his hands clasped under his chin. "GENIUS!" he cried. "Where's my writer? Get him in here so I can fire him for not thinking of this, because this is *genius*."

The security guards stumbled and shimmied and pirouetted in the wings, unable to continue the chase.

Khan saw Bertie spin and dip Sylvia. They had stopped fleeing. The impulse was too strong for them to control themselves.

Khan leaped toward them as gracefully as he could and scooped them into his arms. The compulsion to dance was powerful in his simian brain; it must have been overwhelming in theirs. He stutter-stepped to the exit, while they both arched their backs and extended their arms, nearly unbalancing him.

Cross stood just inside the exit, his heels together, his spine as straight as a broomstick, and a rose clenched in his teeth. Khan had gotten far enough from the sonic pulses to regain some control of his limbs, so he slapped the flower out of the detective's mouth.

"Thank you!" Cross said. Khan shoved the three of them out into the sunlight.

There was a fire ax hanging beside the exit. Khan grabbed it and ran outside. Bertie slammed the door shut, and the Professor swung, sinking the axe blade deep into the door and jamb. It wouldn't hold their pursuers forever, but any delay was a welcome one.

The building muffled the sonic pulse enough that Khan no longer had to dance: he wanted to, but he didn't have to. Sylvia, Bertie, and Cross, however, were all shuffling their feet trying to run and do the Charleston at once.

"My God, this is awful!" Sylvia said. "I never expected it to feel so awful!"

The Professor glanced around. The other actors and workers were all dancing together, and they all seemed to be enjoying themselves. Only the four of them, who knew the source of the compulsion, looked unhappy.

"We gotta get away from that thing," Cross snapped.

Something heavy thumped against the door, making the fire axe quiver. Someone was trying to break through. Professor Khan stepped away from the door. They should flee. Flee!

"But which direction?" Bertie said. "I got so turned around in all these buildings I don't even know where the exits are. We're lost!"

A shotgun boomed, tearing a hole in the wooden door right beside them.

CHAPTER FIFTY-THREE

The blast came so close to Khan's ribs that he felt the breeze of it flutter his voluminous lapels. The shock and terror was so startling that he fell backward onto the asphalt, then rolled over onto his belly.

The sonic device was fading. They could all feel it. The shouting voices of the approaching guards came through the door. They were arguing about whether it was a good idea to shoot blindly through a closed door.

Professor Khan found himself lying at the feet of a couple who were just finishing their dance. It was the tipsy tourists, who had snuck onto the lot with him. They stared down with wide eyes, their mouths hanging open in shock. Then they glanced at the ruined door.

Through the hole, they heard a male voice shout: "We've almost caught the intruders!" in a particularly bloodthirsty way.

The tourists backed slowly away, fading into the crowd. Whatever sneaky fun they'd planned to have, it was all over now.

"This way, my friends!"

It was Blue Hornet, calling to them from the building across the way. He held a door partway open and was waving frantically at them.

How had he gotten away?

Before Khan could ask, the others were running toward him. Professor Khan scrambled to his feet and followed. The guards were close to breaking through the door, and he didn't have anywhere else to go. He pulled his hat brim low and hoped no one would notice him as he raced by a squad of doughboys.

Hornet lit a match as he approached, then lit the fuse of a string of Chinese firecrackers. He threw them as hard as he could past the crowds and the corner of the building, then he pushed Professor Khan through the door and shut it behind them.

They heard the guards streaming into the space between the buildings, but before anyone could speak the firecrackers began their rapid-fire explosions.

Under cover of the noise, Hornet threw the bolt.

"This way!" someone shouted, and footsteps raced by the door like a passing hailstorm. Someone tried the doorknob, but it wouldn't budge. Khan had the sudden image of a second shotgun blast tearing through the door, blowing him wide open, but instead the footsteps retreated.

They all breathed a sigh of relief. Professor Khan glanced around. There was a single dim lamp farther down the corridor and a flight of stairs leading up beside them.

"By Jove," Bertie said, "they sure are enthusiastic about their jobs."

"No," Cross said. "Something ain't right. I don't know who these jokers think they're after, but it's not the usual gate-crashers, not if they're shooting through closed doors."

"What then?" Khan asked. "Gangster assassins?"

"You are wearing that suit," Cross said, pointing at the Professor's blue jacket.

The Professor had gotten dirt all over the front when he'd fallen outside, and he tried to brush it off. "It's good to see you, Blue Hornet," he said, "but how did you escape from Max Devlin and his samurai?"

He pointed at his gray lapels with both thumbs. "I am Blue Hornet."

Sylvia stepped forward. "You didn't hurt that woman, I hope!"

"Señora, I am *Blue Hornet*. I have been a tecnico since the start of my career."

"There's that bally word again," Bertie said, "not that I know what it means."

Cross sniffed as he looked Hornet up and down. "It means he's a white hat. A good guy."

"Yes. I fight with honor. I fight fairly. I do not disgrace myself. Otherwise, I would be a rudos."

"And the samurai?" Sylvia persisted.

"When I escaped, she was unharmed," Hornet said, "but not disarmed. I underestimated her, I admit. She nearly defeated me permanently."

Hornet turned around and showed the back of his mask. The space where the knot had held it together was now fastened by unbent paper clips, their metal ends stabbed through the cotton fabric. His short black hair was already visible through the tear, but the metal clips were also snapping threads. Soon, the mask would become too loose to stay in place.

And here the Professor assumed "defeated me permanently" meant "killed."

"Can't we disguise ourselves like last time?" Bertie said. "I mean, there are costumes everywhere, and Hornet doesn't need to do anything more than take off his mask."

They couldn't see the luchador's expression, but his body language made it clear what he thought about that suggestion. Professor Khan shook his head. "I can't get out of here using a disguise."

"We could commandeer a delivery truck," Bertie said. "Professor, of course we wouldn't leave you behind, but perhaps we could pack you in a wooden crate like precious porcelain, wot?"

"That's... alarming."

"But workable," Sylvia said, "as a backup plan. Let's not forget that I'm still carrying the shrink beam. If we have to, we can carry the Professor out in our pockets."

Khan's hand went to his throat. "Has it been tested on living subjects?"

But the enthusiasm of the others drowned him out: "Capital idea!" "Quite right, señora," "Not in my pocket."

Footsteps ran past the door again, going the other direction. Blue Hornet slid by them to the stairs. "Come, my friends. We should move away from this door."

"Not up," Cross said. "We can't go up."

"I agree," the Professor said. "We don't want to be trapped on an upper floor."

Hornet continued up to the landing. "We must ascend to descend. Come with me, my friends. I have found a surprising solution to our difficulties."

CHAPTER FIFTY-FOUR

The stairs were dark and so was the hall. There were massive electrical outlets low on the walls, but only the most basic lighting. There were no doors, either. Shouldn't there have been office doors or something?

Khan sighed. "It won't be long before they start searching the buildings."

"Keep moving!" Hornet called from the front. "Come along."

At the end of the hall, there was a heavy metal door with a round window in the center. It looked oddly like a porthole. Khan could hear the others going down a set of metal stairs. "What is this?"

"There is a tunnel beneath the buildings," Hornet said. "Obviously, I have not had a chance to explore it, but it is quite long. We will at least come up in another building, hey? Move quickly! Hold the railing!"

"Oh, thank you," Sylvia said.

The Professor slid through the doorway to the stairs. My goodness, it was dark. He held tightly to the railing.

Suddenly, Hornet was right at his shoulder. "I must borrow this, Professor." His hand slid beneath Khan's jacket and snatched the arrow from him. The motion was so quick, and the Professor so surprised, that he didn't have a chance to clap his hand over his jacket until after the arrow was gone.

Hornet backed smoothly toward the door, moving quite quickly. As Khan turned toward him, he saw Max Devlin standing in the hall, his pistol in his hand. The samurai stood behind him.

"Stop right there," Max said. His gun was aimed directly at Hornet's chest. In the darkened room, his voice had an odd echo. "Don't come any closer, or I'm going to start the shooting with you."

CHAPTER FIFTY-FIVE

"You betray me?" Blue Hornet's voice was high and sharp. "I have done what you asked! I thought we had a deal!"

"I don't make deals with burglars!" Max shouted back at him. His voice was raw and strained. "You should have come to me square if you wanted to make a deal, but no, you had to side with them. You had to *break into my place to steal from me*!"

If Hornet felt chastened or embarrassed, he showed no sign of it. "I had no choice!"

"You had a choice." Max's voice dripped with contempt. "You just didn't like your options. Then, when things went south, when you were looking up the barrel of my .38, you made an offer. Well, that's too late, pal."

"Well well," Cross called from nearly the bottom of the stairs. "Max Devlin breaking a deal."

Max glanced down at him. "I had my fingers crossed. Now, I don't want to see any sudden movements or I start squeezing off shots." For the last few words, he raised his voice again. The echo had a metallic quality to it. "In a room like this, who knows where ricochets might end up." He turned to Blue Hornet. "Hand me the arrow, feathers first. Slowly."

The samurai stood at Max's shoulder, her katana held high.

Hornet stood motionless for a second or two. Khan did not doubt the luchador thought himself the match for anyone, armed or unarmed, but two people? He slowly raised the arrow and presented it to Max, who took it cautiously from him.

Max glanced at the arrow head with satisfaction, then slipped it into his jacket pocket.

He waved Hornet back with the gun. As the wrestler came near him, the Professor cleared his throat. "I feel I should warn you—"

Max pointed the pistol directly at Khan's chest. "Talk out of line again and I'm going to shoot you dead. If I do that, I'm going to have to shoot all of you. Get me? If I want to hear from you, I'll ask. And in case you're wondering, considering how many times you've tried to bluff me, I don't plan to put many questions to you. So shut it." He turned to Cross, who stood on the landing below. "Emil, you're next."

"I got no arrows," Cross said, "and I got nothing to say to you."

"I want your gun, flatfoot."

"Or what?" Cross said. "You'll shoot a cop? You can't handle the kind of heat that would bring down."

Max laughed at him. "Not even your gorilla friend could sell me on that line. You think anyone cares about you? In a department full of crooks with badges, you're the one that everyone thinks has gone too far. Oh, the department would 'look into it,' but privately the other detectives would talk about how dirty you were, how many chances you took, and how it was only a matter of time before you ended up face down in the river." As worn as Max looked, he seemed to take some strength from his taunts. "Tell me I'm wrong."

"I got a light touch," Cross said, glaring.

"Maybe they'll carve *Blackmailer, Thug, He could have stolen more* on your tombstone. Now, with two fingers of your left hand, take out your piece, then toss it up here to me. And make it a good throw; if you miss, I'm going to shoot you."

Max held up his empty left hand. Cross took out his gun and tossed it underhand up the length of the stairs.

Perfectly. Max snatched it out of the air and slipped it into his jacket pocket. "You don't have an ankle gun on you, do you?"

Cross lifted his pant legs to show his bare, black socks, then he spat out a curse that made Bertie flush bright red.

"If there's anyone in the world who could arrange that, it would be me." Max turned to Sylvia. "Now your purse. Carry it up here and set it on the landing."

Sylvia did, squeezing by Bertie and Khan on the stairs. When she reached Hornet, she glared at him until he flattened himself against the railing, leaving her enough room to walk by him without touching him.

When she set the bag down, Max waved her back. Then he stepped forward and began to rummage through the bag, taking out the infrapurple flashlight, along with the makeup and change purse, a fistful of notepads and pens, copper wire, fuses, steel brackets, several wrenches and screwdrivers, and a tiny first aid kit.

"What is going on?" he snapped, angry. "I know you found a second arrow."

Sylvia shrugged. "I don't know what you mean."

"Don't lie to me!" he hissed. "I know you collected that arrow from Jameson Lee. I paid the cost of shipping two dozen corpses across the Pacific for that information!"

"Two?" Bertie said, but the Professor gave him a sharp look and he shut up.

Not that Max had noticed. "I'll make you a deal: You turn over all your bafflium arrows and forget about your father's bow, get me? Just walk away. It's only right that I get to keep it; it's mine. Your father made a deal with me for it."

Sylvia's expression was impassive. "For what? The gun he used to kill himself?" Max seemed startled by that, as though she'd guessed correctly. "What do I get in return?"

Max nervously smoothed his tie. "I help you get off the lot. I forget about the fact that you just broke into my office. I leave you alone. You give me the arrows and leave me alone, and I'll let you go. You can all live out the rest of your lives."

"And what if I refuse?"

Max pressed his lips together until they turned white. "I think we both know what will happen if you refuse."

"You can only threaten to shoot us so many times, Max."

"It still works on me," Bertie said.

Sylvia's expression was utterly stoic and her voice was flat. *Lack of affect,* the Professor thought. She didn't look like someone who cared if she lived or died.

Max could see it, too. "What if I started shooting them?" He aimed the gun directly at Khan.

"Shoot the wrestler any time you want," Sylvia said with a careless wave. "As for the Professor and his assistant, I just met them the day before yesterday. Detective Cross I've known for a while. You can shoot him anytime, too."

Bertie took a sharp breath. Professor Khan looked at Max, standing at the top of the stairs. Was he going to call her bluff? Assuming it was a bluff, of course.

"There's one more thing," Sylvia said. "I learned more than a few tricks from my father. You want more arrows? Working arrows? You'll never get them without me."

"We can still make a deal," Max said.

"No." Sylvia sounded like a sick patient refusing treatment. "I know you were there when my father killed himself. I know you stole the bow while his body lay cooling on the carpet. What's more, I know you're sweating like you have a noose around your neck. I don't know why, but you're scared sick, while I don't care about anything you could take from me. You want to bargain with me, I suggest you sweeten the deal."

Max licked his lips while he thought about it. He looked down at Sylvia's purse, then at his gun, then at the samurai beside him. Khan realized he was holding his breath.

If Max started shooting, Khan was going to charge him. Yes, Hornet and Sylvia were both in his way, but they would almost certainly be dead by the time he reached them. Max would kill him, but he hoped it would take a great many bullets to put him down, more bullets than Max had in his gun. Perhaps Bertie could get around the samurai somehow—

"I have a better idea," Max said. He looked at the samurai and nodded toward the door. She retreated into the hallway and he followed. The door slammed shut with a metal clang, followed by a heavy bolt slamming home.

There was no light except for the dim reflection from a long, heavy window high above them. They were trapped.

CHAPTER FIFTY-SIX

"Hey, 'Blue Hornet,'" Cross said, his voice barely louder than a hiss. "I'm going to kill you for ratting us out."

"I am not the betrayer here!" Hornet shouted. "No! You all knew I was looking for the Calicos and you all knew exactly where it was! You, señora, are one of those who stole it from the Princess's tomb!"

"You're wrong," Sylvia said. "I've never even been to Mexico in my life."

"I do not believe you! You recruited me to help retrieve your property, without telling me part of it had been taken from my people! The Princess has been stalking the countryside searching for the jewel. Do you know how many she has killed while you held on to your stolen property? My own cousin was one of them! He had a young wife and a baby on the way. So do not talk to me about betrayal. I am a *tecnico*. I live by my honor. I was not the one who lied first."

"No," Bertie said. "But you're the bloke who joined up with Max."

"Even I have heard of Max Devlin," Hornet said. "His reputation extends all the way to Mexico City. He swore to me that none of you would be hurt, and that he would return the Princess's jewel after only three days. But you ruined that deal, too, with your burglary!"

"That doesn't even make sense," Sylvia snapped.

"He was going to return the jewel to the Princess!"

"You're a fool if you think so," Sylvia said. "Max would never give up that kind of power, not for what you could have offered him."

"You are wrong," Hornet said. "If not for this burglary, I could have worked with Max for the return of the jewel."

"Worked with...? You're holding back the truth," the Professor said. "Max didn't just promise you the jewel in three days, did he? And he didn't just promise not to harm us. He made an additional promise to you, too, didn't he?"

"It is too late to talk that way to me," Hornet said, while waving dismissively.

"Oh no," Khan answered, "you don't get to make a big speech about honor and betrayal, then brush us off like that. Max Devlin offered you something more. Why else would you be willing to wait three days for your jewel? What was it?"

"You speculate," Hornet said, his voice low, "with my honor."

"I do, but I think I speculate correctly. I'll bet he promised you a movie deal. Not the jungle movie?"

Hornet's mask hid his face, but it couldn't hide the sudden quirk of his head.

Cross spat. "I shoulda guessed. You cut a deal that would get your name up in lights and our names in the obits."

"Max gave his word none of you would be hurt. And why should I not make this deal? I have just as much right as anyone. I want to be the ambassador that brings my sport to American audiences. They will marvel at what I can do, they will flock to my matches, and they will love me. Because of me, the luchador scene will expand into this country. Once your people took from mine, but perhaps I can take a little something back. And who will dare to criticize that?"

"I will, old boy," Bertie said. "If we'd managed to grab that device doohickey today, you could have returned your bally jewel before lunchtime. You were willing to push that back by three days."

"You have no right to talk that way to me," Hornet turned his back.

"Maybe not, old chum, but let me ask you this: How many people would your princess have killed in the three days you bartered away for a shortcut to fame?"

Hornet shuddered suddenly, as if Bertie had given him an electric shock.

Lights all around them switched on, flooding the room with light. The walls were made of welded stainless steel that curved at the bottom to join seamlessly to the floor. Each light was covered with thick glass, and there was a loudspeaker mounted just below the gleaming steel ceiling, nearly thirty feet above them.

"Rather odd sort of playroom," Bertie said.

Sylvia pointed toward a set of pipes running from floor to ceiling in the corner beside the long window, which opened at the bottom like the mouth of a drainspout, then toward a large drain below their feet.

"That's right," Max said. His voice was distorted by a speaker set into the wall.

They all turned. The long window above them turned dark, but of course that was only because the lights were on in their big room.

Still, Max was there, visible in the dim light. He raised a microphone to his mouth and said: "I had this giant tank built for some underwater scenes I planned for my jungle picture. Fancy, huh? It wasn't cheap, let me tell you."

"Tell me something, Max," said Professor Khan. Max paused; clearly, there was a microphone inside the tank that allowed him to hear them. "You have so much talent in your pocket, and you help them make so many deals for other people's films, and you make so many preparations, but have you *ever* managed to make one of your own movies you keep talking about?"

Max's expression turned savage and his hand shot out to the side, just beyond the edge of the window on the side where the pipes had been installed. "I got the wheel right here in my hand, you ape. How about I drown the lot of you right now?"

CHAPTER FIFTY-SEVEN

Bertie felt a sudden shiver run through his whole body. He would never eat a kipper again. He didn't even particularly like the awful things, now he was doubly resolved to ditch everything to do with water from his life.

Still, more than anything he wanted to be back home, sitting out in the gazebo with his mother and father, picking at his breakfast while they bored him silly about their gardening or whatnot. He wanted to be with them more than anything, one last time, instead of helpless in the bottom of this blasted mausoleum-shaped swimming pool.

"But that wouldn't get you what you want," the Professor responded. How did Professor Khan manage to keep so cool? Bertie was all aflutter himself.

"No." Max put his hand down to his side as though rethinking a nasty idea. "I want your arrows. All of them."

"You have them," Sylvia said.

Max took a deep breath, then let himself smile. Watching him regain his composure spurred Bertie to do the same. Just because he was completely in control, and Bertie was at his mercy, didn't mean they couldn't show equal measures of bravery, what?

"Now, I know that's not true," Max said. "The Professor had one and you took one from Mr. Lee. Am I right? Irreplaceable, these little babies are." He held up the one he took from Professor Khan. "So I know you have at least one more, plus however many more Anselme built and hid away."

At the mention of her father, Sylvia turned away sharply. The poor thing must have suffered a sudden pang of grief. Bertie laid a gentle hand on her shoulder in hopes of giving her some tiny jot of comfort, but the look she gave him was so brimming with desolation that he withdrew.

"Or what?" called Professor Khan.

"Or I open the floods, Professor."

"I can swim just fine," Cross shouted at the window.

"As can I," Hornet added. "I very seriously doubt that this chamber was designed to fill so completely that there would be no air left in it at all."

"Oh that's very true," Max said, his smirk turning sinister. "There's an overflow drain high up on the wall that prevents this room from overfilling. I'm sure you swim just fine, but for how long? See, this is my building. That's my tank you're in and this is my corridor. I could fill the tank, lock the doors, then take a little trip to San Francisco. Or maybe even farther. How many days can you tread water? With no food, clean water, or sleep, in the dark and the cold—"

Bertie couldn't stand to listen to any more. "We get the thrust of it, old fellow. How about speeding along?" His voice sounded so much braver than he felt. Perhaps that's how the Professor managed it, too? Perhaps he was just putting on a show?

He glanced over at his teacher and saw his bared fangs and furrowed brow. No, the Professor wasn't pretending. He was simply angry.

"Of course you do," Max was saying. "You lot aren't dummies. So here's the deal. You're going to empty your pockets and give me everything you're carrying, Guns, gadgets, keys, everything. You put them at the top of the stairs by the door, then go all the way back down to the bottom. Mr. Wisp opens the door and takes the stuff. If I like what I find, I'll call security in here and have you arrested. If I don't, I drown you."

Cross didn't look away from Max. "You know he ain't gonna keep up his end of the deal. The crook will turn on us as soon as he gets what he wants. I say we refuse."

"I'd rather live," Sylvia said.

"Who wouldn't?" Cross said. "But that don't look like an option any more."

"Don't," Bertie said. He wasn't even sure what he was going to say until the words came out of his mouth. "Don't give in to despair. That's what he wants, eh? He's planning on us giving up hope; he can't defeat us otherwise."

Cross turned and looked up into Bertie's face. The old detective's face was pale and his voice was quiet. "Remember when I said I could swim? I lied."

Bertie nodded. Cross had terrified him from the moment they'd met; being able to show him kindness made his whole body hum with energy. "If it comes to that, chum, stick close. I'll look after you."

The loudspeaker crackled. "I'm not going to wait all day."

"We're doing it!" Cross snapped, then started up the stairs.

Sylvia grabbed the back of Bertie's belt and forced him to walk in front of her. She stayed close as they mounted the steps, but just near the top she stumbled and fell.

"Damn you!" she shouted, turning on Blue Hornet, who was just behind her. "What kind of a clumsy fool are you?"

The luchador was outraged. "Do not try to blame me because you—"

"Be quiet, señor," Khan said. With great reluctance, he was.

Gosh, how Bertie wished he had that ability to command. Perhaps if he spent more time in the gymnasium...

Cross had dropped his keys, wallet, loose change, and blackjack on the top of the landing. He turned to push by Bertie to head down the stairs when Max spoke up.

"Everything."

"That is everything," Cross snapped.

"We both know that isn't so."

Cross glared up at the window, then took out his badge and dropped it onto the metal deck.

Bertie emptied his own pockets and... He felt an absurd dismay at the idea that his things might mix with Cross's. It felt almost indecent and presumptuous. He set his things beside the detective's.

As Sylvia squeezed around him at the top of the stair, Bertie almost fell from the top step. There, hidden beside the top riser where Max couldn't see it, was the infrapurple flashlight that Sylvia had hidden when she pretended to fall.

CHAPTER FIFTY-EIGHT

When they finished, Mr. Wisp opened the door and collected everything into a paper shopping bag. Khan considered charging him, but the man and his gun were too far away. Then Wisp slipped back into the hall as quietly as a ghost, and the door slammed shut and bolted behind him.

No one spoke while Max when through their things. He pocketed every key ring, then went through Sylvia's purse. After that, he went through their wallets, taking out every business card, every receipt, every scrap of paper. He read Khan's note to himself, then slipped it into his breast pocket. The black shoelace it had been tied with he threw onto the floor.

Whatever he was looking for, he didn't find it. He snapped up the microphone.

"Everyone strip."

There were general cries of surprise and outrage from the Professor's companions, and Cross began to back away from the window.

"Why?" Sylvia cried.

"Because you're holding out on me!" Max shouted. He yanked something just out of sight, and water began to flow out of the pipes. After a few seconds, he shut it off. The water had pooled in the center of the room to a depth of two inches above the drain. "Now do it! All of you!"

Hornet began to unbutton his jacket. "The man is a fool. Señora, we could turn our backs if—"

"Don't bother," Sylvia said, her voice flat. "But anyone who touches me loses a hand."

Bertie began to take off his own jacket, and Khan tossed his wide-brimmed hat onto the stairs. Too bad; the suit was stylish, even if it had confirmed his suspicions that pants were overrated.

"I won't do it," Cross said.

The other stopped and started at him, incredulous. "Why not?" Sylvia asked. "If I have to undress, so do you."

"Nix that," Cross said, stubbornly. "I'd rather drown."

The others stared at him, utterly flummoxed.

"What's the holdup?" Max said. "Everyone strips down to their unmentionables. Now. Or I'll make you feel like all those animals that didn't get passage on Noah's ship."

Cross bared his teeth, then crossed his arms. He wasn't going to do it.

"What's the matter, Detective," Blue Hornet said, "are you hiding a 'war wound'?"

Sylvia stepped close to him and looked him frankly in the eye. "Detective Cross, it's not just your life on the line. And even if it was—"

"Fine." Cross threw his fedora onto the stair's beside Khan's hat. "For you, kid, because Jim had a soft spot for you. And because they would undress my corpse anyway."

Reluctantly, the detective began to undress, his pale, flabby face flushed bright red. The Professor did the same, tossing aside his tie and shirt.

Blue Hornet and Bertie also unclothed. Bertie had a body like a piece of pulled taffy, but the luchador was as chiseled as any Greek statue. Both of their gazes kept flitting from Sylvia, now wearing nothing more than a slip and hose, and Cross.

Khan had to admit that he was also curious about the detective's unwillingness to undress. So he watched out of the corner of his eye as the old fellow took off his tie, his pants, and finally unbuttoned his shirt.

There was an elastic band, at least a foot wide, wrapped around his rib cage. At first, the Professor didn't quite know what he was seeing. Then he realized the elastic was there to compress part of the detective's body.

The others all stared at Cross in surprise. The detective glared red-faced at the puddle on the floor.

"It can't be true," Max said into the microphone. "Am I dreaming or is this the craziest thing I've seen yet in this whole screwy business?" He cut loose with a loud, jeering laugh. "Is that Emil Cross, or is it Emily? Who would have thought that the most vicious, corrupt cop in all the L.A.P.D. was actually a dame?"

Max cut loose with his awful laugh again, and Cross glared up at him with raw hatred. Finally, Max stopped long enough to order Blue Hornet to turn out everyone's pockets, searching for anything at all.

He did. He couldn't find anything but lint.

Professor Khan crossed the room and began to dress; the others followed his example. "What exactly are you hoping for here? You already know we aren't carrying any more arrows."

"A key for a bus locker," Max answered. "A pawn slip. A safe deposit box number. A receipt from a messenger service. If I have to, I'll break into all of your homes and search them from top to bottom. But that will take time I don't have." He absent-mindedly glanced over his shoulder.

By Jove, suddenly it all made sense. "You have another deal going, don't you, Max? That's why you haven't offered us one today. I've been waiting for you to do exactly that, but you haven't, because..." A sudden thought occurred to the Professor, and he changed tactics. "Tell me, Max: What does it feel like to make a deal?"

Max looked startled by that question. "What are you talking about? It feels good."

"Humor me, please, just for a moment." The Professor pulled on his pants and picked up his tie. "In what way does it feel good?"

Max looked uncertain for a moment, as though he was being asked, for the first time in his life, to speak about one of the basic facts of his existence. "It feels like breaking glass," he said. "No, like tearing a cloth or a sheet of paper. No, it... When I have a rube beside me, he has all these connections to the rest of the world: family, friends, work, whatever. Then he makes a deal with me and he gets cut loose from some, maybe all of them. He's adrift, with nothing for him to grab hold of." He released the switch on the microphone, letting it fall to his side. Then he lifted it to his mouth again and said: "It feels like power."

When I'm in my shop, inventing something, I feel like I'm connected with everything at once. Sally Slick had said. It was just as the Professor suspected: whatever she and the other Centurions were, this fellow was one of their exact opposite.

"And so does this," Max said. He yanked on something just beyond the edge of the window pane and the water began to flow again. "I'll find that last arrow on my own."

He turned and walked away from the window.

CHAPTER FIFTY-NINE

Sylvia immediately raced to the stairs, snatching up the flashlight and something very small beside it. Coins?

Blue Hornet vaulted over her on the way to the door. He struggled desperately with the handle, but it would not budge.

Sylvia hurried down the steps. "Bertie! Professor! Come quickly!"

They did. Sylvia placed something in Khan's open palm. He bent to look at it; it was about the size of a marble, but it wasn't round. Then she shone the infrapurple light on it.

The device suddenly resumed its normal size, and the weight of it nearly made him fall over. "The shrinking beam! I'd completely forgotten."

"Well, I couldn't leave it in the car. It has a self-reduce mode..." Sylvia leaned in and threw a switch. "Which is now off. Stay close."

She turned to Bertie and shined the light into his hand.

Hornet stood at the top of the stairs, looking down at Cross. "What do we call the little detective now?"

Cross looked up at him with raw hate and shouted: "What do you think?"

"We all have our secrets," Khan said. "Let the detective keep his."

The tiny object in Bertie's palm grew into a glass and metal disk with spools of wires mounted on top.

"That's the shrink ray?" Cross said, standing at the bottom of the stairs. "Well, point it at the door! You can shrink it down and we'll just walk right out of here."

"It won't work," Sylvia said, as she adjusted the spools on the disk.

"Then the window pane!" Hornet said. "We can float right out of here!"

"It won't work," Sylvia insisted. "The shrinking process doesn't exert force. You can't tear off the hinges or break those rivets. It simply won't work. We'll have to shrink something free-standing."

Hornet leaned close to Khan. "Try it on the door, anyway, Professor Simio."

"Besides," Sylvia said. "It's not charged. Bertie, you're tallest so I'm going to need you to boost me up to that light." She pointed to a glass dome set into the wall at least ten feet above the first landing.

By this point, the water at the center of the room was a full six inches deep, and it almost reached the walls. Hornet backed toward the door, while Detective Cross stepped up onto the lower steps to keep his shoes dry.

Bertie knelt down and braced his hands against the wall. Sylvia stepped onto his knee, then onto his shoulders. "Pass it up," she told him, and he gave her the disk. Then Bertie straightened up, while Sylvia walked up the wall with her hands.

That put her directly beside the glass dome over the light. She took a small screwdriver from the bottom of the disk and pressed it against the first screw. With a motorized whirr, the screw began to spin outward. "Don't look up, Bertie."

"Wouldn't dare, old thing."

"Sylvia," the Professor called. "What exactly is the plan?"

"I've reached the bottom of my bag of tricks, Professor. This is it. This recharger should suck enough power out of the local grid to give us one more shot with the shrinking beam. But we'll have to use it on one of us."

Bertie cried out "I say!" but Hornet's and Cross's objections were lost in the clash of their voices. Sylvia ignored them while she removed the screws. Khan cut through all of their voices to ask: "This came up before but I don't recall an answer: Has it been tested on living organisms?"

"It has," Sylvia answered. "And there's been one test on a human, too." She glanced away from her work, showing Khan a guilty expression. "Father could be so insufferable sometimes. Whoever gets the treatment will have to climb the pipes to that air vent."

They all turned and looked into the upper corner of the room. There, just below the roof but above the bend of the pipes, was a small grill. It was barely one foot square; not even Sylvia could have slipped through it at full size.

"I see," The Professor said. "Whoever gets through will turn off the water from the outside."

"Then open the drain," Sylvia said. "Then open the door. In that order. Ah, here we are."

She tossed the glass dome over her shoulder, where it splashed into the deepest part of the water. Then she began to unspool wires from the disk.

"Oh, I say, old thing," Bertie called. "You aren't doing anything dangerous, are you?"

"You mean playing with live current," she answered, "while you stand knee-deep in water with your hands on a steel wall? I can't imagine what you're worried about."

"Just checking!" Bertie said, relieved.

Cross took another step up to avoid the water. "Did your daddy teach you how to handle this stuff safely?"

She stopped working. "Do you trust me? I guess I have to ask this, after all we've been through together, so let me have it out before I switch this on. Do you all trust me?"

"Implicitly," Khan answered.

"Yes, of course," Bertie added.

Sylvia didn't wait for a response from Cross or Hornet. She jabbed a wire into the light fixture and, with a loud, growing electrical whine that lasted for several seconds, all the lights went out.

CHAPTER SIXTY

The darkness was not quite complete. Every light inside the tank had gone out, and so had the dim source on the other side of the window where Max had stood. However, tiny bulbs on the instant recharger gave off enough of a glow for them to see what they were doing.

Sylvia stepped close to him. "Professor, open the back panel, please."

"Awfully clever," he said, "to install working lights on a recharging device."

Sylvia smiled crookedly. "Lessons learned. Here we go."

The electrical whine began again, but this time it grew more slowly.

"I assume," the Professor said, "that the drawdown of power can be nearly instantaneous, but pushing that power into another device, like the shrink beam, has to be slow to avoid overloading it."

Sylvia nodded. "It's fully insulated, though. We'll be fine right up until the moment the water level gets high enough to swamp the devices."

"Ingenious," the Professor said, and he meant it.

"It must be me," Hornet announced.

"What must be you, old stick?" Bertie asked.

"I must be the one to be shrunk and to make the climb. I am not afraid."

"Forget it!" Cross snapped.

Bertie said: "It has to be Professor Khan."

"I can climb better than any of you," Hornet said. "Even Khan. I must be the one to save us."

"You're the reason we're in here!" Cross shouted. "I ain't giving you the chance to betray us again."

"Both of you be quiet!" Bertie shouted, his voice echoing against the metal walls. "It has to be the Professor. He can't swim."

"Neither can I," Cross growled.

"You don't understand," Bertie said. They all began to climb the stairs to escape the rising water. "He's not human and he doesn't float. Detective, you will. I can help you stay above water. Professor Khan weighs four hundred pounds; once the water got above the door he wouldn't last two minutes. There's no argument. He can make the climb and he can't survive the water, so he's going. Are we clear?"

The last tinny echoes of his high voice faded, and there were a few moments in which the only sound was water swirling around the stairwell.

Finally, Hornet said: "Of course. The Professor must be the one."

No one else spoke while the shrink device charged up. They kept moving up the stairs, staying above the water, until finally it flowed over the top landing. There was nothing left to climb, so Sylvia and Khan stood beside each other as the water rose over their ankles.

"That's about it," Sylvia said. "We're out of time and the charge has nearly been exhausted."

By the blinking white light of the recharger, Khan could see that the power supply dial of the shrink device showed an eighty percent charge, barely in the green. "Will this be enough?"

"We don't want you too small," she said, handing the recharger to Cross. Professor Khan gave her the shrink device, and she began to adjust the switches and dials with practiced ease.

"Bertie," the Professor said. "I wonder if I might borrow that fine silk tie of yours."

"Of course, sir." He slid it from beneath his collar and gave it to Khan.

"Out of the water, Professor," Sylvia said. By this time, the water had reached their knees. Professor Khan climbed onto the metal railing and perched there. He felt like a clumsy bird.

"Whenever you're ready, my dear."

Sylvia aimed the ungainly device at him. By Jove, it was unnerving to stare down the barrel of a device like this, even if the "barrel" was nothing more than a lilac-tinted lens. This was their only shot. The Professor closed his eyes tried not to think of all the ways the shrinking process could go horribly wrong.

The beam shone onto him, he could feel it, like a wave of chilled air. He opened his eyes to see that, through the lilac glow, the entire world seemed to suddenly grow huge.

Being shrunk was a profoundly disorienting experience and he lost his balance, sliding back off the round railing. The smooth curved metal offered him no purchase, and he fell at a shocking speed into the icy dark water.

CHAPTER SIXTY-ONE

Professor Khan pumped his arms and legs, desperate to find the surface again.

There was no use, none at all. He was too dense, and his clothes—that most excellent zoot suit Jorje had given him—only dragged him down. Worse, it was so dark he couldn't even be sure he was stroking upward.

No. No, he was *not* going to die here, drowning in a swimming tank while shrunk to the size of a child's doll. Not after he'd fought supernatural terrors, invaded alien fortresses, and battled entire armies. No, it was not right for him to die this way. There was no justice in it.

But it seemed to be happening anyway.

A sudden roar filled his ears, but he couldn't recognize the sound. Was it the drain opening? His lungs ached, but it was too soon. He'd just plunged into the water moments before and he hadn't had time to take a real breath. There was so little time left—

Then he felt something rise up from beneath him and press against his body. It was so startling and terrifying, like being attacked from below, that he expelled all of his air into one despairing yelp.

But it wasn't a predator rising up to destroy him. A moment after contact, Khan broke the surface.

Air—beautiful air!—filled his lungs. He had been lifted out of the water by a pair of hands. They seemed so massive, but no, they were normal-sized. He was the small one.

He looked up and, in the dim glow of the shrink beam button, saw Bertie's huge face looming over him, his hair plastered wet over his forehead. "Professor, is everything jake?"

Khan took another deep breath. How could his shrunken lungs still absorb oxygen? He didn't know, but it was happening, thank goodness. "Yes, Bertie. I am. Thank you." The Professor had to repeat his answer at a shout.

"My pleasure, sir," he answered. "Here is your hat."

Bertie and his hats. He plucked Khan's wide-brimmed hat from the surface of the water and set it on his palm. It was no larger than his pinkie fingernail. Khan realized he had been shrunk so small that he was not even as long as his pupil's hand. Eight inches? Less? He set the wet hat on his head.

He glanced up toward the faint source of light above. Sylvia stood waist deep in water at the landing rail, and Blue Hornet and Detective Cross were beside her, looking down at him with concern.

The silk tie was still in his hand, having been shrunk with him. "Bertie, to the pipes!"

"Of course, sir." Bertie began slogging through the deep water. "Awfully strange to see you like this, sir. You're no longer than a rasher of bacon."

"By Jove, my boy! You mustn't compare me to food with this size difference between us!"

"Ah. Of course, sir. Here you go." Bertie held him beside the nearest pipe. Professor Khan wrapped the silk tie around the metal and grabbed the other end. He braced his feet against the near side—goodness, it was cold—and began to inch toward the ceiling. "I'll stay here, sir, in case you fall."

"No!" Khan shouted. "Send Hornet over here for that! You have to keep your promise to the detective!"

The boy arranged it, but the Professor didn't pay attention to their shouting and splashing. His clothes were still dripping wet and cold, but the sudden frightful shock had jolted him. He felt strong and alive, and he climbed with furious purpose. He reached the top of the pipe before the flowing water could rise to the level of the window pane.

"Changed your minds yet?" Max called, his voice tinny through the loudspeaker. When had he returned? "It doesn't have to be this way! Just give me what I want."

The desperation in his voice was clear. Interesting.

Khan climbed onto the top of the bent pipe and balanced against the wall. No light shone through the grate, but he could still feel air flowing through the flat metal strips. The gaps in the grate were wide enough for him to put his arm through, but not his whole body.

From below, he heard Sylvia cry: "We have nothing to give you!"

Khan laid both hands on the flat louver and, with all his considerable strength and inconsiderable weight, yanked down on it. The metal bent. It wasn't a tremendous gap, but it ought to be enough to squeeze through. He tied the end of the tie around the lowest louver, dropped it onto the other side, and squeezed his prodigious belly through the gap.

By Jove, the drop on the other side could stop a fellow's heart, if he hadn't been prepared for it. What would have been a ten-foot drop for his fully-grown self now appeared to be the cliffs of Dover.

But this was no time for a weak heart. A metal wheel was set into the wall beside the window; obviously, that was the shutoff. Unfortunately, Max Devlin was right beside it, running his fingers nervously through his hair. Khan could have leapt down onto his shoulder, but he couldn't have done it and survived.

Max raised the microphone to his lips and then let it fall to his side again. He spat out a string of curses that would have made Detective Cross blanche, then glanced to his left. There was a heavy wooden door there, and he seemed to regard it with dread. The Professor watched him work up his courage, grasp the knob, then open it.

Khan had to clamber up the louvers of the grate to avoid the top corner of the door as it slammed against the wall, and by the time he was convinced of his safety, the door had started to rebound closed, blocking his view of the room beyond.

"I need more time!" Max pleaded from the other room. Khan immediately froze, hoping to hear both sides of that conversation. But no, the other voice was too soft. "I've done everything you've asked of me! I even gave you that corroded arrow. I only need to shoot a few more times—No!"

A brilliant turquoise light shone through the doorway, and Max screamed. It was a terrible, agonized sound that made goosebumps run down Khan's back.

CHAPTER SIXTY-TWO

Khan tugged twice on the end of Bertie's tie; the wet silk held the knot tightly. Then he began to climb down.

The necktie wasn't long enough to reach the shut off wheel, of course, but it let him reach the top of the windowpane. The huge aquarium window was extremely thick, and the riveted frame that held it in place was substantial. At his normal size, the rim of the frame would have provided little more than a bare finger hold, but now he could stand on it comfortably. The pipes, water gurgling through them, were just off to the right—too far to reach by any means he could work out.

He lowered himself to the first rivet, then the next. It was slippery, scary work, and he didn't have the reassurance of a cushioning pool of water and a friendly rescuing hand below. Still, he had to keep moving, no matter how many butterflies filled his belly. Bertie and the others would die if he failed here.

Then, despite all of his caution, his foot slipped, and he over-balanced to his left. The metal was too slick for his fingers to gain any purchase, and he felt himself falling away, toward the water shut-off wheel below. At the last moment, he pushed off from the rivet.

By Jove, how far was this fall? Twenty feet? He plummeted at a shocking speed, his last-moment push-off from the edge of the window bringing him out over the top of the wheel. Then he hit, the rounded metal edge of the wheel taking him across the chest.

But it didn't cave his chest in. It hurt, yes, but much less than it should have, by any sensible measure. As he wrapped his arms around the rim and felt it wrench against the insides of his elbows as he arrested his momentum, he marveled at the fact that his rib cage had not shattered. Could he be in shock and unable to feel the pain?

Not if his arms were still able to hold on. Then he felt his slight weight slowly begin to spin the wheel—to the right, in fact, which was the correct direction. It came to him suddenly that he hadn't killed himself in the fall because he hadn't fallen anywhere near twenty feet. He still wasn't used to his new size. The fall had almost certainly been less than two.

What's more, like a fly striking a window at full speed and buzzing away unharmed, the kinetic force of his collision with the shutoff was much lessened by his new, smaller mass. He wasn't four hundred pounds anymore.

His hat had fallen off, though. Bertie would be quite distressed.

The well-oiled shut off wheel began to spin faster—someone kept it well maintained—and the Professor had to wrap his legs around a spoke so he wouldn't fall off when he turned upside down. Still, it was a long way to the metal deck below; long enough to kill him? He wasn't certain what stresses his new body could handle, and he didn't want to take the chance.

How marvelous it all was! He was overcome by a desperate urge to ask Sylvia what had happened to the body mass he had shed. Marvelous.

Righty tighty, lefty loosey, that was the rule. The Professor clambered up onto the wheel and began climbing the right side as though the spokes made a crooked ladder. His weight, slight as it was, was still enough to continue to turn the wheel and slowly close the valve. It was dodgy, uncertain work, but it was also nice to have spokes to grip that were almost small enough to wrap his hands and feet around.

The pain across his chest let him know that he would have terrible bruises tomorrow, and his shoulders ached from the strain of so much climbing. Still, he kept going. Where was Max? That was the worst thing. He'd heard the man plead and then scream. Was he dead? Was he going to step through that door at any moment and stamp on Khan like a roach? What had that flash of turquoise light been?

The Professor's curiosity was powerful, but if he climbed down to investigate before the job was done, he'd never get back up to the wheel to finish closing it, so he kept climbing that crooked ladder, feeling increasingly exposed and vulnerable with each passing second.

Eventually the gurgling noise in the pipes became more pinched. At the same time the wheel began to spin less easily. Encouraged, Khan climbed higher. It was only when he was reduced to jumping up and down on the spokes until they would no longer budge that he felt satisfied. The gurgling noise in the pipes had stopped, too.

He was a bit too close to the wall to see the window clearly, but it appeared that the water level was above the glass. Had it really taken him so long? There was only one other control mechanism that he could see: a small lever set just below and to the left of the wheel. That had to be the drain.

A light swept across him. Someone had just opened the door at the other end of the hall.

It was Mr. Wisp, and his gun was in his hand.

CHAPTER SIXTY-THREE

For some reason, Wisp seemed hesitant. He advanced slowly toward the partly-open door. Could he see into the next room, whatever it was? Khan had no idea what could make the gunman nervous, but the feeling was contagious.

The real question was whether Wisp could see him crouching inside the wheel, and if so whether he would recognize him at this size. The shadow cast by the door worked in his favor, but his dripping wet zoot suit wasn't what anyone would call inconspicuous. He moved toward the hub of the wheel as slowly as he could.

It didn't work. His movement caught Wisp's attention when the man was ten feet away. The gunman dropped into a crouch and trained the weapon on him. Wisp squinted, leaning forward. Clearly, he could see Khan's tiny form but his brain couldn't make sense of the shape and color.

There was no longer a reason to move slowly. The Professor stepped onto the axle—nearly slipping in grease—and hurried to the left side of the shut-off wheel.

A gunshot echoed inside the narrow corridor. At the same instant, the metal wheel rang under the impact of a bullet. It vibrated so strongly that it stung the Professor's hands and feet, nearly making him lose his grip.

He glanced worriedly back at Wisp. The man's lip was curled in disgust as though he was looking at a sewer rat. He took a step toward Khan, making the Professor's blood freeze; the man could kill him with a single, careless kick. But Wisp immediately stepped back, turning his shoulders toward the door he'd entered through. How strange. It was almost as if he couldn't bear to move toward his enemy, only away.

No matter. Khan took two quick steps and leapt from the edge of the wheel to the drain control. He tried to land on top of it, but overshot slightly, letting his weight fall onto the far side and catching hold with his arms.

The lever sat inside a little notch; Khan would have to lift it before he could pull it all the way down and open. He braced his feet against the metal panel and tried to push it up, but his greased left foot couldn't find any friction, and he could only dangle uselessly.

Wisp aimed carefully. The Professor glanced into that dark, empty gun barrel and wondered if Wisp knew who he was or if he was shooting at vermin in the shadows.

He fired but the bullet sparked off the end of the drain lever. It jolted up and out of the notch, and as the vibration made his grip start to slip away, his weight pulled the lever all the way down.

It hit the bottom of the track and Khan fell helplessly from it. His impact with the floor was not too jarring, but then he'd fallen farther when he'd slipped off the rivet in the wall above. Without any delay, he rolled to his feet, snatching up his hat, and sprinted toward the door, then dropped and rolled under it.

Wisp did not follow him. Chasing seemed to be against his nature. Khan ran as hard as he could through the doorway into the room where Max had gone.

It was a large, bright room, and it took a moment for him to realize where he was standing. There were two carpenters' stations before him, and beyond that he saw the miniature jumbled skyline of the false Manhattan. He was looking at the set Max had been building for that child star. What was her name?

Before it came to him, Khan saw Max stretched out on the floor. For a moment, he looked like a creature from another world: pale, hairless and wide-eyed, but no, that was his suit and there was his narrow, thin-lipped chin, now devoid of its pencil mustache and customary smirk.

It was just as Cross described. All of his hair had fallen out, and he looked comatose. Khan stood directly in front of his wide, staring eyes, but it was clear he could see nothing.

There was a low rumble from behind him. Khan turned, then looked up.

A jaguar, its fur as dark as the void between the stars, stood over him, fangs bared.

CHAPTER SIXTY-FOUR

Khan's skin prickled and his stomach felt leaden. By Jove, one quick bite and everything would be over. To such a creature, he would barely qualify as a morning snack.

This is not a real jaguar. This was Blue Hornet's mummy princess, and she was not hunting meat.

She stepped toward him, lowering her face and widening her nostrils. Fear ran through Khan's guts in great terrible waves. He fought the urge to shout at her and wave his arms. He could not spook this predator.

Just then Mr. Wisp stepped into the doorway.

"Him!" Khan shouted, pointing at the gunman. "He has the gem you're searching for! Can't you smell it on him?"

The jaguar turned its luminous eyes toward Wisp. Could it smell the Calicos on him? Had he been close enough when Max shot the bow to pick up the scent?

It almost didn't matter. Wisp went wide-eyed when he saw the big cat turn its attention to him, and he spun on his heel and fled. The Princess, true jaguar or not, chased him like he was prey.

Khan turned back toward the set. There were no workers about, but whether they had been driven off by the Princess or the gunfire he couldn't be sure. Unless it was still too early for them to start their day. What time was it, anyway?

There it was, in the middle of the floor: the arrow Hornet took was lying mid way between Max's body and the false skyline. All at once he realized where Max had hidden the bow. Not in his office, where anyone would think to look, but here, inside one of these false skyscrapers.

First thing first. Khan couldn't shoot his message to his past self until he was normal sized, and for that he either had to wait out the effects of the shrink ray—at least another forty minutes—or he needed to free Sylvia and her infrapurple light. And that assumed he could find an undamaged arrow.

The Professor hurried to Max's body and pulled his jacket open. It was like dragging a tarp off a hill, but he managed it. His note half stuck out of the inside pocket but he was too small to do anything with it.

He was also too small for Max's gun, but he didn't have any choice. He heaved it out of the shoulder holster with aching muscles—the satin lining of that red suit jacket turned out to be the perfect place to wipe the axle grease from his foot—then dragged it across the carpet and through the doorway. The exit from the water tank was barred with yet another wheel, like you'd find on a submarine hatch. There was no way for the Professor to climb up to it, but Wisp had given him an idea...

It took only a few moments to cock the gun and lift it upright. Goodness knows it was a heavy chunk of metal, but even shrunk down he had a gorilla's strength. The hardest part was holding the aim true while squeezing the trigger.

But he did it. The shot rolled the wheel back, pulling the bar free of the catch. The axle was so well greased that it nearly bounced into the locked position again, but he was lucky. At glance at the window showed someone's legs kicking on the other side of the glass. The room was draining. Good.

The ricochet had punched a hole in the door behind him but the impact hadn't pushed it all the way closed. Khan sprinted toward the bafflium arrow lying in the middle of the floor. He had to drag it somewhere out of sight until he was ready to collect and repair it. Then he would retrieve his note from Max, who had begun to twitch as though he was coming around. Then—

He heard a woman's voice from up ahead, but he couldn't understand what she was saying. Before he even looked up at her, he knew who it was.

The samurai came toward him, her long katana held low before her.

CHAPTER SIXTY-FIVE

Professor Khan glanced around, hoping that the Princess had returned. She hadn't, not that he would have felt good about pitting this pregnant young woman against that ageless dead creature.

Still, he was helpless. He tried sprinting to one side, but she matched him with three side-steps. She may have been so pregnant as to be waddling, but her strides were gigantic compared to his. Max's gun was still behind him in the hall, but he didn't have time to aim it, even if he was willing to point it at the samurai. Threaten Max with it? That would probably work, but he didn't have time for that, either.

She took a long, clumsy step toward him, and he scampered away as well as his aching muscles allowed. Could he avoid her long enough for Sylvia and the others to get free?

The young woman took three sudden steps toward him and slashed. Her sword work was intricate—she twisted her wrist this way and that, making short deadly attacks. Khan only survived because he stumbled and rolled onto his back, then took off in another direction. The samurai had bent her knees outward as if she were riding a horse, but she still found it difficult to bend low enough to strike him. Luck. Only luck saved him.

Khan sprinted away on all fours. Maybe if he made it into the faux skyline he would be able to hide from her.

But she matched his pace. By Jove, if only he weren't so small. What could he possibly do to a woman—a pregnant woman he did not want to harm who had apparently been tricked into working for an evil man—when he could not even reach her knee by jumping?

Then he remembered an odd book he'd read in the Oxford library. It had come from the Far East and it had been full of unusual diagrams of the human body.

And just like that, he had a plan. The Professor moved slowly away from the samurai, not wanting to keep away from her anymore, but not wanting to put her on guard by charging. Let her make the first move.

She did. As she stamped toward him in her wooden sandals, Khan first dodged to the side, but when he saw the katana flash he started directly toward her.

In a moment, he had hidden himself below her protruding belly. He leapt to the side—correctly anticipating that she would try to stomp on him— then bounded onto her foot.

He didn't have acupuncture needles, of course. However, according to the book, simple direct pressure could be almost as effective. So he drew back his good right arm and, with all the gorilla strength he still had, punched her hard in the calf in the spot those ancient Chinese diagrams insisted would bring on labor.

She shook him off, sending him skidding across the floor toward the carpenters' stations. Khan did his best to find his feet quickly, but it didn't matter. The samurai stood opposite him, her teeth bared in discomfort. She seemed dizzy for a moment, and he thought she might drop her sword, but as soon as she recovered she sheathed it.

Then she cried out and pressed her hands against the front of her robe. Her water had broken. She slowly sank down to the floor, and while Khan couldn't understand what she said, her tone made it sound as though she was saying *Finally!*

Max suddenly rolled onto his side, then pushed himself up to his knees. Without his hair, he seemed skinny and harmless. "It's not my fault."

Khan retreated to the nearest carpentry station, quite close to the minia-ture buildings. "Don't play this game with me, Max." He practically had to shout so his voice would carry. Where were the others? "You said it yourself: Everyone has a choice."

"Not me!" He said, kneeling on the concrete floor. "You don't know the pressures I've been under. You don't know how terrifying—I never meant it to go this far, I swear. I never wanted to kill anyone!"

"But you have. We all have limits, Max. Appetites and limits. They're what define us. Any adult should understand this. We're defined by what we must do and by what we refuse to do. I myself have been living by other people's expectations for too long, but you... What awful thing would make you say *Enough*? What line would you never cross?"

"Anyone would do what I did!" Max shouted. "Any man, woman, or child—even you—if they had a demon riding them."

Demon? Oh, no. "What are you talking about?"

Max ran his hand over his bare scalp, then swept his fingers through the black hair scattered on the floor. "No man can make a deal with a demon, not even me. It's not even a deal, my God, it's just *Give me what I want right now!* I even built all this! I can't—"

"Max!" Khan interrupted. "What demon are you talking about?"

Max looked at something behind the Professor. "The demon Calicos," he said, and pointed toward the faux skyline.

CHAPTER SIXTY-SIX

Khan spun around and saw the little child actress peeking out from behind the nearest tall building. Her hair was curled into perfect ringlets and her eyes were wide with innocent fear. Shirley, that was her name. "Have the gunshots stopped yet, Mr. Devlin?"

Then her eyes flashed the same turquoise color that had shone through the door when Max screamed.

By Jove, the child was possessed.

CHAPTER SIXTY-SEVEN

"He's the one!" Max shouted. He pointed toward the Professor, who was standing at the base of a saw horse. "The enemy I told you about! He's right there!"

She turned toward him, and as soon as their gazes met, her face lit up with malice. A chill ran down the Professor's back. This wasn't the mischievous cruelty of a child; this was old and knowing.

"Well, well," the girl said. "Preliminary host suitability: point four percent. You're an ugly little thing, aren't you? Ugly and brutish and, at the moment, extraordinarily weak. I would not have thought the locals capable of this feat."

"What are you?" Khan shouted.

"Didn't you hear? I'm the demon Calicos. The question you should ask yourself is this: What are you? Because you aren't widely loved. You don't instill a protective urge in others. And now that you have been reduced in size, you can no longer terrify them into treating you with respect. Even this host can destroy you."

She lunged across the top of the saw horse, but Khan had already dodged between its legs, dashing through a disordered pile of planks. One kick from Shirley or Calicos or whatever he should be calling her could have crushed him beneath the shifting planks, but it didn't happen. He dashed out of the other side of the pile, leapt over a bandsaw power cord, and dashed between two buildings.

No stamping feet followed him, so he crept back to the corner of the fake office building and peered back the way he'd come.

Shirley—he was determined to call her that, because he could not bear to dehumanize this enemy—was still standing by the saw horses, searching the ground around her. Her little fists were balled up in frustration.

Max had managed to gain his feet and stumbled toward her.

"Get that," Shirley demanded harshly. She pointed toward the spot where the bafflium arrow lay. "It belongs to me now. Another mistake and I'll shine the info beam on you until there's nothing left of you but the capacity to drool."

There was a loud banging of fists against metal from beyond the door. Max spun toward it, terrified. "They couldn't have gotten out already!"

"Protect me!" Shirley screeched. She ran toward the mini-Manhattan.

Khan turned and did the same, sprinting deeper into the maze of buildings. No, Sylvia, Bertie and the others couldn't have gotten out already. If they had, they wouldn't have to bang on the door. Soon, he hoped. Soon.

The "streets" around him were not to his scale. If anything, they were slightly too small. When he stood against a building his head reached midway through to the second floor. The "people" were of many different mismatched sorts: some were rag dolls, some fashion dolls, some die cast railroad figures. The largest ones barely came up to the Professor's shoulder, and the die-cast cars were only half as long as he was tall.

There would be no hiding in plain sight here, no pretending to be a doll while "Shirley" passed him by.

"Where are you?" she screeched. Her voice echoed through the canyons, making it impossible to tell where she was.

And that gave the Professor an idea.

"Calicos!" he shouted, facing away from where he thought she must be. "You're not fooling anyone! Demon? Hah!"

"Silence!" the little girl shouted. A pair of metal cars bounced through an intersection two blocks away. Shirley's saddle shoes made furious stamping noises as she stalked between the buildings.

He turned and ran back the way she had just come, waiting until she had passed the nearest intersection before crossing in the opposite direction. "What self-respecting demon threatens someone with an 'info beam'?

They don't! What's more, this jewel of yours doesn't have a curse on it. It's an advanced analytical engine, isn't it? Of the sort Charles Babbage created. You didn't steal the idea from him, did you?"

As expected, that elicited an incoherent scream of rage. A die-cast car flew between the tops of the buildings, but not in Khan's direction. Was the alien prone to childish tantrums? How much did the little girl's biology affect it?

"My people traveled the stars while yours were fighting over mammoth carcasses! We have stolen nothing from you!"

"I suppose not. It's much too old for that. But what do you need all this bafflium for, eh? I heard about the thefts."

"Your primitive mind would never understand."

Her voice sounded closer this time. Best to move to a new spot.

As Khan raced between the buildings, he almost ran directly in front of Max Devlin, only jumping back just as Max's gigantic foot clomped down in front of him. The man was slipping between the buildings, crouching behind the larger ones so he could stay out of sight. He, too, was hiding from Shirley.

The temptation to shout *Oh, there you are, Max!* was powerful, but it would at best get him squashed. Besides, he was curious what the man was up to.

Max glanced around the corner of a building, then leapt across the street. The building beside him was one of the tallest—the Chrysler building? Max jammed his fingers through the open windows and yanked the entire side of the building off.

And there it was. The Improbability Bow.

Shirley appeared in the intersection a few blocks away. Max saw her immediately, and he lifted the huge, heavy facade and threw it the length of the street. Shirley barely managed to dodge out of the way as the massive piece of wood wedged between two buildings.

"I'll shoot you, Calicos!" Max shouted. He'd recovered his pistol, and now held it in his left hand. "I don't care any more! I don't care!"

Shirley did not respond. She must have heard the desperation in Max's voice and realized he'd been pushed too far.

Max reached into the building and drew out the headset. The Professor's mind raced. What could he do to stop him? If Max shot the bow, he could doom them all. Khan had no weapons, no strength—it wouldn't even make a difference if he shouted for Calicos to come stop him. The alien was keeping its distance from that damnable gun. Khan could have bit the man's ankle, but what would that have gained him but the heel of Max's shoe.

The Professor's mind raced. Could he pull a nail from the facade beside him? But of course there wasn't time. Max nocked the arrow and drew it back. "I want to hit the target," Max said, "that will eliminate all of my enemies without doing any harm of any kind to me."

CHAPTER SIXTY-EIGHT

As Max shut his eyes to concentrate on that thought, the Professor remembered that his arrow was the same one Khan had used to parry the katana. There was a slender notch in the foil shielding, which Max clearly hadn't noticed.

Stop Max Devlin, the Professor thought with all his considerable mental might. In his little film, Leveque had explained that the headset transmitted the shooter's will into the bafflium core, but the shielding prevented other thoughts in Universal Thought Space from affecting the arrow's flight.

Stop Max Devlin.

The bow went off with a pleasant metallic tone that surprised the Professor. The arrow instantly disappearing into a dark hole in the air. Surely there were a great many people beside Khan who wanted Max Devlin stopped. Calicos, certainly. Everyone he'd trapped in the tank. Everyone he'd ever insulted or given a raw deal. Surely their will, unfocused for the moment but numerous and potent, would aid Khan's. *Stop Max Devlin.*

A hole appeared and the arrow emerged from it at great speed. It struck Max in the back, killing him so quickly that he didn't even have time to gasp.

He collapsed forward, his head crashing against the floor just a few inches from the Professor's hiding spot.

Waves of shame and regret passed through Khan's body like nausea. He had wanted to stop Max, not kill him. Khan had seen too much war—too much death—to think that life was cheap, even the life of a murderous creep like Max Devlin.

The sound of toys skidding along the concrete spurred him to hurry back behind cover. Shirley stood beside Max's corpse with a malicious gleam of triumph in her eyes. She took a moment to scan the ground around her, her head bent low. "I remember what really happened, little gorilla," Shirley called in no particular direction. "I remember the truth about your people's war against the humans, and that will seem like a beach vacation compared to what's coming!" Then she reached for the arrow.

The Professor ran away from her. He had no desire to watch that little girl pull the arrow out of Max's corpse. Besides, she'd given him an idea. She was searching for him by looking down at the ground. He only needed to hide from her until the water drained enough for Sylvia and the others to get free, and the best place to wait for them would be above Shirley's head. Best of all, Max had given him a quick way to get there.

The wooden facade Max had torn from the Chrysler Building had fallen against the largest building in the display, the Empire State Building. Khan leapt onto the bottom of the facade and sprinted up the ramp, climbing four feet off the ground in the span of a few seconds.

Then he found himself on one of the lower decks with the bulk of the building still above him. He stuck his hand into the nearest window and began to climb.

CHAPTER SIXTY-NINE

He felt terribly exposed on the side of the building, but Calicos—no, *Shirley*, didn't swat him like a bug or slap him off the side of the facade. Where was she? Where were the others? Surely they should have gotten free of the water tank by now.

The Professor reached the upper deck and stopped. There was something inside the false shell of the Empire State Building, but the windows did not provide enough light to see by. He circled the building until he had the nearest overhead lights behind him.

He could see the dark glint of bafflium in there. That much was clear. There were bare copper wires, too, but he couldn't see how they were connected. He climbed a bit higher and saw that, unlike the rest of the display, the building's spire was not wood painted to look like steel: it actually was steel. Just below it was a dish of some sort.

He looked across the tops of the buildings and saw little Shirley had climbed one of the taller buildings at the corner of the display. It wasn't as high as the Empire State Building, but it did rise above the others near it. And it had an antenna atop it.

She peeled the foil from the arrow, drew out the bafflium core and slid it into the top of the building.

The Professor turned, scanning the top of the pretend cityscape Max had ordered built. There was a tall building at each corner of the display, and each of them had an identical antenna on the top.

By Jove, it all made sense. Calicos truly was an extra-terrestrial being, and these miniature skyscrapers concealed the communications array that would allow it to send a signal into space.

But to whom?

"I know where you can get another arrow," the Professor called.

Shirley's only response was to smile without pausing in her work. Silence was the answer that he feared. If she was no longer looking for bafflium, that meant her device was complete.

CHAPTER SEVENTY

His first instinct was to begin disassembling the device, but how? He couldn't see it very clearly, and not even a child would grab hold of uninsulated copper wire.

"I've been thinking about you, Calicos," Khan shouted. From this vantage point, his voice didn't echo as much as it had before, but it would have to do. "Why hide yourself in a little girl? She doesn't have money of her own, can't travel freely without a chaperone, and can't issue effective orders. If I were going to possess someone, it would be the CEO of a scientific firm, or a U.S. Senator. Someone with authority and influence. But you chose an adorable little girl. And I think I understand why."

The smile had vanished from Shirley's face. Finished with whatever assembly she needed to do for her device, she began to climb down.

"I think you're a coward. You leapt into the body of the Princess, thinking that no one would harm a daughter of the royal family, right? You didn't realize she'd offered to sacrifice herself. And now you're hiding in this little moppet."

Shirley was below the level of the buildings now. While she wouldn't find him while he was off the ground, he couldn't see her, either. He had to goad her into answering.

"Your silence confirms it," he shouted. "Not even a creep and killer like Max would raise a hand against you in that body. He knew it would be a national scandal if he so much as bruised your delicate skin. And you know what? Only the lowest, meanest, weakest coward uses a child as a shield."

There was no answer. The Professor began to circle the top deck, keeping careful watch for the little girl.

"What are you, anyway? Are you a germ? An energy lattice? Maybe you're some sort of burrowing worm. You have a worm's courage."

"You'll never guess what I am, primitive!"

The echoes were working against him now; her voice seemed to come from everywhere at once. Still, they were never going to drive Calicos out of the little actress if they couldn't even figure out what it was.

The door at the far end of the room suddenly swung open and Sylvia came through with Bertie, Hornet and Cross. Thank goodness. They rushed forward, directly toward the supine and helpless samurai. The young woman reached for her weapons, but Sylvia held up her empty hands. The samurai did not bare her steel, and Sylvia shoved Blue Hornet toward her. His body language suggested he was about to protest, but instead he stripped off his jacket and made a pillow for her head.

Cross, Bertie, and Sylvia rushed toward the skyline.

"Maybe you're a gas," Khan shouted. "When you said *point four percent* I thought you might be a computational machine, but perhaps you are both! An artificially intelligent gas so delicate a strong breeze would carry you away. That's why you hide inside a little girl, dissolved in her blood." Again there was no answer. "That's it, isn't it! You're the flatulence from space!"

Without warning, a huge, baby-soft hand wrapped around the Professor's body from behind, and he felt himself lifted off the top deck.

CHAPTER SEVENTY-ONE

Shirley moved him close enough to her face that for a moment Khan was afraid she would bite him in two. "What an interesting doll!" she exclaimed. "A talking doll, no less. Tell me, talking doll: Do you know what little girls like to do to dolls?"

She turned him sideways and reached up with her other hand. She was going to pull his head off.

CHAPTER SEVENTY-TWO

Wilson Oswald Wisp was in a bad spot. He'd played The Game with animals many times, but this was no ordinary animal. He'd led it into traffic and seen it struck by a Red Line trolley. He'd led it through a bank lobby, where the security guard's bullets passed through it like it was a figment of the imagination. He'd even led it into a construction zone—the deadly possibilities of an unfinished building were almost too high to calculate.

But when a bucket of red-hot rivets fell ten stories onto the thing's back, it turned into a damp mist—a hopeful sign, Wisp first thought—then solidified into the figure of a beautiful, dark-eyed woman in the most garish film costume he'd ever seen.

After that, he'd led her up onto the girders.

That was dangerous, yes, but The Game was played by feel. Wisp had something of a sixth sense for finding deadly situations, and for slipping out of them. He was an expert at leading others into circumstances where they could be broken off and dropped out of the world. Now his sense was urging him upward, along a bare girder on what would one day be the seventh floor, with no safety harness around his waist and no net below him.

The dark-eyed woman was just a few feet behind. Despite all of his careful moves, she was winning The Game, coming so close.

Then her foot slipped from the bare iron and she plummeted toward the bare concrete below.

Wisp grabbed hold of a nearby upright and peered down through the building. He couldn't see a body, but maybe—

A hand gripped his sleeve, and he was so startled that he nearly fell himself. As he turned, he saw that his pursuer had, for the first time in his whole life, actually caught him unaware. At the same moment, the young woman transformed once more, from a beautiful young woman into a shriveled, hairless dead thing like a dried-up bee hive.

His first instinct was to jump. The fall would kill him instantly, but that was better than whatever this *thing* would do to him.

He didn't. He couldn't. They'd played The Game and, for the first time in his life, he had lost. It was his turn to be shattered. She had hold of him and it seemed wrong to keep struggling. It felt like cheating.

He held up his empty hands. Damn that little ape for siccing this thing on him.

The dead girl stared at him, if you could say that something with empty eye sockets could stare. Wisp withstood her attention for one second, then two, then more. Was she going to kill him? What did she want?

Whatever it was, she seemed to realize he didn't have it. She flew apart, becoming a wet mist that blew horribly through his hair and into his open mouth.

She was gone. *Catch and release,* he thought, and would have laughed if a dizzy spell hadn't made his head swoon and his knees tremble.

My God, he thought as he squeezed the cold iron girder, grateful to be alive. *My God. My God. My God.*

CHAPTER SEVENTY-THREE

Sylvia leapt onto the side of the building and lunged toward them, flashlight in hand. The infrapurple beam was blinding.

The little girl reeled back and cried out at the sudden bright light, but thankfully she didn't drop him. Her hand seemed to shrink around Khan's midsection... No, he was growing. He was returning to his true size.

Shirley lost her hold on him, and he grabbed her wrist as soon as his hand was big enough to encompass it. His toes dug for purchase in the window holes on the side of the facade. With his other hand, he grabbed hold of the base of the spire.

It took, at most, three seconds for him to resume his original size, but it was an astonishing rush of power and potency. The world shrank around him and the little girl became a rag doll in his hand. He felt like a giant.

Blue Hornet and the samurai were staring into each other's eyes, their hands clasped, as they took fast, shallow breaths together. Bertie and Cross both stepped into the "street" near Max Devlin's body.

Cross kicked his corpse. Even from this distance, the Professor heard him say: "That's for Jim."

Shirley turned toward Khan, and her eyes began to glow turquoise.

"There'll be none of that now, young lady," Khan said. He shifted position so he could take hold of the child's chin and direct the blue-green beam of light toward the ceiling.

"Curse you!" the girl said. "You will not master me! I am older than your entire civilization!"

"And yet," Khan said, "you look adorable in those saddle shoes."

"You will never harm me," Shirley hissed, her tiny, even baby teeth bared. "You do not even know how to draw me from my host."

"Not yet we don't," Sylvia said. "But I know a secret lab where we can take our own sweet time figuring it out. An intelligent gas, did you say, Professor?"

Good Lord, was she bluffing? One couldn't simply kidnap children, not even actresses. Professor Khan crossed his fingers and played along. "It's my leading theory," he admitted, "but we'll have to test it carefully. After we've examined the Calicos Jewel again. Wasn't that instrumental in trapping it before?"

"I won't!" the girl shrieked. "I won't spend any more time trapped on this planet. The time for conquest is here! Mommy! MOOOMMMMMMMYYY! Activate!"

There was sudden movement against the far wall, as empty crates and old rags suddenly rose up and fell away. A woman in a modest brown dress—the same one the Professor had assumed was Shirley's mother—rose out of the detritus like a living corpse from a coffin.

"Mommy!" Shirley called once the woman had gained her feet. "Commence host defense phase!"

Shirley's mother bent down to dig through the refuse around her feet, and when she straightened again, she was holding a tommy gun.

"GUN!" Khan shouted, and Bertie immediately squatted low and hurried toward him. Cross grabbed Max's pistol off the ground, then crept in the direction Sylvia pointed.

The tommy gun fired, the reports echoing off the high, hard ceiling. A row of bullet holes punched through the buildings above Cross's head. His skull would have been blasted open if he hadn't been so short. Khan glanced out onto the floor and saw that Hornet had thrown himself across the samurai's body to shield her from the bullets.

A shot ricocheted off the spire and brushed the brim of the Professor's hat. His reflexive flinch made him lose his balance, toppling back from the building.

Shirley, her chin no longer restrained, spun and bit Khan hard on the thumb. His hand sprung open and he lost his hold on her. Only then did he realize, to his horror, that they were still seven feet off the concrete floor.

But they were already falling away from the building. Khan dug his fingers into the false windows of the facade, arresting his descent. The little girl dropped onto the flat roof of a blocky office building across the little street, and she immediately fled from rooftop to rooftop, bounding from one lower elevation to another.

Finally, she spun around, her eyes glowing like lamps. Khan released his hold on the side of the building, dropping to the hard concrete below just as the info beam passed overhead.

Had he really sprinted through these pretend streets? At full size they were so cramped he could barely turn around. He glanced over the top of the nearest building and saw that Shirley had gone. She was somewhere inside this cramped maze of buildings. At the intersection, he checked the streets in every direction to ensure the little girl was not waiting in ambush, then hurried around the corner to where Sylvia was crouching.

"That little girl shot a beam from her eyes," Sylvia said. She had a hunted expression. "*Her eyes.*"

Professor Khan laid his hand on her shoulder in what he hoped was a comforting gesture. "She called it an info beam."

"Really?" She blinked a few times, recovering herself. "That sounds interesting, actu—"

A rattle of tommy gun fire struck the Empire State Building. Khan heard bullets ricochet off the alien device within, and marveled at the alien's lack of concern for it. Perhaps bullets couldn't damage it?

Sylvia had taken hold of Khan's hand, squeezing it with all her might. "This whole escapade has become rather appalling, hasn't it?"

"I agree, my dear. We need—" There were a string of pistols shots. Khan shouted: "Don't harm her! She's not in control of herself!"

"I am sick and tired," Cross shouted back from somewhere in the maze, "of not being allowed to fight back!"

Khan lowered his voice. "We need to wrap this up, my dear. I assume you have more arrows?"

Sylvia took a barrette from her hair and laid it on the floor. She shone the infrapurple light on it. "When did you guess I was holding them back?"

"When you hid the flashlight on the stair," he answered.

Two arrows appeared at their feet in a matter of seconds. One had come from Jameson Lee, but the other...? Sylvia offered him one. "You still need to a message to yourself in the past, don't you?"

He took it. "I do, but the note is still on Max's body."

"Well, do it quickly," Sylvia said. "Because I intend to put an end to this. All of it."

Bertie joined them. His long, lanky body didn't fold well in these narrow spaces, and he bumped his head hard against the broken wooden facade of a nearby building. "I saw the little girl's eye... *thingy*. This whole place is a loony bin!"

As though talking about her had summoned her, Shirley appeared above them, leaning out from the roof of the building just above Sylvia.

The bright turquoise beam flashed.

CHAPTER SEVENTY-FOUR

Bertie dove forward, blocking the beam with his body.

All of his hair fell out.

He screamed.

Professor Khan reacted instantly, throwing his shoulder against the wooden facade of the building. Shirley squealed in surprise and panic as the entire structure rocked back. The turquoise beam winked out and she skittered back out of sight.

Bertie fell heavily against Professor Khan, who eased him to the floor.

"My boy! Bertie, speak to me!" By Jove, he was as hairless as an eel. Khan was terrified and furious all at once.

"So many numbers," Bertie mumbled. "So many numbers." He shut his eyes and became still. The Professor nearly shouted in dismay, but the boy's breathing was regular and even. He was merely unconscious, for now.

"The beam must overload the human brain," Sylvia said. Her hands were trembling. Even her glacial cool had cracked a bit. "We should try to avoid that."

"Sylvia, we must hurry."

Together, they crawled down the street toward Max's body. There was nothing to do for Bertie at the moment, but Khan was ashamed to leave him behind anyway.

They hurried, knowing a sudden bark of the tommy gun or the appearance of the little girl would mean the end of them. Who knew what Calicos would do if they failed to stop it now? *The time for conquest is here.*

A hostile alien. A huge communication array. Technology so advanced it resembled supernatural evil out of a horror film. How thick could Khan be that it only now dawned on him that the fate of the entire world rested on them?

Sylvia stopped suddenly at an intersection, and Khan was so wrapped in his thoughts that he nearly knocked her out of her hiding place. She sat back on her haunches and mimed a tommy gun.

"We can't delay," Khan whispered helplessly. His fear had grown unbearable. They had to finish, no matter the risk. Perhaps if he tried to lead the mother away, Sylvia could shoot both arrows. Khan had little chance of evading submachine gun fire in these cramped quarters that offered concealment but not cover, but if he had to—

Sylvia started forward again, quickly and quietly, and the Professor was glad to follow. The woman in the brown dress was standing some blocks away, facing in the other direction. Her broad back completely blocked the street, and Khan caught a glimpse of something metallic on the back of her neck, hidden below her hair.

Then they had reached the Chrysler Building. Now that he was at full size, the missing side of the building and the Bow within looked impossibly cramped, but he could still make it work.

And there was Max's body. The Professor opened the man's jacket and drew out the note. There was no blood on it. He began to roll it tightly around the arrow shaft.

"You shoot first," Sylvia said.

"But—"

"Don't argue. Shoot. Is there something I can do to help?" Sylvia whispered.

As soon as she said it, Khan thought of the black shoelace. Max had taken it from him and thrown it onto the hall floor. He couldn't send the same one looping back in time, assuming he could even get to it, but he needed to tie the note to the arrow somehow.

Then he glanced down at Max's shoes. "One of Max's shoelaces, if you would, please."

She set to work untying and unlacing. The Professor tried to remember whether the note had been closer to the feathers or to the head, but he supposed it didn't matter. Whichever was correct, he would end up doing it. Or someone else would, assuming he was suddenly struck dead.

"Here," Sylvia said, tossing him the shoelace. The Professor didn't remember the knot he'd untied, either, but he used a slipknot now, for the convenience of his past self.

Then he stood, put the headset on, and nocked the arrow. Sylvia stood beside him, fidgeting with her own arrow. No. Don't pay attention to her.

He focused on the target he would need to hit to send himself this message. The wood of the bench and the hem of his kilt.

Then the little girl's mother stepped out from between two buildings and fired the tommy gun at him.

CHAPTER SEVENTY-FIVE

The tommy gun made a cruel din in the big, echoing room. What the bullets did to one's body was bad enough, but the noise was insult to injury.

Not that Khan was ready to accept injury. Arrow in hand, he dove for the floor, knocking Sylvia down as the first volley passed overhead.

For all the good that would do. The gunwoman was too close and he too exposed for her to miss again.

But miss she did. Somehow the expected spray of bullets tearing through his flesh never came. There was a clatter of heavy metal on concrete, and the gunfire was done.

The Professor stood. Detective Cross stood over the prone form of the woman in the brown dress. He was bleeding from the shoulder, but she was unconscious.

He bared his yellowed teeth. "The day I can't take a dame, no matter what kinda iron she's packing..."

Bullets had struck the Chrysler Building, knocking splinters into the machinery of the Improbability Bow and collapsing part of the roof. Khan slapped the wooden facade away, knocking the walls into the street and against the nearby buildings until the Improbability Bow stood exposed.

No more delays. He nocked the arrow again and drew it back... Suddenly it occurred to him that he could aim for any target. Any at all. He could shoot this arrow and be reunited with his queen. The foolish error he'd made so many months before out of a misguided sense of propriety could be undone.

She had told him to return to her, and this was his chance to do it. Finally. He could be with her again.

There was nothing he wanted more.

CHAPTER SEVENTY-SIX

"I want to hit the target," he said, "that will deliver this message to me in the past in the exact way I received it."

As he said it—as he *thought* it—the strangest feeling overcame him. He was *connected* to the bow in the same way as when he was deep in a serendipitous moment in his library. It was the same connection he had spoken of with Sally Slick during their conversation in the deli.

Then, through the bow, he felt that connection extend outward to everything everywhere. The building, the city, the continent, the world, and then farther still—Every molecule, every curvature in space, every jot of momentum now and throughout all of time. How Sally Slick would marvel! His thoughts had become too large for him to hold and control, and he seemed almost to be erased as he connected with All.

CHAPTER SEVENTY-SEVEN

The arrow loosed without a conscious command that it do so, and as it slid through the bow his sense of connection was pulled away with it like a net being drawn by a line. The universe opened up in front of him and the arrow passed out of all space, all time, all thought.

Sylvia had to take the headset off of him. He turned to her, astonished. "My God..."

"It's an experience," she said. "Nothing else carries the same kick."

The light in the room dimmed. They looked up and saw a thick fog swirling near the ceiling.

Sylvia scowled. "What is our little darling doing now?"

"I don't think this is the alien's doing," the Professor said. "I think our Aztec Princess is returning for her jewel."

"Then let's not keep her waiting," Sylvia said. She put the headset on herself and nocked her own arrow. Khan undid Max's tie and hurried over to Cross. The little detective had slumped to the floor, his face ashen. The Professor used Max's tie and his own to staunch the flow of blood.

"NO!" a little girl screamed. Khan spun and saw Shirley sprinting down the street, running toward Sylvia and the bow. "No, you won't stop me!"

CHAPTER SEVENTY-EIGHT

But Sylvia had already nocked and drawn the arrow. Her lips moved as she whispered the intended target aloud, then she released the bow string.

Shirley leaped at Sylvia, her eyes already glowing bright blue-green.

The arrow passed into the opening in the universe. At the same moment, another opening appeared and the same arrow shot in the other direction, but two inches to the right.

The incoming arrow struck the front of the bow at the very base of the mount for the Calicos Jewel. The gem bounced out of the setting and flipped, end over end between Shirley and Sylvia—directly into the path of the info beam.

The turquoise gem froze in mid air while the info beam shone on it. Facets flashed in complicated, ever-changing patterns, as though the data in the beam were being processed and fed back.

Shirley screamed. It wasn't the shriek of a frightened little girl; it was the scream of an old and terrible thing. Just as the jewel was suspended in mid air, so was the little girl. The two of them were locked in spacetime. She screamed again, and Khan realized she wasn't attacking with her info beam any longer; the beam was being drawn out of her.

Finally, the turquoise light sputtered and faded. Whatever had powered it had been drained of its power.

Shirley dropped to the floor, coughing. The gem fell onto the concrete, too, shattering into ten thousand shards.

Sylvia staggered back, the wires yanking the headset off her. Then she began to weep. That feeling of shooting the bow—and the sense of universal connection it had inspired—was gone and would never return.

Professor Khan raced to Shirley's side, holding her tiny body while it heaved and wracked with each cough. Eventually, she began to sneeze—adorable little chirps that sprayed a bluish fluid on the concrete floor.

It took less than a minute for the stuff to clear her system. Khan looked down at the wet mess smeared around her. That was all that was left of Calicos, a centuries-old alien intelligence and would-be conqueror. "Sic Semper Tyrannis."

"I'm only a little sick," Shirley said. She looked up into the Professor's eyes with wide-eyed innocence. "But I feel better now. Who are you? Where's my mommy?"

From not too far away, a woman's voice called: "Shirley? Honey?"

Shirley ran to her, and mother and child shared a fervent embrace. Sylvia stepped forward, drying her tears. "Warms your heart a little, doesn't it? The parent-child bond can be awfully strong. Sometimes."

"Nothing stronger," Khan said, "or so I'm told."

Sylvia pointed at the piece of metal on the back of the mother's neck. "What are we going to do about that?"

Professor Khan approached the couple. "One moment, my good woman." He drew back her hair to expose a metal box with a circular antenna sticking out of it. The indicator lights on the side were dark. It was inert. Still, it had been surgically attached to the poor woman's flesh. "There might be some way to remove—"

The Professor's fingertip barely grazed the metal surface of the box, but it fell to the floor and broke into pieces. All that remained was a tiny rectangular plate at the base of her skull.

The Professor was unsure what could be done about that. "Er..."

"Wear your hair long, Mrs. Temple," Sylvia said. "And high collars."

The woman looked momentarily alarmed, but didn't say anything. It was going to take some time for her to adjust to the world again.

Little Shirley bounced back with the energy and resilience of a child. "What is this place? I want to play here!"

"I'm sorry, my dear," the Professor said kindly, "but there is some equipment in these some of these buildings which would be dangerous for small hands. I recommend that you and your mother return home as quickly as you can."

Shirley pouted at that. "Well, if you insist."

"I'm afraid I must. Goodbye, young lady. I suspect we will never meet again, but I do wish you much happiness. Be a good little girl."

At this, she became haughty. "Of *course* I'll be good. I'm a very good girl. My mommy says so." She took her mother's hand and they started toward the exit.

"Khan," Cross said quietly. The detective caught the Professor's eye and then nodded toward the Improbability Bow.

The Aztec Princess stood beside the machine. She had not taken the form of a jaguar, or a swirl of mist, or of a pretty young woman. She was herself, an ancient mummy in ritual funeral garb.

Her head was bowed as she stared at the floor, and it was a long moment before the Professor realized she was looking at the shattered jewel. Then she seemed to sag, as though a terrible burden had been lifted from her. She quietly, carefully lay on her back and was still.

"Bertie!" The Professor raced along the narrow pathways toward the Empire State Building. He found Bertie already sitting up, looking nearly revived. "Bertie, my boy, are you well?"

"I think so, sir," Bertie lifted his hand, brown hair falling from it. He touched his bare scalp. "I'm an egg, aren't I, sir? How awful is it?"

"My boy, you're alive and well. Hair grows back."

"I certainly hope so."

"I don't give a damn how it looks." With that, Khan embraced Bertie, pulling him to his feet.

"My word!" Bertie said. "I hadn't expected such an effusive display, sir."

"What can I say, Bertie, my boy? You saved Sylvia from the alien's info beam, and Sylvia saved us all. Without you, none of us would have survived."

"So it's done, then? We stopped Calicos and Devlin, saved the little girl, and disabled the bow, with no lives lost?"

Khan clapped him on the shoulder. "None but Max Devlin and the alien itself. My boy, I do believe we have saved the world."

"Gosh," Bertie said. The Professor could not get over how odd he looked. A bald scalp was one thing, but the lack of eyebrows changed the appearance of his face profoundly. "Just think, sir: Everything we've done, and no one will ever know about it."

Khan laughed. "Well, Bertie, if you like, you could always write up our adventure yourself."

CHAPTER SEVENTY-NINE

Bertram Wellington Blinkersly, man among men, did not have to raise his voice to capture the attention of the stout fellows on his team. Simply opening his mouth to speak was enough to make them fall into silence.

"One moment, my good boys! This adventure isn't over yet! We've defeated the scout, but what about this long-distance radio machine?"

Khan, Bertram's loyal gorilla sidekick, was characteristically confused. "What do you mean, sir? Now that you've single-handedly defeated the alien, there's no one to send any broadcasts, hey?"

"True, stalwart companion! But that devil Calicos wouldn't have built the bally thing just to broadcast the latest jazz hits! There must be someone out there awaiting the signal!"

Bertram leapt forward and, with barely a strain of his mighty sinews, began ripping the facade from the Empire State Building.

"But sir!" Khan whined. "I don't understand."

Sylvia stared up at him in awe, her hands pressed against her perfect pink cheeks. *"Très brillante!"*

"There!" Bertram declared, having stripped the machine of its camouflage. "The infernal device lies exposed!"

"Wreck it!" Detective Cross cried from where he lay bleeding upon the floor.

"Not yet!" Bertram declared, then he turned to Cross. The man's bloody wound was ugly but superficial. "Fear not, chum. I haven't forgotten your plight."

"Do what you must and don't spare a thought for me, sir," Cross said. "I put aside fear when I entered your service."

Bertram favored him with a friendly wink, then turned back to the task at hand. The alien machine was the color of cheap iron, and looked to have been built by fusing metal cubes together... not that Our Hero was fooled by the inert appearance of the thing.

"Aha!" Bertram called, and snatched up a headset in his energetic hands.

"Sir!" Khan cried. "Don't put that on! It might not be safe!"

"Hang the danger!" Bertram said, then mashed the headset to his mighty brow.

Immediately he was assailed by strange signals from beyond the ether. //PING// was the first of them, and with it came of flood of impatience and relief. //Commence transmission// //Commence report//

With those signals, Our Hero also caught a glimpse of that distant cor-respondent: *an entire fleet of alien warships!*

//Stand by// Bertram signaled.

"Blast!" he said, ripping the headset from his long, heroic locks. "I shouldn't have done that, fellows. Now they're expecting a report from their vile scout!"

Sylvia glanced at the smoking green corpse of their alien adversary. "But you've already slain him with his own razor laser!"

"I know, Sylvia!" Bertram snapped. "Dash it all, just like a woman to state the obvious when there's thinking to be done."

At that very moment, a flood of sunlight rushed in as a narrow-chested fellow pushed a cart full of equipment into the room. He seemed surprised to find people inside, not to mention the obvious signs of battle. "You guys," he whined with his peculiar American accent, "I don't think you're allowed in here."

"You!" Bertram called. "Stay where you are!" Our Hero raced across the room, confronting the man almost before he could prepare himself. "Delivering some equipment, eh? And I'll bet you customarily use this aban-doned warehouse as a shortcut!" Without waiting for an obviously unneces-sary confirmation, Bertram began to examine the contents of the cart. "I've never seen this equipment before, but I surmise it is used in editing film, yes?

Of course it is: here is the splicer, the viewing screen, the crank. And here are the films being delivered to the editing office, hey? Tell me, my American friend. What films have you laden this cart with?"

Bertram's patter was certainly too fast for the laconic temperament of the Western American, but to his credit the sickly fellow inferred the gist of Our Hero's interrogative. "Films? Why, this one here is an Inspector Wong mystery—"

"Useless," Bertram pronounced. "Go on."

"There's Jojo the Jungle Boy Swings Again."

"Worse than useless. Next."

"This is Rick Radley, Space Cadet."

"Ah!" Bertram's lightning-quick analytical mind considered that one for a moment, but only a moment. "No. Forget that one. Next."

"Well, the only other thing we have here is a stack of these Stooges shorts, but—"

"THAT'S IT!" Bertram seized the man by his shoulders. "My good fellow, you may have saved the world!"

The fellow was understandably overwhelmed, but he allowed himself to be steered toward the ugly alien device.

"I see something in you, my boy," Bertram said, flattering the man with a confiding tone. "You are a man of ambition. Not content pushing carts around studio lots, you! You're destined for great things! It's no secret, one just has to look at you. I'm sure that your dream is to become... an editor of film!"

"Well, actually—"

"Perfect!" Bertram exclaimed. "I am going to give you your big shot. Today is your date with destiny, my boy. Today you and I are going to edit those slapstick jackanapes into the most important film in the history of humankind!"

No ordinary man could have made such a convincing case that a day laborer would endanger the valuable capital of his dread corporate masters by subjecting it to an amateur edit, but so winning was Bertram's British vigour and flawless complexion that the wide-eyed American rustic was overcome with fellow feeling and, like so many before him, pitched in to help.

Within only two quarter hours, the new-found companions had identified and "spliced" together the most extreme and violent of the slapstick scenes. There was no sound, of course; that was beyond the hapless American's meager skills and equipment, but Bertram would make do, as always.

Together they wheeled the cart closer to the dread transmission device... Only to see that Bertram's gorilla companion had hung a dirty drop cloth crookedly in their way.

"You're making a film, aren't you sir?" the loyal but thoughtless gorilla said. "So I hung a screen for you to show it on!"

"Er, quite," Bertram said, knowing he must unhappily puncture his servant's pride. "But we don't have a projector, you see, so I'll be playing the film here in the equipment. See the bulb and the viewer?"

Under other circumstances, the gorilla's disappointment might have been comic, but there was not time for diverting amusements. "But sir," the gorilla insisted. "I wanted to be of some use this time. Just once, sir."

"Of course you can," Bertram said kindly. "Stand by me, good fellow, for I must counterfeit abject terror, and I will need an inspiration."

Khan proudly marched over to them, taking up position beside the cart.

"But I do not comprehend!" Sylvia said in her adorable breathless way. "How do we win the fight with ze leetle movie?"

"Oh, for heaven—Isn't it obvious?" Tears welled in Miss Leveque's innocent eyes, and Bertram immediately regretted the harshness of his response. "I guess it wouldn't be to you, dear thing. Briefly: we have already established that our alien enemies are powerful and carry frightfully advanced weaponry."

"Oui."

"But they are also cowards! They hide behind children rather than risk themselves. They plot in secret. They have even delayed their invasion for centuries while awaiting this report from their scout."

"But sir," Khan said, "What if they do not experience time the same way that we—"

"Cowards, I say!" Bertram declared, picking up the alien headset. "So I am going to broadcast a report that will frighten them out of their little green skins! I'm going to show them proof that human kind are unkillable monsters!"

//Begin report// Bertram thought into the radio machine, then he pressed his face to the viewer and began cranking the wheel. Before his eyes played the worst sorts of horrors: men striking each other with shovels, wood saws, and crowbars. Men shooting each other in the rear ends. Men plummeting terrible heights into marble fountains.

And walking away unscathed.

He ran the loop three times, doing his best to summon the single cold and distant memory of the time he'd been frightened of a darkened bedroom closet when he was a lad of three.

It worked. The alien fleet began to turn around immediately, and just before they zoomed off into the stars, they sent the message:

//No rendezvous. No pickup. Your sacrifice will be honored//

Then they were gone.

"Hah!" Bertram shouted with a hearty laugh as he threw the headset to the floor. "Success!"

It was then, when all danger had passed and all enemies had been vanquished, that the local constabulary made bold enough to enter the warehouse, pistols at the ready. Of course the colonial authorities crumbled before the assured tone and masterful accent of the English nobility, and their senior officer was quickly moved to take orders from Bertram himself.

Our Hero kindly consented to an appointment at the police station on the morrow, after he and his team had celebrated with a proper feast. An ambulance was summoned for brave Detective Cross, and for the newborn child as well.

Bertram looked across the room where the young swordswoman sat on a comfortable day bed, her shoulders supported by the muscular masked wrestler. "I just knew it," he said. Every face turned toward him with a worshipful expression. The new mother raised a weary arm to give him a wave of gratitude. "They do make a dashed cute couple."

CHAPTER EIGHTY

"I say," Bertie exclaimed, as he emerged from Anselme's office to search for more typewriter paper. "This is an awfully fun thing. I wonder that I've never had a dash at it before!" He'd been pounding at the keys for hours, apparently absorbed in his work.

For Professor Khan, it had been a less joyful time. There had been a good half hour when he was certain the LAPD were going to shoot him because they were afraid to approach with handcuffs. It was Detective Cross who had cooled things down with the phrase "blue folder." After that, no one wanted to be involved in their case at all.

Mr. Wisp was still on the loose; he was currently the only suspect in Max Devlin's murder. The communications array was being dismantled by the local authorities without delay or further investigation, ostensibly to return the stolen bafflium but in truth because it scared the holy hell out of them.

Cross and Hornet were concerned that Wisp might try to get some sort of payback from Sylvia, or raid her father's lab, so they all escorted her home. Of course her collapsed, water-damaged house was still marked off as a crime scene, so for the next few days she decided to stay at her father's place. After all, it would be hers once the probate was settled.

First they had checked the house to make sure it was empty and safe, then they had settled down for a silent meal in which they gorged themselves on the entire contents of Anselme's ice box. Afterwards, they lingered. No one seemed ready to move on. Not yet.

Blue Hornet and Detective Cross sat across from each other on the living room couches, talking in low voices. It was clear that, whatever they were saying, no one else was invited to listen.

Khan himself was standing in the doorway to library. Sylvia was there, a strong drink sitting neglected on the bar before her. A pleasant but wholly unnecessary fire crackled in the fireplace. Bertie drew another small stack of paper from a cabinet below a window seat, then paused at the door beside the Professor to watch Cross's and Hornet's conversation. Khan was surprised to see the oddest expression on Bertie's face.

Just then, Blue Hornet extended his hand and Cross shook it. To Khan it seemed like a goodbye, so he took hold of Bertie's arm and drew him back into the library. They were standing beside Sylvia at the bar when the luchador entered.

"It has been an honor to become acquainted with all of you—" he turned to the Professor "—especially you, sir. You are a truly exemplary fellow."

Khan bowed his head. "Thank you, señor."

"As for you, Señora Leveque, your cool-headed bravery is an inspiration. I am truly blessed to have met you."

She touched the side of her tumbler, moving it slightly. "What will you do next?"

"I must first return the Princess to her resting place, of course, so she might enjoy a lasting peace. Then, I return to Mexico City, to... I am ashamed to say that you have all taught me something about myself that I do not like. I thought that being a tecnico meant that I was a good person, but I now realize I have not lived up to my ideals. That must change. I must rededicate myself to behaving as an honorable man, and I must do so with humility, so I will not begin to backslide at the first moment of comfort."

With a click of his heels and a tiny bow worthy of a German military officer, he turned on his heels and marched out of the room.

"Well," Sylvia said, "that was an unexpected—"

Bertie spun and marched out of the room. A few moments later he returned, his expression pinched, with the stack of pages he'd spent the whole day typing. He flung them all into the unnecessary fire.

"Humility," he said. "No backsliding. Living up to my—"

A sudden fervor came over his face and he raced into the living room where Detective Cross was carefully draping his jacket over his injured shoulder. Bertie fell to one knee in front of him.

"Please," Bertie called. "Please come back to England with me! Please don't let us be apart! I love you!"

"Shaddap," Cross snapped.

"I can't! I'll go mad if I don't confess the truth of my feelings. I love you and I don't care who knows! Come with me to England and we'll live on my estate. I know I don't seem like much but I have money and a title and—"

Cross backhanded Bertie across the mouth, knocking him to the floor. Then the detective touched his injured shoulder with a wince; it would be a while before he could comfortably rough someone up. "Say another word and I'll plug you. The answer's 'Get lost.'"

Bertie scrambled to his feet, blood running from the corner of his mouth, then retreated toward the bathroom.

Cross stalked into the library. "Time I was gone."

"I'm surprised," Sylvia said. "I thought you'd soak Bertie for a few thousand before cutting him loose."

"Psh. I don't need that stick of half-chewed gum for my money. Why do you think I've been working so hard all these years rolling pimps and fleecing johns? I got more than enough to buy a nice place on the beach right now. As for his title, he can wave that in front of somebody what cares."

Sylvia's expression was cool. "Still, I'm willing to bet his parents would have cut you a fat check to make you go away."

"There ain't enough money in the world to make me throw over my best girl for that lump."

The Professor interrupted. "At least you had the opportunity to revenge yourself on Max for your partner."

"Because of you two," Cross said, his voice quiet. "Don't think I'm not grateful."

"Are you grateful enough," Sylvia asked, "to drop the blackmail against me?"

Cross sighed. "Yeah. I guess I am. Truth is, it's time to hang up my badge. What's the use of scamming a nice nest egg if I don't live long enough to enjoy it?" With that, he took his leave.

Khan was thoughtful. "It's about time that someone broke Bertie's heart. He was overdue."

Sylvia stared down into her drink. "Professor, would you stay for a late supper? I'm not sure I'm ready to be alone in my father's empty house."

"Of course, my dear. In fact, I would be quite obliged if you would allow Bertie and me to stay the night. I'm sure there is an eastbound train we could catch in the morning."

"Thank you," she said, then laughed a little.

"What is it?"

"Oh, it's Bertie and Cross," Sylvia said. "I confess I didn't see that coming. To be honest, I was dreading the idea that he would make a scene like that to me. I've been the Pretty Girl on this little adventure, haven't I?"

Khan looked at her sharply. Her tone had been ironic, but it had been strained, too. "Sylvia—"

But she talked over him so he would not have a chance to finish. "Hornet was right, though, Professor. You had the headset on and an arrow drawn back in the bow."

"It was a singular experience."

"You could have hit any target in the universe. You could have had anything at all. Anything. You could have been reunited with your great love."

"It's true."

"And yet, you chose to come here to save my life, a woman you barely know. Do you understand how rare that is?"

"I don't think it's as rare as all of that," the Professor said humbly.

"You're wrong." Sylvia's tone was flat. "Not one in a hundred thousand would have used their one and only wish for the benefit of someone else. Not one in a million."

Khan almost objected that he hadn't really had a choice, but of course that hadn't been true. "Los Angeles is a city where people realize their dreams," he said, "but I'm only a visitor here. However, you, my dear, must do better than this."

Sylvia lifted her drink to her lips to hide the ghost of a smile. "Look around you," she said, her voice hollow. "Don't you think I'm doing pretty well?"

"I do not. I know the truth about you, Sylvia Leveque, and I don't want you to continue this way. It's hurtful to yourself and to everyone else. To me."

"Hurtful? How do you mean?"

"I've told you I respected your father because he was a brilliant theoretical scientist—emphasis on 'theory,' yes? He could never have built the Improbability Bow. You did that."

"That's nonsense," Sylvia said. "My father—"

"Didn't have the background. Oh, the truth was clear to anyone paying attention. Poor Mrs. Flewellyn, murdered because she saw the thieves who stole the bow, wasn't looking through your father's bedroom window. It was your house the bow was stolen from. And there have been little tells from you: small delays in the way you answered questions and the way you spoke. But the clincher was that second shrunk-down arrow in your purse."

"I took it from the lab."

"My dear, you must not lie to me. Max Devlin took the arrows and he wasted them on his silly deals or turned them over to Calicos. You had no arrows until you took that one from Jameson Lee. Then, while I was up here in the office drafting the note to myself, you were down in the lab, creating another."

"No," she insisted. "My father's legacy—"

"Belongs to him! I'm sorry that Max killed him; he contributed so much to the scientific world, but this is your work, my dear. You are capable of creating wonders! You, yourself, are a wonder. Embrace that!"

Sylvia pushed away from the bar and went to a shelf full of old reference books. She pulled one down, flipped it open, and removed a sheet of stationery from it.

Her hands were trembling as she offered the paper to him. Khan accepted it and unfolded it. The writing in black ink was instantly recognizable as Anselme's hand, but before he could begin to read it Sylvia snatched it away.

She pressed it against her breast, obviously regretting that she'd taken it out at all. Then she shoved it into a drawer and slammed it shut.

"Sylvia, what is that?"

"My father's suicide note," she answered. "God, it seems so odd to just say that out loud. It's his suicide note. See, I know that Max didn't kill him. I did."

"What are you talking about?"

"That insta-recharger? I invented that when I was eight. Father was amazed and delighted of course, but as the months went on and I began to fill his lab with devices that…"

She didn't seem to want to go on, so Khan prompted her. "Devices that he couldn't even understand."

"I want it to be clear that my father was a brilliant man. Brilliant. He was one of the top five men in his particular field."

"But you outshone him."

"I don't even know how. I was ten years old when I realized no one else could see the world the same way I did. My father marveled at my creations, he told me how wonderful and amazing they were, and then he locked them away in his lab. He didn't want anyone to know about them. He wanted my input on his papers but he would never put my name under his."

"But he couldn't hide the Improbability Bow."

"No, the bow was too big. He couldn't hide that. But he wanted credit for it, too. Sole credit. I couldn't stand it. I was furious. He'd done so much for me, bought me the science books I craved, the tools and materials I needed, raised me all by himself after mother died—it couldn't have been easy to live with a morose 16 year old girl with a shrink gun under her bed. He gave me everything, and… I hated him, Professor. I hated him for putting his name on my work. I told him that, if he sent out that film—the one you watched downstairs—I would go public. I said I wouldn't help him with his work anymore, and once people realized what I could do, his name would always be tainted. No one would ever be sure where his genius ended and mine began. That night, he…."

"My God, his note."

"Yes," Sylvia said. "He did give me the credit I asked for. In his suicide note. That's what I couldn't bear to have you read. He was scrupulously fair to me in in the end, but he couldn't bear to live with the shame that he'd relied on his own *daughter*. You see, Professor? Max Devlin didn't kill my father. I did."

"No!" Khan shouted, unable to contain himself. "No, Sylvia, that is not fair. Anselme should never have done this to you! You have a gift! Your brilliance is a boon to the entire world, and your father should never have tried to hide it away."

"He did what he thought was best."

"Best for *him*," Khan said, and the vehemence in his voice startled even him. "Best for... Listen to me, my dear, please: You could do so much."

"And yet, it feels like so little. I'm more than a little tempted to lock up the lab downstairs and let everything rust away to dust."

"Sylvia, my God. Please don't do that. Why not—I know, come with me to Oxford!"

She managed a crooked smile. "Do they let women teach at Oxford?"

That stopped the Professor cold. "Full professorships? I'm afraid not. New York, then! I have a friend there—"

"Professor, I couldn't. Not right away."

"But—"

"Whatever you think of Anselme Leveque, he was my father. Someone has to settle his estate." She sighed. "We all have flaws, Professor. I was very angry with him, but I loved him and now he's gone. I'll never get to argue with him again about California reds, or neutrinos, or how I keep my tools in the lab." She lifted her drink to her lips but lowered it without tasting it. "You know, I almost brought him back. I could have shot an arrow that saved his life but I stopped Calicos instead, and now I don't even have the Improbability Bow anymore. Without that jewel—"

They sat in silence for a few moments. Khan wanted to muster an argument that would break through her grief and convince her to share her work with the world. Nothing came to mind. Worse, he knew it would be dreadful manners. "My dear, is there anything I can do to make things easier for you?"

She took his hand and squeezed it. "I know you were planning to return east in the morning, but can I convince you to stay on for a little while to help me sort my father's papers? There may be publishable work there."

"It would be my great honor."

"Thank you."

"And I hope you will not consider it tiresome if I continue to suggest, with utmost diplomacy, that the world needs you and your gifts."

She managed a tired smile. "If living in Los Angeles has taught me anything, it's this: Not everyone gets to see their dreams come true."

"The world is changing. If someone like me can find a place in it, you certainly can."

"We'll see, Professor." She drained her drink in one go. "Now you'd better go and check on Bertie. If this really is his first heartbreak, he's liable to do something dramatic."

"Quite." Khan slid from the stool and started toward the main room.

"Professor!" He turned in the doorway toward her.

"Yes?"

She was just as cool and composed as she had always been. "Thank you."

He nodded to her and headed toward the stairs, leaving the library door wide open.

AUTHOR'S NOTE

Of course it is as absurd to suggest that Jimmy Durante, Alan Hale (Sr.), or Joe E. Brown were middling talents that would need the help of a Max Devlin to sustain their careers as it would be to suggest that Shirley Temple was ever possessed by an invading alien AI. Durante was a widely-respected performer, composer and radio personality, Hale was one of the busiest character actors of his day, and Brown, best known now for delivering the final line of SOME LIKE IT HOT ("Nobody's Perfect!"), was a huge star in the thirties with a string of hit comedies to his name.

No disrespect is meant to them or any of the actual people mentioned in this story.

MORE BOOKS FROM
SPIRIT OF THE CENTURY™
PRESENTS

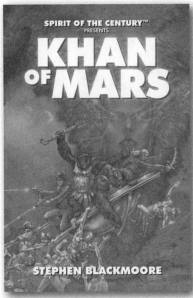

The *Spirit of the Century* adventure continues in these titles, available now or coming soon!

- The Dinocalypse Trilogy by Chuck Wendig: *Dinocalypse Now, Beyond Dinocalypse*, and *Dinocalypse Forever*
- *Khan of Mars* by Stephen Blackmoore
- *King Khan* by Harry Connolly
- *The Pharaoh of Hong Kong* by Brian Clevinger
- *Stone's Throw* by C.E. Murphy
- *Sally Slick and the Steel Syndicate* by Carrie Harris

RACE TO ADVENTURE!

THE SPIRIT OF THE CENTURY™ EXPLORATION GAME

Every year, a worldwide scavenger hunt brings together daring adventurers from all parts of the globe—members of the famed Century Club. Their adventures are filled with danger, excitement, and wonder! Centurions race to be the first to complete every mission, stamp their passports, and cross the Century Club finish line. Will this be your year to win?

Race to Adventure!™ is easy to learn and quick to play. Players take turns selecting exciting items to help them on their quest, like the Jet Pack, Zeppelin, or Lightning Gun! Then everyone moves and takes action at exotic locations.

Be the first player to collect every stamp on your passport, return to the Century Club, and declare victory!

**Find out more at www.racetoadventuregame.com —
and follow the race on twitter: @racetoadventure**

**2-5 Players
Ages 8 and up
Plays in 30 minutes**

www.evilhat.com
ISBN 978-1-61317-008-3
EHP2003 • US $30.00

EVIL HAT
PRODUCTIONS

ABOUT THE PUBLISHER

Evil Hat Productions believes that passion makes the best stuff—from games to novels and more. It's our passion that's made Evil Hat what it is today: an award-winning publisher of games and, now, fiction. We aim to give you the best of experiences—full of laughter, story-telling, and memorable moments—whether you're sitting down with a good book, rolling some dice, or playing a card.

We started, simply, as gamers, running games at small conventions under the Evil Hat banner, making face to face connections with some of the same people who've worked on these products. Player to player, gamer to gamer, we've passed our passion along to the gaming community that has already given us so many years of lasting entertainment.

Today, we are turning that passion into fiction based on the games we love. And, much like the games we make and play, we need and *want* you to be part of that process.

That's the Evil Hat mission, and we're happy to have you along on it.

You can find out more about us and the stuff we make at *www.evilhat.com*.

ABOUT THE AUTHOR

Child of Fire, Harry Connolly's debut novel and the first in The Twenty Palaces series, was named to *Publishers Weekly's* Best 100 Novels of 2009. The sequel, *Game of Cages*, was released in 2010 and the third book, *Circle of Enemies*, came out in the fall of 2011.

Harry lives in Seattle with his beloved wife, his beloved son, and his beloved library system.

You can find him online at: http://www.harryjconnolly.com